The Malevolent Witch

The Book of Khayin
Volume One

By

M.R. Gross

Copyright © 2017 M.R. Gross

Cover Art by Dent Niggemeyer

Author Photo by Doug Geiger

All rights reserved.

First Edition: June 2017

This is a work of fiction. Any resemblance of characters to actual persons, living or dead, is purely coincidental. The author holds exclusive rights to this work. Unauthorized duplication is prohibited.

This book is licensed for your personal enjoyment only. If you would like to share this book with another person, please purchase an additional copy for each reader. Thank you for respecting the hard work of this author.

ISBN-13: 978-1547151721

ISBN-10: 1547151722

m.r.grossauthor@gmail.com

To my daughter Kirsten,

you are an inspiration in more ways than I can count.

To my wife Ruth,

for putting up with me while I obsessed over this book. I love you.

Acknowledgments

To Joie, thank you so much for cluing me in on what goes on in a woman's head, though I'm sure I still got it wrong.

To Dent, for the many hours you poured into doing my cover, I just hope the book is as good as the art.

To my peeps in writer's group; Jason, Jen, Tuesday, Nat, and Brian, you have all been instrumental in the writing process for this book and I can't thank you enough, hopefully this is a reflection of what I have learned and not a reflection of what I have ignored.

PowerHouse Summit Members: Thank you for all the little stuff, that was not all that little.

A big thank you to all my Beta Readers, your feedback made this work better, thank you for taking the time to read through the first iteration of this book.

And lastly; To all of you who bought this. This is my first of hopefully many. I cut my teeth on this book and I am so glad to share it with you.

Thank You!

Chapter 1 The Bet

It had been hours. The room stank of smoke, booze and bodies that hadn't seen soap or clean water for some time. There was a quiet that fell over the place, only the sound of breathing and the occasional mug hitting a table. The two men stared at first each other and then the cards in front of them. No Limit Texas Hold'em was the game, and the game had gone on through the night. Dawn was breaking and only two players remained.

The table was in the corner of the large open room and Khayin sat with his back to the wall, his chair balanced on its back legs. A cigarette hung from his mouth, with ash over an inch long barely winning the fight against gravity. He had a wide brimmed hat and a loose fitting white button down shirt. A leather cord with a pentacle hung around his neck. Over the shirt he wore a black leather vest. Two holsters lie empty on either thigh. He had to check all his weapons at the door before entering El Diablo's. His opponent was every bit the Mexican stereotype and he wore it like a badge of honor. His large sombrero covered his eyes, making it difficult to read his facial expressions.

"Your bet, pendejo," Juan said in thick accented Spanish.

The quiet in the room was so absolute and so long that the words startled Khayin. He lost his balance and the front of the chair came crashing down to the floor. The sudden jerk in movement made the ash from his cigarette fall into his lap. The comical slapping at his crotch to rid his pants from ash drew a thunderous burst of laughter from the few spectators that managed to stay awake.

"Balls!" Khayin yelped. He smirked while he tried to regain some composure.

Khayin was undoubtedly the chip leader and Juan was a terrible player. Khayin purposefully stretched the game, winning and losing hands in hopes of keeping all his opponents in the game long enough to bleed them dry. He lifted the corner of his down cards.

He let the cards snap back and eyed the community cards in the middle of the table: an Ace of clubs, a Ten of clubs, and a Five of diamonds.

He studied the cards in front of him and then Juan's face. He had to keep Juan in the game so he didn't want to bet big. The Mexican's pile of chips was small, but winning it would net Khayin an even 50,000 chips. That amount could get him back to Chicago in time to catch the original Star Wars trilogy. He loved those movies and was thankful that the wizard who magicked them back to life loved them as well. Someone else would have done it eventually; it was a money maker, and they were clearly the favorites among the people of Chi-Town.

The Great Cataclysm, or 'The Day Magic Returned', as some have coined it, was over 200 years ago, and magic wasn't the only thing that returned. The creatures that relied on it returned as well. Dragons, faerie folk, mermaids, unicorns--everything from fantasy come to life. Atlantis popped up in the middle of the Bermuda Triangle. Mysterious islands and isolated lands that were once totally uninhabitable became populated overnight with people that have been living there for centuries or millennia. The down side, and there was always a down side, was that the electricity went out all across the world, but some ingenious wizards had figured out a way to use magical energy rather than electrical.

Khayin glanced at the community cards then back to Juan. After a moment he tapped the table to signify that he checked his bet before picking up his glass and downing the last of his whiskey. He had asked for top shelf, but if it wasn't tequila it wasn't really top shelf. He grimaced from the hard liquor then turned his attention back to the game and his opponent's face.

"Check?" Juan smirked. "You checked? You not very confident in your hand, bounty hunter. Maybe luck is turning around?" He peeked at his down cards and adjusted his glasses. The Mexican glared at Khayin while he fiddled with his chips. Counting out his bet, he slid it across the table adding their number to the pile of chips already sitting at its center.

"Player bets one thousand chips," the dealer said in a

monotone voice. He was middle aged and wore green coveralls. He'd been stoic the entire evening; he even remained neutral during Khayin's display with his cigarette and chair. "The bet is to you, sir." He stared at Khayin.

The bounty hunter shivered, trying to shake the creepiness away. He counted out a thousand chips from the large pile he had neatly stacked according to denomination. Khayin winked at Juan and slid his bet to the pot. *Juan must have a pair. Most likely a pair of Aces.* He stifled a smile. He didn't want to give away to the others what he suspected.

"Player calls," the dealer said plainly, picked up the deck of cards and dealt 'the turn'. An Ace of hearts was added to the community.

Khayin could see the excitement in Juan's face, though he tried to hide it. The bounty hunter peeked at his down cards just for something to do. He knew the cards and he knew what he needed. He looked at the Mexican and that ridiculous sombrero. Out of the corner of his eye he could see the dealer staring at him. The bounty hunter picked up his glass and motioned for the waitress, a pretty girl wearing a summer dress that came to about mid-thigh. Khayin had been flirting with her all night and she was more than eager to refill his tumbler. When she bent down he lightly brushed her long black hair back from her face, letting his hand glide down the curve of her jaw, down her neck, and along her back resting on her left cheek. She breathed heavily.

"Maria, what might you be doing after this?" Khayin whispered softly into her ear. She smiled coyly.

"You done playing grab-ass with senorita? We continue?" Juan was definitely anxious to move the hand along.

"Don't be jealous, Juan. It doesn't become you," the bounty hunter said with a devilish grin.

The waitress lingered longer than was appropriate before she slowly backed away. Khayin lifted the whiskey to his lips, sipped and checked his bet at the same time. He never took his eyes off Juan. Gently he placed the glass on the table.

"Check?!" The Mexican was obviously frustrated, but also overjoyed; the bounty hunter could see it in his eyes. Juan adjusted his glasses and counted out his bet, then pushed it to the center of the table. The stack fell over and spilled chips onto the column of community cards. The dealer, more than a little annoyed, re-stacked the chips and shot a glare toward Juan that screamed murder. Khayin stifled a laugh.

"Player bets one thousand chips," the dealer said through clinched teeth. That was the most emotion that the bounty hunter had seen out of the dealer all night.

"You got, what? Another two-thousand chips over there? Juan, buddy, I wouldn't be so flippant with your money." He made a little tsk, tsk, tsk noise with his tongue as he shook his head a bit and counted out some chips. The pot grew a little more.

"Player calls," the dealer announced.

The anxiety was radiating off of Juan; Khayin could feel it from across the table. The Mexican played with his glasses again. Khayin knew Juan had a good hand. He wasn't worried about losing, but it would definitely be his last hand; he needed to sleep. The saloon was deafeningly quiet. Everyone seemed to anticipate that the next card flipped was going to be the last card played.

The dealer dealt and flipped 'the river'. A Queen of clubs. Khayin fought down every emotion that threatened to make itself known. He had to play the betting carefully as to not scare Juan off. He looked at the Mexican, trying to read his partially covered face. His face didn't change. The Queen meant nothing to Juan, but he looked confident in the hand he held.

The dealer looked again at Khayin, who picked up his tumbler and casually sipped his whiskey. He tried to find some redeeming quality in the liquor and just grimaced with disappointment. He checked his bet a third time.

Juan slammed the table with his fist. "Check! Check! Check!" he yelled. "Is all you do?" Khayin remained stoic. The Mexican shook his head and glared at the bounty hunter. He gathered all of his remaining chips and pushed them violently to the center of the table.

The normally calm dealer seemed agitated at Juan's display. "Player bets two-thousand five-hundred chips," he spat.

Hiding his amusement, Khayin looked at Juan, then at the

community cards, sneaking a peek at his down cards and praying to whatever god was listening that his cards hadn't mysteriously changed. He counted out his bet and looked at Juan.

"I call your twenty-five hundred and I'll raise you...five thousand more." He smiled.

"What?!" Juan panicked. "But, I don't have any more money."

The dealer looked at Juan. "Your own house rules, Senor. If you can't match the bet you forfeit the game."

"Well then," Khayin replied, "looks like I win." He reached for the pot.

"No, wait!" the Mexican exclaimed. "I...I..."

He rummaged around in his traveling pack that rested on the floor beside him. After a minute he produced a crumpled piece of paper, smoothing it and slapping it down on top of the scattered cards on the table. It was clearly a wanted poster, though the woman pictured in the crude drawing could be just about anyone. The reward offered was 10,000 chips, and further reading revealed that the woman was a witch--a Nighthag or a Schadovitch to be more precise.

Khayin looked at Juan quizzically. "What am I supposed to do with that?"

"Tis bounty worth ten grand, senor," he said matter-of-factly.

"No shit, Sherlock," he teased. "It ain't worth nothin' to me." He was a little perturbed by the vagueness of the poster. "It ain't worth more than the paper it's printed on."

"Ahh..." The Mexican smiled. "But, girl is in carriage outside." He waited a moment, watching Khayin examine the parchment. "You accept bet?"

The bounty hunter ruminated. He had come on a single horse, and had no way of taking a bounty anywhere. There was also no way of knowing for sure that Juan had what he claimed he did, even if Khayin went out to look at the merchandise. The rumored Nighthags were just that: rumors. No one had ever lived to tell about an encounter with one. And how the hell would an amateur like Juan get his hands on one? The Mexican only dabbled at the bounty hunting trade; a skilled hunter he was not. Maybe Khayin could sweeten the deal.

"OK Juan, tell you what." He didn't want a negotiation, so he tried to sound as firm as he could. "I have no way of transporting a bounty. I was actually on my way to Chi-Town from a pretty hectic job, so you throw in a horse or that carriage with the bet and I'll accept."

"Whoa, wait a minute..." Juan didn't get a chance to finish.

"There's no way of verifying what you've got out there is a Schadovitch, or hag. You know as well as I do that that's subject to the person that posted the bounty." Khayin explained. Juan nodded in agreement.

"Fair enough, pendejo." The Mexican relented. "I got a extra horse. She's a good horse. All this is pointless though, Bounty Hunter, because I win." Juan flipped his down cards over and tossed them into the center of the table. Two Aces.

Bastard's got four of a kind.

Juan realized his mistake after he revealed his cards. Khayin never called the Mexican's raise. He slapped the table, then smiled and shook his head. The tension in the room grew, those who were still awake fidgeting with anticipation. Maria stood very close to Khayin's side.

Milking the moment for all that it was worth, the bounty hunter peeked at his cards. He met Juan's gaze, then a devilish grin grew across his face. He picked up his cards and tossed them just as the Mexican had, a King of clubs and a Jack of clubs. A royal flush.

Juan's face went pale, then flashed to a brilliant shade of red. He stood up so fast that his chair flew back and crashed to the floor. The Mexican grabbed his sombrero and threw it across the room, a move that was more comical than intimidating. Khayin chuckled and stood, scooping up all his winnings into his traveling sack. He tossed a couple chips and tipped his hat to the dealer. Maria grabbed his face and kissed him hard on the mouth. She tasted just as nice as she looked.

****

Khayin followed Juan outside. "So, wait a minute, you had a

bounty out here the whole time we were playing poker? Weren't you afraid of someone stealing her?" A falcon flew overhead and landed in a tree in front of the bar.

"No, pendejo. It's magiked. My carriage has special alarm." Juan held out a plastic square about three inches wide and an inch thick to Khayin. When he looked at it more closely Khayin could see little light bulbs inside.

They walked to a carriage that was covered in a tarp, and the Mexican pulled the tarp away just enough to open the door and reveal what was essentially a traveling jail cell. The bounty hunter noticed the anti-magic sigils etched on the bars as well as the floor and ceiling, but most striking was the female form stretched out in the middle of the cell. Her head was covered in a sack. She wore a light sleeveless tunic and short pants that fell in tatters on her thin frame, and her arms and hands were wrapped in strips of shredded cloth. Her feet were bare. She sat upright in a flash and moved to the bars in front of the two men, as if she could see them through the hood.

Khayin, wasting no time, reached in and pulled the hood off her head. Her long, blood red dreadlocks spilled out of the hood and over her shoulders and back. The pale skin of her face was etched with light blue tattoos matching the color of her eyes. The tattoos didn't mar her beauty, but accentuated it. She stared at him. Khayin could see the fury in her eyes and it only seemed to make them all the more beautiful.

"Damn," was all that Khayin could say.

Chapter 2   The Dream

The darkness was absolute. Young Kira'Tal awoke lying on a hard uneven surface. She opened her eyes, or at least she thought she did. She pushed herself up into a sitting position, acutely aware of the deep ache in her bones. A rocky floor wasn't an ideal place to sleep. She lifted her right hand in front of her face. Nothing. *Am I blind?* A sudden wave of panic washed over her. She shuddered. *No, the Crone and my sisters wouldn't have blinded me.* She sat motionless and meditated, steadying her breathing until the panic and jitters melted away.

Upon centering herself mentally she concentrated on listening to her surroundings. Far off she heard water dripping into...what? A pool? Cave lake? She wasn't entirely sure. She heard no other sound. Kira opened her eyes once again and she saw a faint glow, some kind of luminescence in the direction of the dripping water that wasn't there before. Or was it? The young witch stood, brushed some blood red dreadlocks out of her face and took stock of her possessions. All she had were the clothes on her back. Her feet were bare and she wore only a light tunic and pants that came down to mid-calf.

It was the night of her Gnoxel, a rite of passage into adulthood. The cave in which she awoke was home to a very ancient dragon. The witches believed the Dragon-Mother to be the last of her kind, for over many millennia no other had ever been discovered. Kira knew she had to find the beast somewhere in the labyrinth of tunnels in the cave; then her trial would truly begin.

Kira was the daughter of the tribe's leader, the Crone. There was much expected of her. Life to this point hadn't been easy for the young witch. Her natural magical abilities had yet to manifest and her twin sister, who was younger by minutes, had bloomed and passed her Gnoxel early. The siblings hated each other; it was much more than a simple rivalry. Kira by rights would inherit leadership of the tribe, but if she didn't develop any power that right would go to her sister, Brianna'Tal. The young witch shook her head as if to clear her mind with the motion alone. She breathed in deep and exhaled through her nose trying to find peace within herself.

She walked toward the glow in the distance, making every footfall careful and deliberate. She moved slowly and held her arms outstretched, probing for walls and cautious not to run into something in the total black before her. The pale yellow glow grew brighter as she got closer, and she fought her growing anticipation to keep her mind focused on her task. Her walk through the tunnel produced little noise, only the occasional stone kicked as she slid her feet along the floor.

She finally stepped inside the circle of light. It was beautiful. Fungi and moss festooned the open cavern. A pool of water sat at its center. The air was damp and the walls wore a sheet of water. The cavern was as bright as a starry night sky. Kira walked to the edge of the pool and peered inside. Luminous fish swam through the water. From her vantage point she couldn't tell how deep the pool was, or whether it continued to other hidden caverns within the cave. She examined her surroundings and only allowed herself the briefest moment of elation that she was able to see it at all. She focused more on the issue at hand: the cavity appeared to be a dead end. Kira saw no opening other than the one she had come from.

The young witch took a moment and looked herself over. Her pale skin was covered in dirt and grime, her feet even more so. She squatted down closer to the water and looked at her reflection. She looked like she hadn't slept for days though she had just woken up. She scooped some water into her cupped hands and splashed her face. It was cool and refreshing, and she licked a finger to taste. The water was clean, not bitter. She cupped her hands once more, but this time she lifted the water to her mouth and drank. Kira had no idea water could taste so good; it was unlike any water she had before. She stood up, closed her eyes and jumped in.

The water was colder than she initially thought. She waited a moment for her body to adjust before she dove to find another way out of the cave. Totally submerged, she opened her eyes and looked around. To her surprise she could see clearly. The fish had scattered when she entered, but slowly started to swim around her like she was one of them. She swam the circumference of the pool and found a small opening almost directly beneath where she had stood a moment before. Kira surfaced, then took a deep breath before diving down and entering the small underwater passage.

The tunnel was long and she started to feel the pressure, her body begging for some air. She could not see an end in sight and she could feel herself beginning to panic. The pressure grew more intense, like some creature was trying to burst out of her chest. It hurt. She had to calm herself or she would drown. She closed her eyes and forced herself to relax, pulling herself along at a much faster pace. She held to the walls on either side to reassure herself a bit, but in her haste she scraped and bumped her already sore arms. She felt like her lungs were going to burst. She started to tremble.

The passage finally opened up to another pool, and Kira reached for the surface. Every stroke got her closer, and finally her fingers felt open air. She let out a loud gasp as she broke the surface of the water. Her lungs hungrily took in air and the young witch paused just to orient herself. The pool and new chamber looked almost identical to the one she had just left, except this one had two passages heading in opposite directions. She made her way to the edge of the pool, hauled herself out, scraping her knees along the way. She stood dripping wet, her clothes clung to her body like a second skin. She closed her eyes and meditated. She absorbed everything around her. The smell of the cave moss. The sound of dripping water from the stalactites.

After a moment she reached out a little further, pushing back the sound of water and smell of moss and searched for something, anything else. She heard a faint sound coming from her left, too far away, too distant to make out. To her right she heard nothing, an unnatural nothing. She opened her eyes. Kira took the right passage.

The tunnel was dark, just as dark as the first passage she had taken. She walked just as carefully, but this time she probed ahead with her arms as well since there was no glow to guide her. She stopped when she kicked something on the floor that didn't feel like a rock. She squatted down and felt for the object with her hands. Kira picked it up and used her hands to identify it. She found a smooth rounded surface with a faint crack, and as she glided her hand along she found two large holes side by side. Beneath and directly between those holes she felt...

Shit! It's a skull!!

She dropped it quickly, startled. She took a moment to collect herself and then moved further along, more slowly than she did before. The young witch felt several more skulls and other bones scattered haphazardly. She didn't bother to pick them up to verify. She had a sense that she was now in another large cavity and when she reached a dozen or so feet in she found a pile of bones and skulls. She only touched them long enough to know what laid before her. *My ancestors who failed their Gnoxel. Here to scare me?* It worked. She was unsure why this chamber was so deafeningly quiet, but she knew she didn't want to be in there any longer. Fear started to crawl ever so slowly up her spine and she started to break out into a cold sweat. Kira turned around and as quickly as she could she backtracked her way to the pool.

She stopped in the middle of the cavern and looked back over her shoulder, even though she knew she wouldn't be able to see anything. She exhaled. *When did I hold my breath?* She closed her eyes again. This time she counted to ten and opened them. She looked at the remaining passage and moved forward, making her way down it just like she had with the others.

Kira followed the distant sound she heard from the pool chamber. The noise became louder. It was a buzzing, or maybe a humming. It grew louder and more distinct the closer she got.

Snoring? She approached another cavern, this one much larger than the previous two, cave moss and fungi illuminated this chamber as well, but she didn't notice it until she was inside. Upon entering the cavern the humming, buzzing, snoring sound ceased to another unnatural quiet. A shiver ran up her spine, but she wasn't cold.

"Have you come to subdue me, or are you here to sate mine hunger?" The voice was many, it came from nowhere yet everywhere. It was sensual, frightening, exotic and definitely feminine.

Kira looked around her frantically, though she tried to look unfazed by the disembodied voice. "Where...where are you?" She tried to sound authoritative and commanding, but it came out just as frazzled as she looked. "Show yourself, beast," she said with better control.

Laughter filled the chamber. "There's...there's something different about you, little one. Come closer, I want to see you more closely. My eyes are not what they used to be."

The young witch cautiously took a few more steps into the cavern. Most of the stalactites and stalagmites were on the outer edges of the chamber, leaving the center unobstructed. When she reached the center of the cavern she saw a pair of large glowing yellow eyes; what those eyes were attached to she couldn't see. She breathed in heavily as goose bumps ran up her arms and legs and she could feel the tiny hairs on the back of her neck rise. This place felt ancient. The smell of old dust and a faint odor of blood filled the air.

"Oh my, you are a beauty." The head came into view. "Much more pretty than your sister."

The dragon's head was large and had a mane of black and gray hair. Kira had a sudden surge of courage and dared to lock eyes with the ancient beast. The two of them stared for what seemed hours though the young witch knew it was only a minute.

The dragon sniffed the air between them. "They sent you here too early. You are not ready, but yet..."

"I am ready!" Kira said defiantly.

"Oh, child, you so are not." The large beast came fully into view. The Dragon-Mother had no wings and had a long body similar to a snake. The mane ran the length of the body along its back to the tip of her tail. She had six legs and claws as long as Kira was tall. The young witch could hardly believe that the beast could fit in the chamber. The Dragon-Mother picked Kira up and held her between two clawed fingers, holding her twenty feet off the ground.

Kira shook, her eyes went wide and she tried to pry herself loose. She was terrified. She didn't want to die. It was supposed to be an honorable death for those who didn't meet the standards of the tribal witches. *To hell with an honorable death, to hell with tradition, I want to live!* She continued to struggle herself free, but she couldn't match the dragon's strength. "I'm not afraid of you!" She blurted out in nervous terror.

A smile stretched across the Dragon-Mother's face, or at least Kira thought it was a smile. "Oh, child. I have been around a very long time. I have been called by many names." She shifted her bulk, which made Kira tense up.

"I have seen generation after generation of your tribe come through here, but you intrigue me." She paused a moment as if to access some hidden compartment in her brain. "The Tal family has always been rich with magic and you will be no different. I sense great power in you, Kira. You will become more powerful then both your sister and mother combined. No, I shall not eat you. The Tal family is stronger with you leading it. Your time will come, child. My eyes see great potential."

The dragon pricked one of its fingers on her other hand and a small bead of blood formed. "Drink, daught'r of the dragon. My gift to you. My life essence will awaken what lies dormant." Kira hesitated. *Why me?* She slowly leaned toward the blood and stopped. *What am I doing?* She shook her head to be rid of her doubts and drank. "Now sleep and when you awaken you will be in your own bed." *What did she mean, "daughter" of the dragon?* Before she could pull her head away from the bloodied claw she was asleep.

****

Kira hadn't dreamt or thought of her Gnoxel in years. She awoke in absolute darkness. This time it was different. She shook her head. Her hands were tied behind her back and there was a hood over her head. She could hear voices, speaking in a slave tongue. Two males, but she couldn't make out what they were talking about. They were referring to a game called poker, but she'd never heard of it. The voices grew closer. *Where am I? Why can't I remember?* She calmed herself with a little meditation. She tried to remove the hood with her knees, but she kept pulling dreads along with the hood; she needed her hands. The voices were almost on top of her. She heard the rustle of fabric, and then a faint hint of light. She sprung toward the light. Kira was only there for a moment before one of the men pulled the hood from her head. The two men stood side-by-side looking at her. The Mexican she remembered, but the other one she didn't know. There was something about him, though--he was no ordinary male. She thought she sensed something.

"Damn," Khayin said in perfect English.

Chapter 3   The Accomplice

The orange light of dawn slowly crept up over the horizon. Khayin could feel the heat of what the day would bring and the sun hadn't even shown its face. Khayin lit another cigarette and glanced at the captive in the cell wagon before nodding to Juan.

"Alright, Juan, let me go settle up and grab my gear." He took a long drag on his cigarette. "Grab that horse and put it next to Chewie over there." Khayin motioned toward his horse that was tied to an old cement pole.

"Chewie?" Juan asked.

"My horse, idjit. Then I'll give you a hand with her." He thumbed to the covered wagon. Juan just nodded.

Khayin finished his cigarette and flicked the butt. He stepped back into El Diablo's dank and stuffy interior. There were three patrons left but all of them seemed they were getting ready to call it a night. Maria hastily cleared off and cleaned tables. The bounty hunter made his way to the bar and tapped the counter to get the bartender's attention.

"How much do I owe ya?" Khayin asked as he untied his money pouch from his belt. Poker chips were the universal currency in the Americas.

The bartender was also the owner. His name was Jesus, which Khayin thought was hilarious considering the name of the bar. Jesus was a short, stout man with a gruff voice. Despite his look, which closely resembled a cartel muscleman, he was actually quite personable and good for conversation. He finished wiping a glass and walked over to Khayin. He stopped short a few feet away and squatted down below the bar. When he resurfaced a second later he held a small duffle bag. Jesus took the last few steps and dropped the bag onto the counter.

"Two hundred fifty chips," he said matter-of-factly.

Khayin fished out a couple chips for that amount plus a little extra and dropped them into Jesus' hand. "Thanks for the hospitality," he said with a tip of his hat. Jesus grinned and then quickly went back to work, disappearing into a back room.

Khayin opened his bag and started to rummage through it. Before he could strap on any gear he felt something wet, soft and heavy hit the back of his neck. A wet rag lay at his feet, and he turned to see Maria standing with her fists on her hips and wearing a scowl. They were the only two left in the bar.

"What's that for?" Khayin asked as he rubbed his now very wet neck.

"What were you thinking, grabbing my ass like that?" She scolded.

"The flirting was your idea, I was just playing the part," he defended.

"The part of what? A dick? An asshole? Come on, you're better than the usual scum that comes in here." The scowl melted from her face.

"Me? You're the one that was hanging all over me, practically shoving your cleavage in my face." He regretted the words before they fully came out of his mouth, but the lack of sleep and being slightly drunk from the horrid whiskey did him no favors.

Her face turned red and she started toward him. "What'd you say?"

"Nothing." Khayin nervously recoiled from her approach, but his back was against the bar and he wasn't going anywhere. "I said nothing. Really. I'm sorry."

"I spent the last seven hours slipping you cards and peeking at hands and you have the nerve..."

He didn't let her finish. "I'm stupid and all the other things you called me. I'm sorry. You were a great partner and I couldn't have done this without you." His expression was pleading. He truly was sorry and this episode was just a reminder of why he didn't make it a habit of prolonging games—he got stupid.

"Khayin, if I didn't know you as well as I do..." she started.

"I know, you don't have to say it." He reached behind him and grabbed one of the bags of chips. He handed the bag to her. "Here, take it. You earned it."

"Don't insult me. You can't buy me off like some puta." Her face remained fierce, but her fists relaxed and fell from her hips.

"That's not what I'm trying to do and you know it."

"Yep, I know it, but you will not live this one down, gilipollas." Maria swiftly closed the gap between them and grabbed the bag. "Is there really a bounty of a Hag out there?"

"I don't know what she is, but there's something fishy about that poster. Whoever or whatever she is, she is better off with me than with Juan." He looked toward the door.

"I agree. You planning on taking her in?" she asked.

"Where?" Khayin shook his head. "No, I think I'll check in with Codex, see if she knows anything."

"Sounds like a good idea." She bent over and picked up the wet rag she threw at him earlier. "I'm not apologizing for throwing this at you. I should kick your culo."

"And I'd deserve it."

"Damn straight." She smiled and went back to work.

Khayin wondered if in another time, another place, if circumstances were different, if he and Maria would have ended up together. He liked her, maybe too much, but...He shook his head to clear his mind of a life of love and settling down.

Khayin started to pull out weapons from his bag and strapped them on. Two .44 Magnum Revolvers, six throwing knives, two bolas for those pesky runaway marks, two kukri daggers, and an ancient looking dagger made of a human femur. All but the bolas had a secure and efficient place on his body. His weapons were too valuable to him to leave them with his horse. Things had a way of disappearing in this town.

Before he walked out the door Khayin got a sudden flash of images. His falcon showed him what chaos was starting to brew outside. The falcon had been a gift from a Native American medicine man, and he and the falcon had bonded almost immediately. Khayin could see through his eyes and give him simple commands. The bird of prey was just out front watching a fight unfold. He saw Juan lying prone on the ground beneath the now open door to the cell wagon and two men dragging out a kicking and flailing woman, the Schadovitch Hag. One other man stood back toward the entrance to the bar watching.

Khayin checked himself over one last time before he exited. The dawn's morning sun peeked out just a bit over the horizon. It was much brighter than it had been earlier. He squinted toward the scene just as the woman screamed. It was clear that she was screaming not out of fear, but in anger. No, rage. She was yelling something at the top of her lungs, but Khayin couldn't make it out, even with his magic earring, a wonder that translated all languages spoken from him or to him. He wasn't going to wait to find out what she was saying.

Khayin stood there, twenty paces from the entrance to the bar. Thanks to his falcon he saw everything and everyone.

"So, which one of you idjits thought that this was a good idea?" Khayin lit another cigarette. The two men who carried the woman did a poor job. She was putting up one hell of a fight. One of the men, wearing a cowboy hat, held her upper body. He hooked his arms under her armpits and lifted her. The other man, who wore pea green coveralls, was trying to hold her feet. His face was a bloody mess and he only had a grip on one leg. Khayin had to stifle a laugh. The two men just glared at the bounty hunter.

"She killed Juan, bounty hunter." The voice came from behind him, but Khayin didn't turn around. "She deserves to be punished," the voice said as if that was the only explanation required.

Khayin looked at Juan's body splayed out on the ground beneath the wagon. He took a drag from his cigarette and flicked some ash onto the ground. "A captive who seizes an opportunity to take out their captor..." he said plainly. "You'd do the same if roles were reversed, would you not?"

"If there was a bounty on her then there must be a reason. In this case a criminal killed a lawman." The voice sounded confident.

"Juan was far from a lawman. He was barely a bounty hunter." He took another drag.

"Doesn't give her the right to kill him," the voice said in disgust.

"But you're no lawman neither, and I see no judge and jury. Who are you to be passing off judgment? Besides, she is my bounty, and therefore my responsibility, not yours." The tip of the cigarette glowed orange as he inhaled.

"Sorry, senor. This is happening. Don't," there was a slight pause, "get in our way."

Khayin closed his eyes to see through the falcon's. The man behind him held a crossbow aimed at the back of his neck. Khayin shook his head.

"Here's how this is going to go down," Khayin began. "Mr. Voice is going to come down with a lethal case of lead poisoning. Mr. Hat is going to find it hard to see though steel. And, if Mr. Coveralls is smart, he'd run as soon as I drop my cigarette butt." There was a long moment of silence. Even the witch was speechless and let her body go slack.

The air was still. The morning light painted beautiful colors in the eastern sky. A small bead of sweat formed on Khayin's brow. *Man I need a shower.* He dropped the butt and he followed the cigarette down until he was in a squatting position drawing a pistol and a knife along the way. He aimed up at Mr. Voice's head. He pulled the trigger. The bullet shot from the barrel and only slowed when passing through his target's skull. A brilliant spray of blood and gray matter painted the sky behind Mr. Voice, leaving nothing in its wake. Khayin spun around to face the other two men. He threw the knife in his other hand and it flew true. The throwing knife embedded itself in Mr. Hat's left eye, killing him instantly.

Mr. Coveralls wasted no time. He dropped the girl's leg and ran as soon as he heard the pistol fire, but he didn't foresee how fast the bounty hunter was. Before he could get more than a few feet his partner fell, which freed the witch. She hit the ground, but immediately pounced on the man, taking him down. She punched him repeatedly in the head, then clasped her hands around his throat and squeezed the life out of him. His eyes bulged as he gasped for air.

Khayin reloaded his pistol as he walked toward the woman strangling Mr. Coveralls. The body stopped twitching by the time he reached them. She sat there a moment with her hands still around his neck as if she wasn't entirely sure if he was dead. Khayin looked at her more closely now that there was better light. Her red dreads fell down to mid-back and he noticed a collar around her neck with the same anti-magic sigils as the cell wagon.

She snapped her gaze to Khayin, her hair whipping her face. He could see that same rage as before. He lit another cigarette, and held out his tin to her.

"Want one?" he asked. She just stared. "Suit yourself." He put the tin in an inner pocket. "Let's say we get out of here before any locals come to see what happened." She remained still and never took her gaze off of Khayin. "Look, I've got no clue why you're here or how on god's green earth that hack Juan even captured you, but we need to get out of here. I know you've no reason to trust me, but how about I don't put you back in that cage and I'll let you ride with me." She said nothing.

"I know you understand me, the magic in my earring translates it. You look like you've a good head on your shoulders and probably can spot a liar, so," he squatted down next to her, "look into my eyes and see if I'm lying." He made a focused effort to look directly into her eyes. "You're safe with me. Besides, where are you going to go? Let's get out of here before more people than I can handle show up. I know a place we can hang low."

The witch nodded. Khayin knew better than to try to help her up. The two of them walked to his horses. The horse he had won from Juan was a young white and brown mare. The witch jumped up into the saddle like a pro. Khayin couldn't help but grin. He secured his duffle bag to his saddle and climbed up.

"My name is Khayin, but most people call me 'Caine'. This here," he patted his horse, "is Chewie. And this..." He whistled and his falcon flew over and landed on a leather bracer Khayin was wearing on his right forearm. "This is Millennium." His smile couldn't get any bigger. He was obviously amused with himself. "Get it?" He waited a moment. She just stared at him. "His name is Millennium, and he's a falcon. Millennium falcon, the Millennium Falcon." As if repeating himself was going to help her understand. She only stared at him. "Never mind," he said in defeat. "Let's go." They spurred their mounts and headed north.

Chapter 4 The Church

As the odd pair traveled north, Mexico City shrank behind them. She didn't know how she felt...relieved, nervous, scared. Kira had no idea where she was, let alone where this man was taking her. To his credit though, he didn't try talking to her. She was unsure of her situation. Unsure of him. Khayin. She looked at him. Kira was riding slightly behind and on his left. She could see his profile, though some of his face was obscured by his hat. This man, Khayin, wasn't as cruel as the Mexican. Maybe he might help. Help get her home. For now she would wait.

As they rode, a large shadow covered them. Kira looked up and saw a large winged dragon flying overhead. It had dark blue scales that glistened in the sun above it. The large beast was a breathtaking sight and it paid them no mind. *I've never seen a winged dragon.* She was nearly awestruck; her eyes widened and her mouth fell slightly open.

A few hours went by and the only sound was the wind and their horses' shoes. They hadn't run into any other travelers; they were completely alone. She reached up and touched the collar around her neck. It was cold, and she traced the sigils with her fingers. She tugged and played with it, more out of anxiety than any hopes of taking it off.

Khayin grabbed a knife from his belt and handed it to her. She just looked at it then him. "For your collar." He gestured with the knife. "I doubt it'll work, but you could give it a try." She took the knife and attempted to cut the collar off to no avail. She handed him the knife back and shook her head. "Well, now we know." He took the knife and sheathed it.

"There's a word. A...magic word, or key word, whatever you want to call it. Unfortunately I don't have the word. Juan, the Mexican with the big-ass hat?" Khayin paused. She looked up at him and gave a very small nod. "He knew the word." She frowned. As if he caught her expression he said, "Don't worry though, we'll figure it out. I got some pretty cool friends, or at least people who owe me favors." He winked at her.

"Why?" she asked in an almost whisper. She betrayed no emotion. She wasn't sure she could, or even wanted to trust him.

"Why what?" Khayin caught her eyes. "You're smart enough to know why he slapped that necklace around your pretty little neck."

Pretty? "No." She kept the eye contact. "Why did you help me?" Her accent was exotic, a cross between Brazilian, Spanish, and something more ancient. She still showed no emotion, despite her anxiety. "You killed those men and put yourself at risk for me. Why?"

"Tell you what. I'll be more than happy to answer your questions. In fact I'd be giddy as a school girl, because I've got questions for you too. But not here. Let's not talk on the road. The village is just ahead and I can get us some food, water and a much needed bath. I can probably persuade the Padre for some clean clothes too, and then we can talk all night if you want." Khayin smiled. She liked his smile, but she stifled any betrayal of that before it surfaced. Kira just stared at him.

He was right, they were at the small village within minutes. The largest building was a church, she found out later--a place where people go to worship their god. The other buildings were mostly huts or shacks that were used as homes. There were people out and working and some even playing. She could feel their eyes on her. The midday sun was high in the sky. Khayin led them to the large building before jumping off his horse and tying the tethers to a pole outside the church. Kira did the same.

"Padre!?" Khayin called as he walked through the doors.

The building consisted of only a few rooms, the largest of

which they currently were standing in. The room was furnished with long benches all facing a small platform on the other end of the room. A large man entered from a door near the platform. He wore long pants and a short sleeved button down shirt. He had a pistol holstered on his hip and a very large knife strapped to his other hip. The man smiled as soon as he saw them.

"Khayin," he said enthusiastically. The two men embraced. Kira grunted. She was not used to seeing men so...happy. It kind of disgusted her. Men were slaves. They lived only to serve and mate. This was all wrong and it made her even more homesick.

"Padre, this is my...er...friend? Uh...traveling companion? Balls! I never got your name, sweetheart." Khayin gestured toward her.

"What did you call me?" she snapped. Her hands balled up into fists and her face flashed red.

"Fuck, sorry. I just never asked you your name and I...you know what? Nevermind." He turned his attention back to the holy man. "We need shelter, food, rest and a bath. Uh, yes please, a bath."

"Sure, friend. Follow me." He led them to one of the rooms in the back. The holy man muttered something to Khayin as they walked that Kira couldn't make out. "I'm sorry, all I have is the one room. I use the other one." He looked at Kira when he said that. Her anger melted some. "I can run you a hot bath and get some food and water for you as you wash. I'll also procure some fresher clothes. Nobody wants to put dirty clothes on after getting clean." He smiled and walked off.

While Khayin unloaded a handful of things from his horse, the holy man made the first bath. After he left the room Kira didn't wait, she disrobed immediately and stepped in to the warm water. She noticed a small pile of clothing set to the side as she lowered herself into the liquid heaven. She had neglected to close the door and when she heard a noise, she managed to catch a quick glimpse of Khayin closing the door and taking care not to look at her. *Hmm, he didn't bother to stare.*

Kira just laid back and relaxed. She closed her eyes and succumbed to the tranquility of the quiet and pleasure of the pseudo freedom. After a few minutes she washed and rinsed. She took great care to wash her dreads thoroughly and dried them carefully. Kira stood in the room stark naked. The room was warm and a light breeze came from an open window. She glided over to the stack of clothes and found a pair of camouflage pants, a white tank top, a t-shirt with a drawing of a hairy muscular man with metal blades coming out of his hands, a pair of socks and a pair of boots. They all fit remarkably well.

She entered the big room to see the holy man and Khayin talking. They both stopped and looked at her.

"Damn, girl. You clean up well," Khayin remarked. She frowned.

The holy man broke the budding tension. "I have a collection of bras in the room where you'll be sleeping. I wasn't about to guess your...uh...size." She looked at him quizzically. "Bras?" He gestured by cupping his hands where breasts would be on himself. "We used to get missionaries come through here and leave clothes and other amenities, so keep whatever you use," he said joyfully. "While you," he looked at Khayin, "take a bath I'll get some food together." He stood up.

"Thanks, Padre." Khayin nodded. The padre shrugged and exited the church.

Khayin stood and walked over to the bathroom, but stopped and looked at Kira. They stood only a few feet apart. Khayin was around six foot she guessed, which made him about five inches taller than her. She had to look up slightly to catch his gaze. They just stared a moment. She saw no malice, no ill feelings toward her at all. He must be hiding it. He wants something. He smiled.

"Kira," she said as she walked away.

Kira examined the bras and after many trial and error attempts she found a few that fit. She both disliked and liked them. They weren't the most comfortable articles of clothing, but she thought she understood their purpose. Some of them were still in their original packaging, but she couldn't read the language, so she only had the pictures to go by. She decided to try one for a while before she discarded the idea altogether. Khayin had finished his bath and knocked on the door to the room she was in.

"Kira," he called from beyond the closed door. "Are you decent?"

"Come in," she responded, a little too nice than what she would have liked. *Cursed. I won't start liking him.* He is male.

He opened the door and stood just outside it. He wore blue jeans and a white long sleeved shirt. He had the same black leather vest from before, but only carried a few of his weapons. He had also put on his old pair of boots and his hat.

"The padre has some food. He set up a table outside. Come on out when you're ready," he said.

Kira just nodded and she watched him turn and leave. She looked around the room, finally taking notice of it. It was a small room compared to the central room and there were two beds and a dresser. She walked over to the single window in the room and looked outside.

"Why can't I remember what happened to me? Why am I here? Who was that Mexican? And who is Khayin?" She balled her hands into fists. "I have to convince him to get me home. I don't like it here. I need my sisters. I must get home," she said in frustration, "but I have no idea where home is." She took a deep breath to calm herself then went outside to join the men.

****

Sometime later, well after the meal, the holy man retired and left Kira and Khayin alone. The night air was beginning to cool and Khayin had started a fire. Some of the kids in the village came over to the fire and Khayin was roasting some treats for them. It was only when most of the village had retreated to their homes for the evening that Kira initiated the inevitable conversation.

"Why?" she repeated from their earlier talk, as though no time had passed.

"Oh yeah," he responded like he was just remembering. He pulled a folded sheet of paper from a pocket and handed it to her.

She took the paper and unfolded it to see a crude drawing of a woman. She recognized numbers, but she couldn't read the words. Khayin handed her a pair of glasses. She shrugged and put them on before looking back to the parchment. The words suddenly legible, she saw that it was a wanted poster that offered a reward to the individual who brought in the 'Nighthag'. She had heard that term for her people before.

Her gaze fell on Khayin. "Is this supposed to be me?" she asked.

"Hell should I know. Juan seemed to think so." Khayin rolled a cigarette and lit it with the fire between them.

She looked back to the poster. "Is this a lot of money?"

"Decent amount. I've collected bounties much higher, but they were pretty high profile. The Schadovitch are a myth, legend, folklore. I've never heard a believable story from anyone who had supposedly met one." He took a drag from his cigarette.

"They are real." She paused to let that sink in. "I..." She stopped herself, she didn't want to reveal too much, but she knew it really didn't matter.

"No shit. Fuck. I mean, I'd a feeling, but...shit." He was genuinely surprised, she saw it on his face. He hadn't tried to hide it.

A long moment passed. "Well, gorjcha. What does this mean? You planning on collecting this bounty?" She gave him a stare that screamed 'Over my dead body'.

"Every sanctioned bounty has the Syndicate seal, or mark. If you wanted to place a bounty on someone you go through the Syndicate. Not all hunters work for the Syndicate, in fact most don't, but it's the best way to guarantee payment. A bounty hunter sees a poster with the appropriate mark and they know it is a legit hunt so there won't be any complications when receiving payment." He took another drag. "You follow me so far?" She nodded. "Not only does that poster have a kid's drawing of one of your people, but there is no Syndicate mark."

"So it isn't a sanctioned hunt," she deduced, waving the poster in the air.

"Exactly. So my questions are, where'd Juan get it and who posted it? Juan wasn't a very smart man and he was a mediocre hunter at best, so how'd he get the drop on you and where was he taking you?" He inhales through his cigarette and blows out circles of smoke. "I've no interest in collecting that bounty, but I do want to know the answers to those questions."

"I can't remember how I ended up in that cell or in the custody of the Mexican." She hated to reveal that to him. Kira was relieved to know that Khayin wasn't going to pick up where the other hunter left off, but she didn't want to expose any kind of weakness to him either. She tried searching for the best way to tell him she wanted to go home and that she could only reach home with some help. She settled on the direct approach.

"I need to get home. You must help me get there. I don't know where I am and I have no idea where to even begin to find my way there." It wasn't a plea. It was more like a command and it didn't go unnoticed.

"Whoa! I don't 'must' take you anywhere. And if you try to leave without me you won't last but a few days out there with that thing around your neck," Khayin snapped.

"I must get home, gorjcha. For someone to make such a poster they know more about us than my sisters wish to be known. I have to warn them." This time it came out a little more like a plea, but it held a commanding tone.

"Look, I have no clue where your people are, so let's take this one step at a time. I know a few people. Let me do some investigating. Also, you are a liability as long as you are wearing that necklace, so we need to get that thing off you. In the meantime...what weapons can you use?"

Chapter 5   The Call

What the fuck am I doing? What've I gotten myself into? This isn't me. This is going to cost me money, not make me any.

Kira slept on a cot across the room with her back to him. He was conflicted. Khayin could just leave her, forget all that had happened and continue to Chi-Town, but no, he couldn't do that. There were too many unanswered questions, and truth be told he had always been a sucker for the damsel in distress, though he knew if he ever called her that she would cut his balls off. He shuddered.

The sun had not risen and the sky was still dark. Khayin was a little apprehensive about sleeping in the same room as her, but something in his gut told him she wouldn't do anything. He was hopeful that he was right. Before they turned in for the night Khayin had given her a bow and a large Bowie knife.

Khayin left the room quietly and went outside. He stretched and called for Millennium, who appeared in the dark sky and flew to his arm. He looked at the bird of prey and smiled. The falcon nodded. Khayin remembered back to the Native American hermit in the northern Michigan woods who had gifted him with the magic that bonded man and bird. Sometimes Khayin would take side jobs. His tracking skills were useful for other things than bounties and Khayin would sometimes take unconventional payments--not everyone had need of chips.

"Looks like we've got a partner, old pal, at least for the short term. I just hope it isn't a ticking time bomb." He jerked his arm ever so slightly and Millennium flew off.

Khayin jogged until the light of dawn decorated the once dark sky. When he arrived back to the village he found the padre cooking breakfast and Kira sitting cross legged on the ground off to the side of the church building in a state of meditation. Despite the coolness of morning Khayin was damp with sweat. He walked past the padre and nodded, then entered the church. He went to the room where he had slept the night before and dried himself. He put on the rest of his clothes and packed the rest of his things.

"You staying for breakfast at least?" the padre asked as he saw Khayin emerge from the building.

"Of course, but then we need to leave. I really appreciate your hospitality, padre." Khayin walked past the man and threw his bags onto Chewie.

Kira had finished her morning meditations and saw Khayin packing his horse. She walked straight for him. The look on her face unnerved Khayin slightly and he had to suppress an urge to reach for one of his many weapons. She stopped only a few feet away from him. Catching a hint of rosemary and sage that scented her hair, he breathed in deeply through the nose.

"We leaving?" she asked pointedly.

"After we eat," he gestured toward the padre. "Then you pack while I make a call." She cocked her head slightly with a raised eyebrow. Khayin's eyes and smile went big while he held up his hands, palms forward, and he wiggled his fingers. "Magic." She snarled and brushed past him.

The three of them ate in silence. The smell of the bacon and the budding of dawn was serene. Khayin and Kira finished then prepared for their journey. Khayin fished out the pre-Cataclysm flip-phone that Codex had given him, flipping it open and pressing the send button like Codex had shown him.

"Snuggly Bear!!!" A girl's voice screeched over the communicator. "OMG. You aren't going to believe this. Some guys came by from Chicago and they were asking all sorts of questions about a hunter named Juan Rodriguez. Do you know him? Anyway, I told them he rarely checks in and that I haven't seen or heard from him in a long time. They didn't want to believe me, but I put my foot down and said 'you better believe me' and they were like 'If you are lying to us we will make your life a living hell.' Can you believe that they had the nerve to threaten me in my domain? Ha! I laughed right in their face." The words came so fast that she was nearly impossible to understand. She paused for what seemed like a long time compared to the pace of her monologue. "So, how can I help you, Snuggly Bear?" she asked in a calm regular clip.

Khayin felt like he had to catch his breath. He spoke to her regularly and he thought that he would be used to it, but every time he ended up breathing hard. "Hey, Baby Doll. I have some questions for you, but I think we need to talk face to face."

"Sure, Snuggly Bear. Believe it or not I have some time right now," she continued in an easily understandable rate.

"I'm just outside Mexico City. There's no way I can get to you today." Khayin said.

"Silly goose. Just hit the 26339 keys on the number pad, then hit send. It'll take you straight to me," she giggled.

"I have a couple of horses and a passenger," Khayin rationalized.

"You have a bounty? I've no record of you taking a job." She sounded confused.

"No. No bounty just..." He wasn't sure how or what he wanted to say, but before he could even finish, a sharp gasp interrupted his thought.

"Do you have a girl with you? I always said you needed a girl. You are such a handsome man, but you live a dangerous life. You need a woman in your life to settle you down. I'd find you someone but I'm always so busy. You travel so much and I find it hard to believe that you would ever settle down, but maybe you should settle down. It might do you some good. You know my mommy used to say that a man needs a good woman to keep him grounded. You need to be grounded." She snorted a laugh then continued her rapid staccato. "I don't really mean grounded, like sent to your room or nothin'. Just grounded like morally and stuff so you don't do anythin' stupid, you know..."

"Codex!" Khayin nearly shouted. "You know I can't do that,"

he said more calmly.

"Can't or won't." She had a bit of a snip in her tone. "It's better to love and lose it, than never to love at all. Isn't that what they use to say?"

"I'm not going to have this conversation again."

"Screw that curse, Khayin. Have you even tried to break it? Cause you never have asked me." He could hear a little pout in her voice.

"Codex, please. Not now."

"Hmpf, fine, Snuggly Bear." She was back to a normal pace again. "The teleport will take you and one other person and some of your gear or all of your gear, depends on how much you have. Just be sure to be touching the other person. Appropriately."

"I'm not going to be popping in there cupping some woman's breasts, Codex," he said with a roll of the eyes.

She laughed loud and genuine. "You always make me laugh. See you in a few minutes then?"

"See you in a few minutes," he confirmed. She giggled and the line went dead.

Khayin turned to see Kira standing behind him. Her face wore a scowl and her arms were crossed across her chest. A couple of long dreads fell in her face and she didn't bother to brush them aside. She wore the same clothes that she had after her bath. The same clothes she slept in. He wasn't sure how much of the conversation she actually heard or even if she were able to hear Codex.

"It was a joke. I wasn't even thinking about touching your breasts." He stopped a moment and rethought what he just said. "OK, so, I have thought about touching your breasts, but I would never touch you without your permission." The scowl remained. "So, you finished packing? Cause we have to leave, like now." He said with a desperate attempt to change the subject.

Kira turned and walked toward the horses. If there was a bright side, she wasn't storming off, and her walk was casual. Khayin followed and despite the awkward moment they had shared a moment ago he couldn't help but watch her walk away.

The padre adjusted the saddles and bags on the horses when

they returned to the church. Nearby, the children of the village were playing soccer, probably waiting for their breakfasts, their mothers having shooed them out the door so they could cook without them underfoot. Khayin paused to watch the children, reminding himself why he never stayed long in the village. He never wanted to take a chance that it would be marked as a safe haven for him, therefore making it a target if anyone ever were to come after him seeking revenge.

"We're not taking the horses, padre," Khayin said as he approached him. "Keep them. Consider them payment for services rendered." Kira shot him a questioning glance. "The teleport is only meant for two." He looked at Kira. "Take whatever you can fit in the saddle bags."

Khayin reached for his bags and flung them over his shoulder. "You can keep anything we leave behind. I won't ask for them back. You're a good friend, Padre." Khayin reached out for a hand shake and got a hug instead.

"Thank you and may the good Lord bless you," the padre said and broke off the embrace with a couple of back slaps.

"I think I could use a blessing or two from any god out there right about now. I have a bad feeling about this." Khayin looked at his old friend. "Codex mumbled something about men from Chicago looking for Juan. That can't be good."

"I can't say I know this Codex or your line of work well, but I do know that it is a risky business. Take care, my friend. And keep that one safe." He motioned toward Kira. "I've a feeling the two of you are going to need each other. The good Lord put the two of you together for a reason." Khayin just nodded.

Kira approached the holy man. Her head was down and she fidgeted, wringing her hands. "Thank you," she said with effort.

"For what, child?" The padre clasped her hand in his.

"For the sage and rosemary." She met his eyes.

"You're welcome, but do me a favor." She remained silent. "Keep an eye on our mutual friend. I fear your journey won't be easy and he is going to need you more than he cares to admit."

She gave the padre a nod. Kira stood with her saddle bags over her shoulder and waited for Khayin. Khayin walked over to

Kira and he smiled. He didn't want her to see any anxiety he might have about their situation. Truth be told, he was starting to reconsider leaving her. *What's going on? Is Chi-Town looking for Kira? What've I gotten myself into?* More questions and still no answers. He looked at the witch. She stood confident, despite her situation. She looked a little annoyed, but Khayin figured that was for lack of understanding and memory. She obviously didn't trust him, but he was starting to think that it wasn't necessarily him she distrusted, but men in general.

"Well, for this teleport to work we need to..." Before he could finish she grabbed his free hand. She was gentle, but firm. She just looked at him, no expression.

"We have to be touching," she said.

He couldn't sense any coldness in her tone, or warmth for that matter, but at least she wasn't pissed. He flipped open the communicator, punched in 26339 and hit send.

Chapter 6   The Strip

The first thing she noticed was a little pain shooting up through her arm from the hand that held Khayin's. Kira looked up at Khayin and noticed a look of unease wash over his face. She couldn't help but smile. Next, she studied the area around her. Tall structures lined the side of the road, some lit with lights so bright that they could still be easily seen in the light of day. Some lights spelled out words in a language she had yet to learn. She could speak several languages, but never bothered to learn to read them. There was always a spell or artifact for that.

The road was paved. There were people everywhere--women dressed in barely-there clothing, men with carts selling food and other wares. There were also men and women dressed in matching outfits carrying batons. Some carried crossbows, others compound bows like hers. She saw a few with guns. Khayin had given her a quick lesson on different types of weaponry and she recognized the firearms right away. She was so enraptured of her surroundings that she didn't realize that she was still holding Khayin's hand. She snatched it away quickly.

"What is this place?" she asked.

"Sin City. The City of Lights. The Entertainment Capital of the World." He threw his hands up in the air and spun around. "The Strip is where we stand. At least that's what it was called before the Cataclysm. Now, well, now it's a shadow of its old self, but still one of the largest cities in North America and probably the city with the most working lights, so I guess 'The City of Lights' is still an accurate name." He looked around before settling his gaze on her. Kira barely noticed as she just absorbed it all.

"Cataclysm. When magic returned to your world?" She asked the question, though she wasn't really all that interested in the answer. There was too much to see.

"Yeah, we'll have to talk about that sometime. I'd like to hear your version of it," he said still looking at her. She only nodded.

"Why are we here?"

"Answers to some of our questions, hopefully." He sounded unsure of himself.

"You don't sound very convincing." She shot him a skeptical eye.

"Yeah sorry, princess. I'm not confidant we're going to get many answers here. That poster wasn't official, which means it was a private contract. If it was private, not too many people will know about it. On the bright side we should be able to get that collar off ya." He started to walk down the street.

"How's any of that going to get me home? And don't call me princess," she said with a little disgust.

"Right. Home. Well, I doubt anyone here would have a clue. You are a myth. Your people..."

"Sisters," she said cutting him off.

"Your sisters," he said with air quotes, "and you only exist in stories. And stories get embellished over time. No one here would have reliable information. I'll have to make contact with another friend of mine. He should have a better idea, especially with you walking in next to me."

He led them across the street. She noticed more than a few of the underdressed women making eyes, both at her and Khayin. A couple of them even tried touching her, but she was quick and managed to dodge most of the gropes except one. When Kira felt someone slap her ass, she turned to retaliate. She was surprised, though, to see only a young girl staring up at her and smiling. Out of the corner of her eye she saw a large man emerging from a nearby alley and walking slowly toward them, his eye not leaving her. It was only then that she noticed her hand raised, ready to strike the girl. Khayin must have noticed too because he grabbed Kira's hand and moved down the street a little more quickly. She didn't protest.

They briskly walked further down the strip, but Khayin slowed when they noticed a couple of big men tossing another man out of an alley. He looked badly beaten. Blood ran from his nose or mouth. It was hard to tell which, so covered was his face with it. When the man stumbled to an upright position, he held a mangled hand against his chest and limped slowly away. The two giant men, their bodies covered in hair and unnaturally muscled, looked casually at Kira and Khayin before disappearing back down the alley.

When Khayin continued walking, Kira was shocked to see him turning down the same alley the men had. She tensed, her hands in fists, but followed him with curiosity. He seemed to know where he was going. The alley was long and well-lit, and about wide enough for four people to walk side by side. It was clean and mostly empty. She could see the two men ahead of them, and they continued to follow at a distance until they reached a simple black door in the side of the building.

Khayin kept walking, Kira following behind, until they were at the door beside the giants. Khayin reached out to open the door, unconcerned by their presence. One of the big guys put his arm out to stop the bounty hunter, but Khayin just looked at him. The other large man nodded his head and they both stepped back, allowing their entrance.

"Ogres," Khayin said. "They're not too bright, but they make excellent guards."

The door opened into a long hall. Kira could see no light source, but the hall was brightly lit. There were no doors on either side, and the hall seemed to go on forever. After a few minutes of walking she finally spotted a door on the far end. The door opened as soon as they approached, and they stepped through.

The room was empty but for a desk that sat at its center and the well-dressed man who sat behind it. He appeared to be wearing a black tuxedo, and the room smelled of fresh flowers. It was lit in the same peculiar way as the hall they had just left. Kira turned to look back the way they came and found herself staring at a blank wall; the door was no longer there. Kira turned back around as a sudden panic washed over her. A quick scan of the room revealed that there were no doors at all.

Kira grabbed Khayin's sleeve and tugged at it. "Where are the doors? How do we get out of here?" Her movements were jerky and she was on high alert. Khayin smiled and patted her arm, trying to reassure her that everything was okay. She moved away so that he ended up patting empty air.

The man behind the desk practically glowed as he greeted Khayin. "There's my handsome man."

"Hey, Stephen. It's been awhile. How's Rocco?" Khayin asked.

"Oh, he's fabulous, but you know I'd drop him like an ugly fedora for you. Just say the word and you and I can travel the world together." He spoke with a child-like voice, as if he had never hit puberty.

"As tempting as that sounds we have two problems: Rocco wouldn't rest till he tracked us down and kicked my ass, which I have no doubt he could and would do. And Codex--well, no one wants to see her bad side and you would probably see more of it than I would," he reasoned.

Stephen's face grew brighter. "Ain't that right." He gave Kira an analyzing look. "And who is this lovely creature? Are you cheating on me?"

"This is Kira. She's why I'm here. And I'm not sure how much I should say right now."

"Hmpf," Stephen grunted, obviously not happy with that answer. He made a little shooing type wave at a door that Kira knew hadn't been there a minute ago. "Go right in; she's waiting for you."

First thing Kira noticed upon entering the office was the overwhelming presence of magic. It was nearly palpable. Beyond that, the room was hopelessly cluttered. Kira wasn't familiar with the tools of cultures outside her own, but the room in which she stood was packed with all sorts of interesting things. She saw strange silver boxes with glass on one side. Devices much like the one Khayin had used to call Codex were scattered about. More of those light signs she saw outside on the buildings sat on the floor and other flat surfaces, but these were much smaller. She didn't know what any of it was or how they worked, and while she was curious, she was far more interested in the person before her.

A girl sat behind a desk looking at one of those boxes and clicking a board with letters on it in front of her. The magic she felt was definitely radiating from this girl.

Finally, a woman of real power! Is the world I'm in now run by men?

The magic woman's hair was blonde and she wore it in side tails. Her make-up was heavy, with dark eyes and red lips. The sweater she wore covered the top half of her torso, leaving her stomach bare. Kira couldn't see through the desk, so she had no idea what this girl-woman wore below the waist. She was chattering quickly into a small black box, and there was no indication that she noticed them.

"No, Mom. I told him he needed to come back with the money. I don't do charity cases. He gave me some sob story about a sick wife. Which was a lie, cause he hits on me every time he sees me. No, he might have a wife. I just find it hard to believe he cares for her if he is hitting on me. And as soon as I told him that, he switched gears and said it was a sick mother. I told him that he told me his mother was dead. And we went in circles for a while, but when he finally realized I wasn't buying his shit he pulled a weapon on me. ME! Can you believe it? So, I kicked his ass out. And had Huey and Dewy rough him up a little for good measure. I can't have people thinking they can get away with pulling weapons on me, like he would've been able to get close enough to use it anyway," she said in one breath.

The rapid speech surprised Kira. She was grateful she understood the language spoken, but disheartened that she still couldn't decipher it on account of how tightly the words were strung together. She looked at Khayin who was smiling at the girl with the blonde hair.

Codex suddenly snapped to attention. "Look, Mommy. I gotta go, bye," she said looking at Khayin. "Snuggly Bear!" She jumped up and over the desk, then wrapped her arms around the bounty

The Malevolent Witch

hunter.

Kira could clearly see the girl now. She was about her height and wore a pleated skirt that stopped mid-thigh. She had knee high stockings and she wore canvas shoes with rubber soles. Kira looked at Khayin, confused. Men were slaves. Servants. This felt so foreign to her and made her all the more homesick.

"OMG! How was your trip? Was it fun? It's always fun, otherwise you wouldn't be doin' what you're doin'. Right? How was Mexico City? I heard the cartel has gotten a lot stronger there. Fernando Sanchez runs a tight ship. He's got a lot bigger army than the government down there, but that isn't sayin' much. The government went to shit after the Cataclysm. The cartel is the true power down there. It will be a scary day when Fernando gets his own wizard." Codex stopped and looked at Kira for the first time, eyeing her up and down. "Well, what do we have here?"

"What are you looking at?" Kira teetered on confusion and anger. She didn't like the expression on Codex's face.

"Oh, you're cute." Codex walked over to her and stopped only a foot from her. Kira watched her eyes scanning her like she was a bauble on display for sale. "Is she for me?" she asked.

"Sorry, Baby Doll."

"Hmm...Too bad." Codex stopped suddenly and went back to her chair behind the desk. "So, what do you have for me?" she said as if Kira wasn't even there. "I assume she is part of what you wanted to talk about?"

Khayin pulled the wanted poster from a pocket inside his vest and handed it to Codex. She unfolded it, studying it for a moment before reaching into a drawer and pulling out a pair of glasses. She flipped it over to look at the blank back with the same scrutiny as she gave the front. She turned it back over and stared at it again, then she looked directly at Kira.

"Hmm...Terrible likeness," she said as she looked from the poster to Kira's face and back again.

"Probably because they've no idea what the Schadovitch look like," Khayin responded.

"This could be anyone." Codex studied the poster and Kira. "Where did you get it? It's not like you to go on an unsanctioned hunt."

"Funny thing. I won it in a poker game," Khayin said smiling. "From Juan Rodriguez."

"You shittin' me?" She gave Khayin an astonished look. "You won a girl in a game?" She said that last part with a frown.

"No." He shook his head slightly. "I'm not shittin' you. And you know I don't look at it that way." He looked at Kira. "I couldn't let Juan keep her. Who knows what he was up to."

"Interesting." She looked back to the poster. "Can you leave this with me? Let me dig into it, see what I can find."

"Sure, it's not like I'm going to need it. How much?" Khayin reached for his money pouch.

"Oh, please." She shook her head.

"Thanks." He put his money away. "Also, can you recommend anyone to remove her collar?"

"Yes, but do you really want to?" Codex finally took her eyes off the poster and looked at Kira. "No offense, sweetheart, but I'm only looking out for my friend. Can we trust you?"

Kira's mouth opened to answer, but Khayin cut her off. "Yeah, I think I can trust her. I think we want the same thing right now. Plus, I can handle myself." Kira didn't know what to think. *Is he for real? He trusts me? Is he that skilled or is he just stupid?*

"Ha! Famous last words." Codex laughed. "Outside Vegas, there's a town called Paradise. There is a spellcaster there who calls himself Merlin. He should be able to help."

"Merlin? Seriously?" Khayin asked in disbelief.

"Not the real Merlin, silly. He's in England. This one will actually help, especially if you drop my name. The real one has a stick up his ass. He'd never help you."

"Thanks, Baby Doll." Khayin was about to turn and leave when Codex stopped him.

"You got something for me, Snuggly Bear?" she asked.

"Oh, yeah." He rifled his pockets until he found what he was looking for. Kira saw a small device similar to the one Codex had just been chattering into. He handed it to Codex.

"Just let me know when you need it back." She took the object from him and placed it in the top drawer of her desk. "I'll let you know if I find anything out. Where're you headed after you take care of the collar issue?"

"Have to find her home." Khayin looked at her. Is that sympathy? "Get her someplace where she is comfortable. Get her back to her sisters."

"You're too good, Khayin. I hope it doesn't kill you one of these days."

"Yeah, me too." Khayin agreed before turning and walking out the door.

Chapter 7 The Question

There was a flicker. Lights? Motion? Then it was gone as if it never happened.

Khayin's eyes swept the alley and found nothing. He gave a nod to the two guards flanking the door and proceeded down the alley. He and Kira walked side-by-side into The Strip. Khayin was amazed by how brightly the neon lights still shone in the sun light. Khayin stopped to roll a cigarette.

"So," Kira began, "you and Codex?"

"What?" he asked, genuinely curious.

"Are the two of you life mates?"

The question startled him and he nearly lost his tobacco. "What?!"

"Look, I am trying to find the right words for it. I know you understand my language, but I don't use the same terminology as you." She explained.

"No, I understood you." He cleared his throat. "No, we're definitely not 'life mates'. She is more like the daughter I never had. And, umm...let's just say I'm not her type," he said in hopes that was enough to satisfy her curiosity. She looked at him quizzically, and he knew he'd have to explain. "She's not into men." Kira continued to stare at him quizzically for a moment before he began to see the light dawn in her eyes. A slight smile cracked her normally stoic expression before she frowned once more. "Then how does she reproduce?"

Khayin erupted in laughter. He laughed so hard that his sides started to hurt. He only stopped his hysteria when he saw Kira's face. She was on the verge of an explosion of her own.

"Whoa, umm...I'm not laughing at you. You just caught me off guard." He focused once again on rolling the cigarette, pausing to compose himself. He lit it and breathed in a long unhealthy drag before answering her question. "That, Kira, is a question you should direct at Codex herself. In practical terms," he paused, "I guess she can't. But that conversation is none of my business, nor do I want to know."

She just stared at him. After a long moment she nodded. She looked at her feet and then she looked back at him. "How does the magic work?" She pointed to the earring in his ear.

"Hell if I know. It translates all language I hear and what others hear from me. So basically I speak in English but you hear it in your native tongue, whatever that is," he explained.

"Are there languages it doesn't know?"

"No, not that I have encountered. Sometimes it takes a while to figure out the language, but in the end I understand. Sometimes if the language is obscure or really old, I'll only understand the basics, and sometimes slang doesn't get translated at all." She nods. "There's a store that we'll hit before we make our way to Paradise. We'll get you a translator as well. That way you won't be left in the dark and I won't have to translate for you."

"One more question," she stated.

"Only one?" he chuckled. "Shoot."

She cocked her head to the side and looked at him curiously. She shook her head. "Magic--how does it work in these lands? I mean, Codex obviously wields a different kind of magic than I do, so are there different types?"

"Well, for 'one question' you sure did pick a big one. Hmm..." Khayin put the cigarette to his mouth and sucked in some hot smoke, holding it for a few long seconds before blowing it out. "Let's walk to the store and I'll tell you on the way." Khayin proceeded down the street heading south. In the distance they could see Stratosphere Casino. The tall tower still stood.

"There are different classes of magic. Codex, for instance, is what they call a Cybermage, or Tech Wizard. She focuses on bringing pre-Cataclysm tech to life. In order to do that she needs to know and understand how the tech worked back then. Not easy." He paused for a cig break. "Then you have this Merlin guy we are going to see. He is a spellcaster. Your typical storybook Wizard. He studied ancient texts and scrolls and learns incantations, cantrips and so on. Basically he learns to alter reality in small ways--bends it to his control--on a limited scale."

Khayin looked at Kira who seemed to be in deep thought. He stopped in front of a store on the strip called The Artificer's Vault. He took one last drag on his cigarette and tossed it before opening the door and motioning for Kira to enter. She walked in and he followed. It was a small shop with shelves of different oddities. A couple of display cases were on one wall and a long glass table-type case rested in the middle of the shop. Khayin proceeded directly to the merchant toward the back of the store.

The merchant was a short stout man with a full black beard that was speckled with gray. He was balding and wore no hat to cover it. He smoked a pipe and didn't take notice of Khayin until he was standing right in front of him. The merchant took his attention away from some metal tubing he was working on and looked at Khayin.

"Ah, how can I help you today, young man?" His voice was almost a whisper.

"I'm looking for a translator. Do you have any?" Khayin flicked his earring.

"Ah, why yes, I do." The merchant walked away and over to a case further down the counter. He pulled out a board lined in royal blue velvet that had rings and earrings on display. He brought it back and laid it in front of Khayin.

"Kira," he called in a voice slightly louder than normal.

Kira walked over to Khayin and the merchant and examined the jewelry in front of them. She picked up a few rings and tried them on, frowning when most did not fit.

The merchant smiled. "Ah, give them a moment, my dear. They will adjust themselves."

She looked at him then back down to the ring in her hand. She tried placing it on her left index finger and it stopped at her middle knuckle. She waited a couple seconds before she tried pushing on it again and magically is re-sized and continued onto her finger without resistance. She held her hand up to look at it in a different light. She liked it. The ring was a plain silver band--nothing remarkable except for a few sigils etched on the inside of the band that no one would see while she wore it.

"Ah, I think we have a winner," said the merchant in a little sing-song tone.

"How much?" Khayin asked plainly.

"Ah, one thousand chips, young man."

Khayin smiled. "Six hundred."

"Ah, why...why, I am insulted," the merchant whined.

"You insulted me first, I'm only playing the game you started." Kira watched the two men haggle. Khayin gave her a wink. She wrinkled her nose.

"Ah, very good, young man. Eight hundred chips and you'll make the young lady happy."

"Seven hundred chips and you'll make us both happy." Khayin pulled out his money purse and started to count out 700 chips.

The merchant slapped the counter in front of him. "Ah, good show, young man, good show." Khayin gave the merchant his money. He put it under the counter without counting it. The merchant eyed Kira's collar. "Ah, young lady, where did you get such a fine piece of artificery?" Kira scowled. The merchant recoiled slightly.

"A glorified slave collar." Khayin explained.

"Ah, may I see?" the merchant asked Kira. She stepped a little closer and the short man examined the leather collar. He nodded and wet his lips. His eyes squinted and then went big. "Ah, fine work it is. Not mine, but very fine work. You can't cut that off, only released by a special word or maybe a balm from an alchemist."

"A balm?" Khayin looked at him with doubt.

"Some alchemists have created such a balm that defuses magic, but it's not always a hundred percent," the merchant explained.

"Hmm. We're headed to see Merlin, in Paradise." He put in

the last bit quickly so as not to mistake that Merlin for the other.

"Ah, yes, Merlin." The merchant nodded. "Ah, he could help. Unfortunately I cannot." The short man put a finger to his lips. "Ah, may I ask where you got it?"

"Yes you may, but I don't have an answer for you. I found her with it on." Khayin stopped himself, he doesn't know this guy. "Anyway, thanks for the ring." With that, Khayin and Kira left.

"Ah, come back again," the merchant called out as he watched them leave.

Kira turned to Khayin the moment they stepped outside. "I will pay you back," she said.

"Don't worry about it," Khayin said as he continued down the street.

Kira grabbed his arm and forced him to stop. She moved to stand in front of him. "I will pay you back." Her tone offered no room for argument.

"OK," was all Khayin said.

"I know sisters that can make items that have special properties, but what do you call this kind of magic?" she continued with their previous conversation.

"Artificery. They know a limited amount of spell magic for their profession, but only what they need to make their wares. There's a lot of money in that kind of magic." Kira nodded. "Then there's the Alchemist. The Alchemist is the master of potions, elixirs, powders, poisons, oils, lotions, that kind of stuff. Things that can give an individual special properties for a limited time."

They walked in silence for a while. They passed the Stratosphere Casino as they left the strip and followed Paradise Road. They were only a few minutes off the strip when Khayin noticed the flicker. This time he recognized it for what it was. Movement. He pulled his kukri from their sheaths and Kira instinctively pulled out her bow.

"We've got company." His eyes darted around.

Khayin wished Millennium were here, but his falcon would still be flying from Mexico. He noticed Kira frantically looking around, her eyes wide and alert. He felt something hot grasp his right forearm. Something really hot. Even after he felt the pressure of the grasp recede, he could still feel the burning. It started to intensify, the pain growing to the point where his arm was nearly useless. It took everything in him to keep a hold of the kukri. He dropped the kukri in his left hand and fished out a potion vial from an inside pocket. His heart beat rapidly.

There was a scream from somewhere behind him. Kira! Trying to remain calm, Khayin flipped the top open on the vial and drained its contents down his throat. He started to feel the effects almost immediately, the pain in his arm beginning to subside. He spun around to see a figure. Man? Woman? He couldn't tell. The person was dressed head to toe in black, a mask with a variation of a skull covering its face. The skeleton had Kira by the throat, holding her a few inches off the ground.

As if their attacker sensed Khayin looking at it, it turned to look at him. Kira took advantage of the slight moment of distraction, grabbed her knife and drove it deep through her attacker's arm. She dropped to the ground and her hands went to her throat. The skeleton grabbed the knife and pulled it free from its arm. It turned its attention back to Kira. Their attacker threw the knife at Kira and narrowly missed as she scrambled for her bow.

The skeleton turned back to Khayin and stretched out its arm. A gout of flame sprung from its finger tips and Khayin quickly rolled out of the flame's path. The skeleton turned back to Kira. With a wave of its hand a chunk of earth broke free from the ground and slammed into the witch. The chunk exploded on impact and laid Kira out sprawled on the ground. The skeleton then sprung into the air and landed, standing over Khayin.

The skull mask almost looked as though it were smiling. Khayin kicked the figure between the legs and to his astonishment he got no reaction. Even if it were female there should have been something, but that damned mask kept smiling at him. The muscles in his neck started to constrict, cutting off his air supply. He couldn't breathe. He started to panic and reached for one of his pistols. The skeleton squatted closer to Khayin. When the mask was only a foot away from his face, Khayin felt a spray of blood and the body fall on top of him.

Khayin pushed the corpse off him and saw Kira standing a few yards away with a bow in her hand panting. She fell to her knees and dropped the bow. Khayin dropped his chin and inhaled deeply. He looked at the dead mage next to him, reaching over and removing the mask. A man? Boy? No, maybe a girl? He still couldn't tell. He saw the veins beneath the skin glowing. Khayin tore open the Lycra fabric of the bodysuit the skeletal mage was wearing and saw the same blue glowing veins all over its torso. No genitalia and no breasts--what is this thing? He searched the body for any identification. What he found was another wanted poster. Khayin recognized the printing company's watermark and knew it had been printed in Chicago.

Codex said something about men from Chicago that were here to question her about Juan. Hmm...What the hell is going on?

Khayin got up and brushed himself off. He grabbed his kukri from the ground and returned them to their respective sheathes. Kira came up next to him and nudged the dead mage with her foot.

"Nice shot," Khayin said. "And thank you."

She ignored what he said. "What was it?"

"There're some other types of wizards out there, more specialized. I think this one is what they call a Battlemage. They specialize in the obvious--battle." He took out his cigarette tin, pulled out one previously rolled and lit it. "Seems the origin of that first poster is Chicago and I think I may be on their target list now as well." He took a long deep drag. "It has been following us since we left Codex's. It must have reported us." He started to walk again. "Shit. We need to get to this Merlin and get you home."

"Are we just going to leave the body?" She was still standing next to the dead Battlemage.

"Yes. No one will know it was us and even if they did I doubt they'd care. Chicago has no jurisdiction here." He continued to walk. "You coming?"

Kira started to walk, leaving her eyes transfixed on the corpse for a few more moments before turning completely away. "Yeah, gorjcha. I'm coming."

Chapter 8 The Collar

The walk to Paradise was uneventful, but Kira couldn't help but notice the drastic difference in the scenery. She definitely knew when she left Las Vegas. The City of Lights was all shiny and busy and the outskirts was everything but. The buildings were abandoned and rundown and what people she did see weren't living the lifestyle of the people of Vegas. They were dirty and wore clothes that were ill-fitting and torn.

"Welcome to Paradise," Khayin said a little too enthusiastically when they entered the city limits.

The town (city, settlement, Kira still wasn't entirely clear on the differences) was slightly more alive than the towns they had walked through. Not all the buildings were occupied, but most were. Kira could surmise that if Las Vegas wasn't so close, Paradise would probably not survive.

Khayin walked through the small town with purpose, Kira at his side. She didn't like the feeling of walking behind him. It felt too much like he were leading and she wasn't OK with that, even though she had no idea where to go or what to do next.

"Do you know this Merlin?" she asked without making eye contact.

"Not at all." He stopped in front of a building that looked abandoned. The windows were boarded up and the walls were covered in art--giant letters and pictures of male and female genitalia. It was things like this that made her long for home.

"We're here."

"In there?" She gestured at the door to the rundown building. A slight shiver ran up her spine.

"Yep." Khayin looked at the door then faced Kira. Kira realized that even though Khayin was a male, she liked his face. It reminded her of an old friend. She shook that thought away. "If there's anything you want to ask, ask now. Once we're in there I think it's best if I do the talking." She scowled slightly, but nodded, then shook her head to signify she had no questions.

Khayin opened the door and the two walked through. They stepped into a lush forest. Kira quickly turned to see from where they had just come and saw the town as she remembered it before they walked through the door. She smiled. Khayin pulled a dagger from his belt and drove it into the door before he closed it. When the door shut Kira saw it disappear and a dagger hilt floating in mid-air.

"So we can find the way out," Khayin explained. She just nodded, still in awe of the level of magic that surrounded them.

They followed what seemed to be a path. The forest around them was well kept and the temperature was a comfortable 70 degrees. There was no sun in the sky, but everything was illuminated as if it were shining brightly at midday. They had only walked for a few minutes when they saw it, in the middle of a clearing stood a log house. Smoke could be seen coming from the top of the structure. Kira just absorbed it all, her heart skipping a beat or two in the excitement. *Powerful magic. All around me. I can feel it.*

As they approached the house the front door opened as if beckoning them to enter. Khayin stepped in without hesitation, and after pausing for just a second, Kira followed.

"Welcome, welcome. Please come in, come in." An old man stood a few feet from the entrance. He wore blue robes and a tall pointy blue hat. He had a long white beard and mustache. "It has been such a long time without visitors." He gestured to a large bench-like seat by a fire. "Please, please take a seat. Can I get you some tea?" Both Kira and Khayin nodded. "Excellent, excellent." He scurried off into another room.

The room in which they sat was large and meant for lounging and entertaining people, Kira guessed. Nothing looked extraordinary. In fact everything looked tame, like a normal home. Slight movement caught her eye and she turned to see a large owl on a perch in the corner of the room. She elbowed Khayin and pointed toward the bird. Khayin nodded.

"Familiar," Khayin said pointedly. "He's probably watching us through its eyes."

"Like your falcon," Kira said.

"Yep." He smiled.

A couple of moments later Merlin walked back into the room. "So, to what do I owe this pleasure?"

Khayin wasted no time. "My friend here has a collar issue." He touched the collar around her neck and to her own surprise she didn't flinch. *Friend? He considers me a friend?*

The old wizard looked at Kira and then the collar. "Could you come closer, young lady? My eyes are not what they used to be." Kira got up and moved closer to Merlin, who donned a pair of glasses and inspected the collar. "Anti-magic neckband," he said plainly.

"Yeah, we figured out that much. We need it off." Khayin was blunt and to the point. Kira wasn't sure if that was because of their present company or because of the matter of the collar.

"Did you try cutting it off?" The old wizard asked with a big smile.

"Yep, first with a butter knife, then I tried a nail file like I saw in a movie once. No good." Khayin shook his head like he was distraught. *We didn't do any of that--why is he lying?* Kira's head bounced between Merlin and Khayin and back again.

Merlin chuckled.

"Codex said you could help us." Khayin said.

The old wizard stopped his inspection and let his gaze wonder off. "Codex," he whispered. "Ah yes, that little spitfire. Well if Codex sent you then I must help." He stood up faster than a man his age should have been able to. "Wait here. I'll be right back." When he left the room, Kira looked at Khayin, who just shrugged his shoulders. A few moments later the wizard returned holding a metal container about as big as a large man's palm. It had a small spout on top with a screw-on cap.

"What are you going to do with spirits, Merlin?" Khayin asked. Kira could tell Khayin didn't like calling him that.

Merlin laughed. "Oh no, dear boy. This is not alcohol. It's an oil. These old flasks make perfect containers."

"I thought you were a spellcaster?" Khayin sounded confused.

"Oh, but I am. That was how I was able to identify the enchantment on the collar. You could have brought the collar to the Artificer that created it and he or she would have had no problem removing it, but I'm guessing you don't know who that is. Hence your visit to me. I keep some oils on hand in case of emergencies." He opened the flask and covered the spout with his index finger before turning it upside down. He then spread the oil from his finger onto the collar. He repeated the process until all of the collar was covered with oil, dark and slick. He stood and waited, Kira and Khayin just watched each other with a look of doubt. When only a moment later, the collar detached and fell to the floor, Kira jumped up.

The dam broke. Magic flooded over and through her like rushing water. Her tattoos radiated. Kira's hands went immediately to her throat and felt the now naked flesh. She felt that old familiar friend wash over her like warmth from the sun. Magic coursed through her veins once again. She could hear the heartbeat of the world. Her skin tingled and she felt alive for the first time in a long time. She smiled big, then quickly stifled the excitement. She bent down and picked up the neckband and without thinking she threw it into the fire. She was a slave no more.

She could barely contain herself. She looked around the room and reality struck her. Kira was still away from home. She was still lost and she still had to rely on a man to get her home. *His company hasn't been that bad. Kind of entertaining, even if I don't understand half his jokes.* She gave Merlin a slight grin.

"Oh, you are welcome, child." He put the cap back on his flask. "You know, I seemed to have misplaced your names."

"My name is Khayin," he said with hand outstretched. "And

this here is..."

"Kira'Tal." She cut him off.

"Well, Kira'Tal. You are a long way from home now, are you not, hmm?" the old wizard asked.

"You know who I am?" Kira nearly knocked the old man over when she sprung toward him.

"Oh, I know of your people, yes."

"I'm lost. And I'm trying to get back home." Her hands fidgeted and her speech was rapid.

"I am sorry, Miss Kira'Tal. I do not know from where you came. I just know you're not from anywhere around here. I think your home is south, further south than Mexico even. I wish I knew exactly. I could learn so much from your people I'm sure, but your sisters are very secretive." He sounded very apologetic. She hung her head. "If you have time I would love to hear about your home and your sisters, hmm?"

"Maybe some other time," Khayin interjected. "What do we owe you for this service?"

"This?" Merlin waved his hand. "For this, nothing. Your company was enough, but tell Codex she must come visit." The old wizard sat down. "Oh, you didn't need to put your dagger through my door; you would have found your way out."

"Well, thanks." Khayin said, he got a nod in response. "One question before we go." The wizard raised an eyebrow. "That owl real?" Khayin pointed to the owl in the corner.

Merlin's face lit up. "Archimedes? Why of course he is real." The owl turned his head toward them and opened his big eyes.

"Archimedes? You named your owl Archimedes." Khayin's expression was wide.

"Yes, why? What is wrong with Archimedes?" Merlin seemed puzzled.

Khayin shook his head and started out the door. "Never mind." Kira followed with one of her hands still touching her bare neck.

The wizard was right--they found their way out easily enough. Khayin retrieved his dagger and the two of them stood outside the rundown building. Khayin reached into an inner pocket of his vest and pulled out his cigarette tin. He sat on the curb of the street in front of Merlin's building and started to roll a cigarette. Kira watched him.

When he had finished, Kira asked, "May I have one?" She sat down next to him.

"Are you sure?" Khayin asked her, his eyes wide. She nodded.

He handed her the cigarette he had just rolled then produced a small rectangular piece of metal, flipping open the top and producing a flame. She waved off the portable flame, lighting the cigarette with her magic and putting it to her lips, smiling in joy at the return of her powers. She breathed in the smoke. He watched her for another moment then started to roll one for himself.

The two of them just sat and smoked. They didn't talk, just enjoying the early afternoon. The sky was clear and the sun was almost directly overhead. They watched a couple dogs fight in the street over a dead bird, only to see a cat sneak in and snatch the bird away.

"So, how's it feel?" Khayin asked.

"What?"

"Magic." He was looking at her and his eyes went big and he feigned putting his hands up.

Kira rolled her eyes. "Wonderful. Fantastic. Marvelous. I feel...alive." Her eyes were now closed, she could feel the world around her. She felt magic flow through the air, through every living thing. When she opened her eyes she saw Khayin looking to the sky.

"Good," was all he said.

"Do you know magic? I mean, do you use it?"

"Ah, that question will cost ya." He never looked away from the sky above and she knew she wouldn't get any more from him on the subject. She could respect that. They didn't know each other well enough.

"How are we going to get me home?" she asked, changing the topic.

"Unexpectedly, we got a lead from Merlin." He took one last drag from his cigarette and flicked the butt away. "We'll head back to Mexico. Probably head to Panama. I know a water sprite down there that might know something."

"You know a faerie?" She was genuinely surprised. The faerie folk she knew only talked to users of magic, and even that was rare.

"I know several actually, but only Tippy might know where your home is."

"Tippy? Did that translate right?" She wanted to laugh, but choked it down.

"Yep, you heard it right." Khayin stood and brushed off his butt of any dirt. "We need to get some horses, or a teleport, but the horses might be more in our price range." He looked at her. "Whatcha think? We could get a port to Mexico City and ride from there, which'll be a little faster. Or, we can ride from here. It is a four thousand mile ride from here. We're looking at a," he looked up and to the left, "three to four month hike."

Is he really asking for my opinion? "If you have the money or the know-how, I'd rather take the quicker route."

"I agree. You ready?"

She stood and flicked away the last of her cigarette. "Yeah, let's go."

Chapter 9   The Port

They walked back to Vegas. Khayin thought that if they could get a teleport back to Mexico City they could get horses there. The idea of a 4000 mile ride on horseback wasn't appealing to either of them. Mexico City wasn't as populated as Las Vegas, but populated enough that a teleport there wouldn't be as costly, seeing as the trip was a little more common than a straight port to Panama. He just hoped Tippy could help and it wouldn't be a wasted trip.

They arrived back in Vegas mid-afternoon. The weather was nice and the skies were a brilliant blue. The Strip started to fill up as more tourists started to appear. Kira stayed at Khayin's side and tried not to make eye contact with anyone. The business he was looking for was an old Travel Agency amply named 'The Port Authority.' Khayin thought it was a pretty clever name.

The Agency's proprietor was a young wizard named Mistress Tao. She had taken over her mentor's business when he fell into some trouble with Codex. People learned after a while not to get on the Cybermage's bad side.

The Port Authority wasn't too far into town and they made good time. Kira seemed to have a bit more pep in her step. He figured not being shackled and her connection to magic being restored had a lot to do with her new found energy. He hoped that she might open up a little more.

"I still can't read this language," Kira stated as she stared at the sign above the agency's door. "What language is it?"

"English," Khayin said, not looking at her.

"I'm not familiar with written...English. Most slaves...people," she corrected herself, "outside my village spoke Latin, or Spanish and some variations of Spanish. We never found much need to learn to write English, but the Crone made us learn to speak different languages, including English, to keep our minds sharp, she'd say." She looked at Khayin.

The two of them stood outside the building. *She's in a good mood and she is talking. Maybe... He decided to risk it.* "You said slaves."

"I did, by mistake," she said, clearly trying to avoid the topic entirely.

Now he looked at her. "No. I heard right, and you tried to cover it up."

"I did. Fine." She paused a moment. "You dodged a question I had for you earlier. You answer that and I'll answer yours."

"Fair enough, but not here. Let's get that port and we'll talk over a meal around a fire." A smile grew across his face. He may yet get in her head and figure out who this mystery woman was-- and her people. "I'm going to try to get us to Mexico City, but I need to be sure we have enough chips for horses and traveling expenses, like food and lodging and stuff. I'm not sure if we will be hunted in the city because of the mayhem we caused at El Diablo's, so we'll have to stay clear of there. I know Maria wouldn't have reported it, but I'm not too sure of Jesus. Better safe than sorry, right?"

Kira just looked at him. She wore no expression. *God, what is going on in that head?* He wondered. Khayin turned and entered The Port Authority.

There was a desk directly across from the front entrance. To Khayin's right was a waiting area with a few chairs and a long red couch. In front of the couch was a short table with piles of magazines. Behind the desk sat an older woman; Khayin guessed she was in her sixties. She wore a business suit and had her gray hair pulled up into a bun. She stared at Kira.

After a moment she said, "Welcome to The Port Authority, where chips can get you anywhere." Her voice was monotone and devoid of emotion. She clearly didn't want to be there. When she noticed Khayin a slight smirk crept onto her face, but she stifled it just as quickly as it appeared. "Khayin, welcome back. How may The Mistress serve you today?"

"Hi, Helen. My, don't you look ever so radiant," Khayin said with a broad grin.

"Oh, cut the shit, Honey, I'm too much woman for you. You wouldn't know what to do with yourself, let alone what to do with me." She waved her hand in a half shooing and half pointing manner. "The Mistress is in her office. I'm sure you know where it is so I don't have to take you back there."

"One of these days, Helen." Khayin said as he walked past her desk and into the hall beyond. Helen just shook her head.

The hallway was short with only two doors. Khayin took the first door on his left. It stood ajar and he could clearly see the large office within. The room was decorated in a Japanese fashion, complete with paper walls segregating a large room into smaller rooms. Just inside stood a full suit of Samurai armor. Khayin saw a pair of expensive shoes sitting outside the door.

Khayin bent down and pulled off his boots. Kira just watched him.

"Mistress Tao is Japanese and she is traditional." Khayin motioned toward Kira's feet with a pointed finger. "It's customary to remove one's shoes before entering." Kira just shrugged and took off her boots. "Don't worry, this is about as traditional as she gets," he said with a smile.

The Mistress's desk sat in the far left of the room, taking it out of the view of the door, though Khayin knew she didn't need to see the door to know all that was happening in her building, let alone her office. Standing beside her desk was Mistress Tao. She was a short woman with a full figure. She wore a black pin-striped skirt suit. She also had her black hair pulled into a ponytail. Khayin saw that she was about as old as Kira and they both looked to be in their mid-twenties.

"Khayin," she purred in a lovely accent. "I've heard so much about you, but never had the pleasure of a proper introduction."

Khayin bowed. "Mistress Tao. It's an honor." Kira just looked at both of them, head shifting between the two. Khayin straightened. "Congratulations on the business and I'm sorry for your loss."

"Nonsense." Tao scowled, then quickly smiled showing a row of perfect white teeth. "Good riddance to that old cretin I say. He got what he deserved."

"I hope you and Codex have a good relationship?" he asked.

"Oh, we...have an understanding." A devilish grin escaped before she could hide it. Khayin only nodded.

I bet you two do.

"So, how can I help you? Where do you need to go?" She asked, straight to business.

"As far south into Mexico as I can get. I need to get to Panama, but I've come down with a case of Lackoffundsitis."

"Panama does not have an established port-link and would be expensive, which you already knew. How much are you willing to spend?" She made her way behind her desk and turned to face the wall. She pulled down several large maps and flipped through them until she found the one she desired. She released the others and displayed a map of Mexico and Central America.

"I've got five thousand chips I can spend on a port, maybe more, but that would cut into chips I have set aside for other expenses." Khayin reached for his money purse. Mistress Tao only nodded.

"Mexico City is the cheapest and I'd only charge you half that, since you are a friend of Codex's." She examined the map. The large map displayed cities and roads. What Khayin really noticed, though, were that some cities were marked with different colors, and that those cities were connected by blue lines that could easily be mistaken for roads, but Khayin knew they were porting connections. "Now, Tuxtla Gutierrez is closer to Panama and in your price range, again with a Codex discount," she said with a white smile as she turned to face him.

"That's not necessary." Khayin shook his head.

"Your honor requires you to turn it down, but mine requires me to insist. I'm sure I'll be using your services sometime in the future and you will remember this." She countered.

"OK. Tuxtla it is. Do they have an established port?"

"Sort of. I know a wizard down there and he has a circle that I use from time to time."

"And he's OK with that?" he asked concerned.

Mistress Tao smiled that pearly smile. It was almost enough to make him melt. "No, and yes. He visits the Mayan ruins that are relatively close and we trade from time to time. That is all you need to know. He is not aggressive and when you show up on his property armed like you are he will not protest. Plus, he is a smart man. He will know that the only way you could port to his home is by me. You can probably purchase some horses from him as well. He has a nice little setup down there."

"Five thousand chips then." He fished out some chips and counted out the desired amount and held it to her hand outstretched.

She pointed a black lacquered fingernail to a bowl on her desk. "It feels so...cheap, accepting chips hand to hand. I do not know why. Anyway, now that business is over." Mistress Tao walked over to Kira and looked her up and down. She circled her as if to take in every inch. Tao stopped when she completed her revolution and they were face to face.

"What is your name, dear?" the Mistress asked.

"Kira'Tal," Kira spoke directly and confidently, and Khayin thought she was either a very good actor or braver than Khayin had thought.

"Of course. Codex told me about you." Tao clicked her teeth with a black nail. "So, you are the witch Hag, one of the mythical Schadovitch?"

"That's what they say. We've never called ourselves by that. What makes a witch different than a wizard?" Kira asked.

"Ooh, good question." Tao was obviously amused. "I really don't know. There are so many different kinds of magic and all its users get blanketed under the same label. What makes the Hags any different?" It was a rhetorical question.

Khayin could see Kira purse her lips and shrug.

"Well, if anyone can get you home, this man can. If only half of what Codex says about him is true, you will be home in no time." She touched Kira's cheek. Kira flinched. Then suddenly Tao turned to Khayin. "Codex told me a little of what is going on. She is worried. Especially after what happened since you left her place earlier today. Do you need..."

"No." Khayin cut her off. "I don't want to bring anyone else into this. Even though technically you are, but no more. I think we'll be safe from those Chicago men when we get into Mexico, hopefully." Khayin tensed. "She heard about the attack?"

Mistress Tao flashed her smile. "Darling, you know there is not much that goes on in this city that she does not know about." She slid between Khayin and Kira and headed to the door. Khayin followed.

Once in the hall they donned their shoes and followed Mistress Tao to another room a little further down. They stepped into a large open room with a circle drawn on the floor. Within the circle were intricate designs of runes and other magic symbols. None of it made any sense to Khayin, but he could see Kira was very interested. The circle and designs within were a permanent part of the floor.

"Go ahead and step into the circle," Tao instructed.

They did what they were told. Khayin saw the Mistress pull some components out of a small bag she had in a pocket. "This is a ritual? I didn't have to step into a circle to teleport to Codex."

She looked a little perturbed. "Codex is...Codex is on a level that most wizards aspire to be and she views spell and ritual magic beneath her. Do not get me wrong. She knows more spells and rituals than any wizard and is probably on even footing with Merlin--the real one--but she will not use it except for her own gains. But don't take offense, it is just how she is. She is like a savant, autistic maybe, maybe not. All I know is that her mind works differently and if she does not like something or if it does not hold her attention, she packs it away." She stopped, obviously in thought. "She is strange, different, beautiful, and powerful. My old mentor found out the hard way." She visibly shuddered. "Ready?"

"Yes," Khayin and Kira said in unison.

"Next stop, Tuxtla Gutierrez. Say hi to Luis Barragan for me," she said as she crushed a red pepper in her left hand.

Chapter 10 The Chief

"The Asset has made contact, Chief," said Dorne. He was a wiry man who had never seen a day of combat in the field. His uniform hung loosely on his skinny frame. He wore glasses and sported a thin mustache.

"And?" The Chief's voice was low, gruff, and demanded attention. The two men were standing in a dark room. Chief Lawrence Rantz stared out through a window that didn't allow any light to come in. Outside sprawled Chicago, a Tech Wizard mecca. The city was alive with lights, vehicles, and other various old world tech.

Joshua Dorne swallowed a lump in his throat. He hated bringing bad news. "The Asset was neutralized, sir." He waited a moment for Chief Rantz to respond, but he said nothing. Dorne continued, "The Asset did confirm the witch's presence and the one she is traveling with." He paused again for any response and still all he got was silence. "She is not with Juan Rodriguez."

Dorne stood in front of the Chief's desk. Chief Rantz had his back to him and the room. He was a tall man, broad shouldered, and had a military style crew cut. Dorne stood nervously. The Chief was not a nice man and did not take bad news easily. Dorne didn't want to be on the receiving end of his rage.

"And who might she be with, Dorne?" he asked in a calm tone.

Dorne hesitated. He was a little surprised of the Chief's tone. He didn't sound upset. He sounded neutral. "The Asset claims she is traveling with..." He paused again even though he knew the Chief was getting impatient.

"Spit it out, Dorne," Chief Rantz said with frustration.

"Khayin, sir. The Asset said she was traveling with Khayin." It was out. He said it. Dorne tensed waiting for the coming storm.

There was a long silence. Dorne began to sweat. He dared not move, but all he wanted to do was get out. He knew he was just the messenger, but that didn't stop the Chief in the past. Dorne himself had never been an eyewitness to his rage, but this was also the first time he personally had ever delivered bad news to the Chief of Security.

After what seemed an eternity the Chief spoke. "You are dismissed, Dorne," the Security Chief said in a smooth calm voice.

Dorne spun on his heel and left. Behind him through the closed door Dorne could hear a yell that was almost inhuman, then the sound of shattering glass. The yelling continued with strings of expletives and one word he could actually make out...Khayin.

Dorne smiled. He looked at Elizabeth, Chief Rantz's secretary and shrugged. The secretary was the Chief's niece. She was a nice girl. She was a ginger. *Too many freckles.* He preferred a woman's skin to be unblemished. She smiled at him.

"Everything OK?" she asked.

"Yes, everything is fine." He winked at her and watched her cheeks blossom into a rosy shade.

He loved getting under people's skin and it thrilled him to do so to the Chief, despite his fear of him. He wasn't sure why the Chief didn't lash out at him, but he was thankful.

One of these days Chief Lawrence Rantz, you will let that rage out on the wrong person and I'll be there to swoop in and stake my claim.

Dorne had only heard tales about this Khayin and he knew how much the Chief hated him. That was part of the reason he wanted to tell him himself. He never understood the hatred. Khayin frequented Chicago often and liked to visit the theater. He had also dropped off a number of bounties in the city.

Dorne left the first floor office and proceeded down to sub-floor thirteen. He didn't like to use the elevators; they were unnatural. He didn't trust them. He didn't trust a lot of magic. He exited the stairwell and walked down the long white hall to his office. The desk in the foyer was empty; he had given his secretary the day off. He sat behind her desk.

A young man wearing a security uniform entered the office. He had blonde hair that he wore short. His face appeared shocked when he saw Dorne sitting at the desk.

"Uh...uh...sir?" he stuttered.

"What is it?" Dorne snapped.

"There was an incident in Mexico City."

"So what? What does that have to do with us?" Dorne was annoyed.

"Juan, sir."

"What about Juan?"

"He was found dead outside a bar called El Diablo's."

Dorne smiled. "Really..."

Chapter 11   The Sleepover

Tuxtla Gutierrez. Once a thriving city in the southeast of Mexico, now it was more of a ghost town. Most buildings were left abandoned. The government fell apart like most cities and looters ran wild. Chaos left Tuxtla a lifeless husk. Scavengers still frequent the ruins, but 200 years has stripped it of anything of usefulness.

Kira had never visited any settlement outside her own community. The few traders she had met in the past had relayed stories and she'd listened with earnest attention. She had always been fascinated with the outside world, but fear had kept her from exploring it. Fear of the unknown and fear of her mother, The Crone, who forbade it. Only a select few could venture beyond their borders and some of those never returned.

She found the contrast of settlements enthralling, from the small villages, to the large cities like Vegas, to the near desolation of Tuxtla. She could only imagine what they were like before the Cataclysm Khayin had mentioned.

The teleport placed them just at the edge of the city. They stood in another circle that looked very similar to the one on Mistress Tao's floor. She checked her companion and noticed his queasy visage. She chuckled inwardly. It's nice to see a crack in his armor. Before them were trees and homes. The trees were too thick to see any great distance, but she had a feeling they were very close to this Luis guy's place, on account of Tao saying they would port in his yard.

The Malevolent Witch

Kira scanned their surroundings and quickly found who they were looking for. An older man wearing coveralls and a curved brim hat approached. He held a bow with a notched arrow in his left hand. Flanking him were two more men, much younger, also carrying bows, but they had them drawn and pointed at them. Khayin put his hands up, so Kira nervously did the same. So much for not being aggressive.

"We come in peace," Khayin said in a voice other than his own. She looked at him quizzically, he only smiled.

There are weapons pointed at us and he is smiling. No fear? Or is he crazy? Both?

The three men stopped about thirty paces from them. The older man just watched them for a long moment. Kira summoned some of her magic. Her fingers started to tingle. She wasn't afraid and she knew she could handle the situation before them, but she wanted to see what Khayin was going to do. With her magic back she didn't need Khayin as a protector. She wouldn't have admitted she had ever needed him for that.

The old man lit a cigarette and motioned for his companions to lower their bows. "Only one soul uses that porting circle. Is it right for me to assume she sent you?"

Khayin never lowered his arms. "You're welcome to assume that. Mistress Tao says hi."

If the old man reacted to the name he didn't show it. "Why are you here?"

"We're on our way to Panama and I was hoping you might put us up for the night and sell us a couple horses, if you have any. Or tell us where we might find some," Khayin said plainly.

"Tell your girlfriend to holster that magic," the old man said with a scowl.

Khayin gave Kira a glance and lowered his hands. She relaxed. She let the magic dissipate and flow back into the elements. The old man waved off the other two men before fixing his gaze onto Kira. She could guess what he was thinking. *My tattoos must be rare. Why else would I stand out?* Then he looked back to Khayin with the same scrutinizing eye he had on Kira.

"Alright, young man. I think I can help ya." He walked toward them and outstretched his hand to Khayin. "The name's Luis Barragan." Khayin took his hand and they shook.

"THE Luis Barragan?" Khayin asked.

"Whattya mean?" He gave him a questioning look.

"The architect and engineer from the twentieth century?"

He chuckled. "No. A many great grandfather. I's named after him. How'd he still be alive? It's been over two-hundred years. No one is immortal, son. Everything and everyone dies. Magic hasn't been able to stop that and lord did they try. How'd you know my many great grandfather?"

Khayin shrugged slightly. "I read a lot."

Luis seemed to be satisfied with his response because he just smiled. "Good. Come. Follow me. I've some rooms you can use for the evening." He looked back to Kira then to Khayin. "Unless you prefer one room?" Kira grimaced. Luis smiled.

The walk was short. There was a small farm, enough to feed a small village. By the looks of it Kira could tell they only grew what they needed, not to trade. Luis led them to a house a couple hundred yards from the teleportation circle. She noticed the home was well kept but rarely lived in. It was simple, with just four rooms: two rooms with beds, a bathroom with a tub and toilet, and a larger room with a table and stove.

"Dinner will be served in a couple of hours. I'll have one of my boys fetch you," Luis said as he walked away.

"That's OK, we really don't…"

"The missus would really appreciate it," Luis said, cutting Khayin off as he turned to face him. Khayin just nodded.

They watched the old man walk across the field to a much larger house. Kira looked at Khayin, who continued to stare after the old man.

"We going to sleep here and leave in the morning?" she asked.

"Yeah." He turned and entered one of the bedrooms. "We'll have to stop somewhere for some clothes and food. If we keep wearing these," he picked at his shirt, "we'll get a little ripe."

Kira stood in the hall that separated the two bedrooms. She looked into one of the bedrooms and noticed it was exactly the same as the other one. She walked down the hall and entered the bathroom. Kira immediately began to strip off her clothing.

"I'm going to bathe," she said.

Naked, she turned the knobs and water began to fill the tub. She reached down and put the rubber stopper in the drain. She heard footsteps in the hall, but when she turned all she saw was the door to the bathroom closing. She smiled and sat in the slowly filling tub. She took care to keep her hair from getting wet by tying it up as best she could with a shirt. Kira then sat back and relaxed, trying to forget where she was and what had happened.

****

The dinner was nice. In fact, it was the best meal Kira had had in a long time. She ignored the stares she got from Luis's boys and she also managed to stay out of the majority of the conversations. Mrs. Barragan invited her to help in the kitchen after they had finished, while the men went and talked business. Kira wasn't fond of that idea at all. Mrs. Barragan did all the cleaning while the men did nothing. Kira tried to hide her displeasure and all she got from Khayin was a smirk, which just made her blood boil and her hands curl into fists.

After a short while Khayin entered the kitchen. Kira was elbows deep in the sink washing dishes. She scowled at him, but he just gave her a helpless shrug. She knew he had no part in what she was doing, but she had to let her anger out on someone and he would do nicely.

"I'm going to turn in early," Khayin stated. "If you are done relatively soon I'll let you know what the plans are, but if I'm asleep when you get back to the house we'll just talk tomorrow." Khayin turned and left.

Kira looked at Mrs. Barragan, who was drying what she had been washing. Before she could even say anything the woman nodded.

"Go, honey. From what I hear you have a long trip ahead of you and this might be the only comfortable night's sleep you'll get for a while." Mrs. Barragan smiled.

Kira instantly dropped everything, afraid that the woman may change her mind. She dried off her arms and left the kitchen. She was out the front door before anyone could try to stop her. She practically ran to the house where she and Khayin were staying. Kira rushed up the stairs to the low porch and swiftly entered the house, slamming and locking the door behind her. *Never again!*

"You knew!" she spat. Khayin was sitting in a chair in one corner of the room. He was laughing. "Somehow you knew."

She marched over to where he sat and punched him square in the nose. He didn't see it coming, because he made no attempt to move or defend himself. Khayin stopped laughing.

"Hey!" His voice was muffled and he chuckled a bit. He cupped his nose with his hands which also covered his mouth. "What's that for?"

"What!?" Her face flashed red and she was ready for a fight. Her hands were balled up into fists, her knuckles were white. "You knew." She repeated.

"Maybe," his nose was bleeding and his hands still covered the lower half of his face, "what could I've done about it?"

Magic started to course through her. Her tattoos started to radiate. She felt humiliated. Never before had she had to do men's work. Kira stared at Khayin. She knew he was right. To refuse would have been an insult to their hosts. The few times there were guests in her village those guest sometimes did things that made them just as uncomfortable. She couldn't wait to get home. Kira spun on her heel and stormed off to her room, slamming the door.

Kira sat cross legged on the floor in meditation. *Why did I get so worked up? And why'd I feel so embarrassed and humiliated in front of Khayin?* Kira was snapped out of her meditation when there was a knock on her bedroom door.

"Come in," she said in a smooth calm voice.

Khayin opened the door, but didn't step in. "Hey, I..."

"Don't say it. You did nothing wrong. If anything, I should apologize for hitting you." She cut him off.

"Thanks, I accept." He had tissue pushed up his left nostril.

"I said I should, I didn't say I would," she snapped. "You could've warned me."

"Fair enough." He said with a little smirk. "But in my defense,

I still know nothing of you or your culture. How was I supposed to know that would offend you?"

Kira looked at him. She wasn't mad any longer and she realized just then that they would have to take a little time to talk. She expected him to respect her and her culture, but she had never told him anything, not even the smallest bit of information for him to even guess. *Well, we do have a long journey ahead. I am sure it will come up.*

She relaxed. "What's the plan?"

Khayin seemed to brighten up. "I got us three horses, two to ride and one to haul supplies. Luis also helped plot out the quickest safe route to Panama. There are some hostile territories between us and our destination, so we tried our best to avoid those. He also marked a few supply stops in case we are unfortunate and don't run into any caravans." He paused and Kira just watched him.

"Luis said we can keep whatever clothes and linens are in the house. I purchased a couple of sleeping bags from him as well," he continued.

"Sleeping bags?"

"Yeah, they are like thick blankets that can zip up around you. It makes sleeping on the ground a little easier. I'll show you when we need them. Other than that we are set to leave whenever we are ready. I figured we'd leave at dawn."

"Sounds good. About how long do you think it will take?" She was anxious to get home, but she knew a safe path instead of a fast path was wiser.

"About a month--give or take a few days--if everything goes well. But to be honest," he paused, she looked at him curiously, "I kinda want to see what you are capable of. I kinda want to run into a little trouble just to see you in action. I can already tell you are a bad-ass without the magic." He reached to his face and almost touched his nose. "I can only imagine what you can do with it."

Chapter 12   The Contract

The morning always comes too early. Khayin hated mornings and he woke up early to get them over with. He went out for his ritual jog before the sun broke the horizon. He got back to see Kira sitting cross legged in the middle of her bedroom floor in meditation. He went to his room, grabbed some clothes from the dresser and brought them into the main living space of the house where he had laid out his saddlebags.

Khayin had finished packing when Kira entered the room with a handful of clothes of her own. He motioned to another set of saddlebags that laid beside his. She walked up beside him and without speaking, softly elbowed him and gestured to his face with a nod of her head. He took it as an apology for hitting him. She then packed her things.

"Mrs. Barragan said she'd set out some food, some to pack and some for breakfast." Kira didn't turn around; she remained focused on packing. "There's a small village about forty miles from here. That'll be our first stop. If it's abandoned we can use one of the shacks for shelter. If not, hopefully we can barter for a roof over our heads. I also got a water purifier from Luis, so we shouldn't have a problem keeping hydrated."

"OK," she said. There was a long moment where the two of them didn't say anything. Khayin wasn't upset. He healed quickly and his nose was just as it had been before she broke it. He was just happy that she didn't unleash any of her magic. Kira hitting him showed that she was warming up to him, which would make their journey a lot easier.

"Khayin." She was facing him now. "Sometime tonight we should talk. We both have questions and I think that our journey will be much more bearable if we knew each other a little better."

"Agreed." He smiled. "Let's put these bags on the horses and see what the missus has for us."

The two of them walked outside. The three horses Khayin had procured the night before stood tethered to a post in front of the house. He approached a tall black stallion and stroked the animal.

"Good morning, Chewie," he said to the horse.

"Wasn't that the name of your other horse?" she asked.

"Yep," he responded, "I call all my horses Chewie."

"Why? Isn't that a little...I don't know, impersonal?"

"Yeah, that's the point. I go through a lot of horses." He continued to fasten the bags onto the beast.

"Why Chewie?" She also fastened her saddlebags to her horse.

He shot her a questioning look. "Why not? Chewie's the best damn co-pilot in the galaxy."

"Galaxy?" He could tell she was completely confused.

He sighed. "Look, if you ever want to visit or hang out after we find your home, I'll take you to go see the best damn movies ever made." It was hard to hold back his excitement just thinking about it.

"Movies?"

"Dear lord, woman. What rock have you been living under?" The look on her face made Khayin change his tone. "Sorry, I didn't mean to offend. We'll talk later, maybe we'll have a better understanding of each other then," he said with a smile.

They walked together to Luis's home. Mrs. Barragan was waiting for them on the front porch, rocking slowly in a wooden rocking chair. A large sack of something sat on the floor of the porch next to a small table. On the table lay some fresh fruits, bread and a couple of glasses of water.

"Khayin, Luis says you're a bounty hunter?" Mrs. Barragan asked.

"That's right."

"And you are heading to Panama?"

"Right again. You going for the hat-trick?" He smirked.

"The what?" she asked, obviously confused.

"Never mind." *I need to get myself back to the states where at least some of my jokes are understood.*

"Our daughter ran away from home, and she's in Panama with her boyfriend. We'd like you to bring her back home." She eyed Khayin. He could tell she was trying to read him. "We'd pay you, of course."

"I'm kinda in the middle of something right now." He actually liked the idea. He may even get some pay up front which they could use, but taking a bounty could get distracting. And on top of that who knew if they were being followed. It could put the Barragan's daughter in danger.

"You are going in that direction anyway. And from what Luis tells me, the only reason you are here with us is that you could not afford a port to Panama, so you could use the chips, yes?" She gently rocked.

Fuck. She's got me there.

"My standard fee for a non-violent bounty is two thousand chips, but Panama is a good month's travel..."

"We'll pay you five thousand now and an additional five when you return her to us. Sound fair?" Her face was deadpan. Khayin was beginning to wonder who was actually in charge on this farm. He liked her.

Khayin closed the gap between himself and the Mrs. Barragan. He outstretched his hand and she shook it, sealing the deal.

"Good," she said, "the money is in the sack with your food." The right corner of her mouth curled up ever-so-slightly. Kira smiled.

"Well played, Mrs. Barragan, well played." He released her hand. "I need details."

"Of course." She reached into the folds of her shirt and produced an envelope. "Inside is a picture of my daughter. Her name is Rosa. You will also find a picture of her boyfriend." Her face turned sour on that last part. "He has ties to the cartel and truth be told, I couldn't care less what happens to him. He has been nothing but trouble." Khayin just nodded.

"You probably won't hear from me for a while."

"I'm aware of that," she responded.

"If you need to get a message to me send it to Mistress Tao. She'll know how to get it to me, and I'll do the same." She nodded in understanding. "Good. It's been a pleasure. Thank you for your hospitality and thank your husband for me too."

"I will. Take care, Khayin." She looked at Kira. "You too." Kira only nodded.

****

Ever since they had left the Barragan estate, Khayin couldn't shake the feeling of them being followed. For three days they hadn't seen a single soul on the road. He'd turn around and nothing. He doubled back and still the feeling remained.

Who would be following us? Are they after me or Kira? And how'd they know where to find us?

He became anxious. He wasn't scared--it took a lot more than a stalker to do that--but he didn't like the unknowns. Every once in a while he'd glance at Kira and he could tell that she sensed it as well. She would occasionally take quick checks behind her. The edginess he was feeling was getting on his nerves. Then it was gone.

The first village they came to was still in Mexico, but hadn't been in existence before the Cataclysm. The sun had just dropped below the horizon. The village's name was Refugio and from what Khayin could tell it was abandoned. Well, most of it was abandoned. A few buildings sheltered some families and it looked as though they were barely surviving.

Khayin and Kira brought their horses to a vacant house on the opposite side of where the villagers had their homes. Well, the word "houses" was overstating what they actually were. They were no more than metal shacks of one room each. The villagers seemed to pay Khayin and Kira no mind. He tethered the horses to a small tree behind the shack.

"Can you bind them so no one steals them?" Khayin asked.

"I think I've got something that might work." Kira walked over to the tree and started to draw a circle in the dirt around it.

Khayin took the saddlebags and put them in the shack. He didn't like the idea of removing all the saddlebags, but he didn't want to take any chances. Kira had finished her spell as Khayin grabbed the last of the supplies. Her eyes glowed slightly and her tattoos were more visible. She looked alive. Not that she wasn't before, but now she seemed more vibrant.

"I'll start a fire," Kira said.

She grabbed some twigs and branches from the small wooded area behind their shack and made a pile a couple of yards in front. She then scoured the area for some large stones and built a makeshift fire pit. With a word, a fire sparked and jumped to life in the pit. Khayin came from the shack with some bread and some beef that had been protected with a preservation spell. He carried a couple of canteens as well.

They settled themselves on some chairs Kira had found in her search for stones. Khayin pulled out his cigarette tin and produced a couple of pre-rolled cigarettes. He offered one to Kira, who accepted. Khayin reclined as much as his chair would let him and stared into the darkening sky.

"My sisters live on an island. The trees on the island are very tall and the branches and leaves block out the sun. It's like night there all the time." She paused for a drag on the cigarette. "There are a dozen tribes. All have the same beliefs, but none really ever got along. We all worship, or take counsel, from a dragon that lives on the island."

"Dragon?"

"That's what she calls herself, though I'm sure she can take the form of anything really. Legends say she was once human, but no one knows for sure and she has gone by hundreds, if not thousands, of names." She took another drag from her cigarette.

Khayin took the opportunity. "You mentioned slaves once."

"I did." She looked at Khayin for the first time during her story. "Women rule the island. Men are slaves. They're there for reproduction and chores we feel are beneath us, like washing dirty dishes," she said with a slight smirk. "It's been that way for centuries or more. Men of our tribes show no affinity to magic and thus are deemed inconsequential, expendable." She made a shooing motion with her hand.

Khayin decided not to comment on that. "Do you have siblings?"

"My mother is the Crone, leader of our tribe. And I have a twin sister a few minutes younger than me. Her name is Brianna'Tal." She turned her gaze to the starry sky.

"Wait, so, you're a princess?" Khayin liked this.

"I guess, technically. I'm heir to be the next Crone." She finished her cigarette and tossed it into the fire pit. "Enough about me. Talk."

"My name is Khayin. I'm a Pisces. I like long walks on the beach," he began.

"Fuck you."

He laughed. He was really beginning to enjoy her company. She didn't irritate him as much as people usually do. "Well, princess. I don't know much. I don't remember ever being a kid. I have no recollection of a family. In fact, my earliest memory is me as an adult." He took a long drag on his cigarette. "They're only fuzzy images, but I remember standing over a man lying in a pool of his own blood and me holding the dagger."

Chapter 13   The Convoy

Kira just stared at him. She wasn't expecting what she just heard and as vague as it was she figured they were even in the "opening up" they had agreed to. She had grown up with such a low opinion of men that she found it hard to appreciate them at all. She liked Khayin though. She could even see herself being attracted to him. She wouldn't let herself pursue that line of thinking though. It's best to leave that alone.

"I'm going to turn in." She stood up. "My ass is hurting from all the riding today and we are still at the beginning of our journey."

"Goodnight, Princess."

"Is that what you're going to call me now?" She stood in the doorway of the shack.

"I might throw in a 'Your Highness' or a 'Your Worship' when the mood hits."

"I have a name," she countered.

"Yep, Princess," he said with a smile.

Kira shook her head in defeat. She smiled and closed the door. That was a fight not worth fighting.

****

The evening passed without a hitch. They checked the horses and found no foul play, so they packed and prepared for their journey. Before they left they had breakfast and found a nearby stream. They filtered some water to refill their canteens and walked their horses out of town a little way before mounting them. They left the village shortly after dawn.

Khayin pointed out on the map that their next stop wouldn't be a village, town, or city. They would have to camp. Their travels that day did bring them through a couple of small settlements. Those settlements had no trade or commerce and barely had enough food or water for themselves. They didn't stop. They didn't talk a whole lot either. She had a ton of questions for this man and she had a distinct feeling he knew more than he was letting on.

The day got hot and there wasn't a lot of shade. Traveling at night would've been more dangerous, so they had to endure the sun. It was midday, just after they stopped for a quick bite to eat when they noticed a skirmish in the road ahead of them.

There were four men and two women armed with crossbows and pistols. A couple of them had bladed weapons sheathed at their sides. They were holding up a caravan. The victims--Kira counted three--were garbed in long robes and they had hoods covering their heads. From her vantage point she couldn't tell if they were male or female.

Khayin stopped, as did Kira. She looked at Khayin.

"Should we intervene?" she asked.

"We probably should. They look defenseless. I hate bullies."

"I could swing around them and try to flank," she strategized.

"If they didn't already know we were here that would be ideal, but we are exposed in the middle of the road. They're just waitin' to see what we'll do." He glared at them. "How good of a shot are you from horseback?"

"Fair, but I can be more effective with my magic." She grinned. "Besides, you said you wanted to see me in action."

Khayin looked at her, a wide smile stretched across his face. "OK, Princess, show me what you've got."

As they got off their horses two of the raiders approached pointing their pistols at them. Kira couldn't see any distinguishing marks to signify that they were part of a larger group. A male and a female addressed them.

"Fuck off, pendejo, unless you want an extra hole in yer head." The woman waved her gun as though shooing away a fly.

"The way I see it," Khayin began, "there are six armed thugs harassing three unarmed people, so we thought we might even the odds."

Khayin shot first. The woman who tried to chase them off laid dead with a hole in her head. At the motion of pulling his gun Kira Pulled from the elements and threw the dead raider's partner. The telekinetic force picked him up and slammed him against a tree. She heard bones break and splinter. The rush of power put a smile on her face.

The others forgot about their prey and turned to try and eliminate the new threat. The three travelers ran and hid behind their wagon. A tall burly man with a pistol took aim at Khayin, who dove and rolled, making the big man miss. Khayin shot as soon as he recovered from his roll and hit the big man in the leg. The man dropped. A crossbow bolt nicked Kira's ear as it flew just wide, and she could feel the sting as blood began to trickle down the side of her neck. Kira Pulled a stone the size of a human skull and hurled it at the man reloading his crossbow. There was a loud crack when the stone collided with the man's head.

A second bolt caught Kira in the shoulder. The bolt sank deep. The impact spun her a bit and she cried out in pain. Her eyes flared and her tattoos glowed brightly. Luckily the bolt head was just a point and not a broad head. She yanked it free from her shoulder with a wince and threw it at the woman who had shot her. She Pulled and propelled the bolt faster than any crossbow and it struck the raider in her chest. The bolt went straight through, knocking her back several feet.

Khayin rose and took aim at one of the two remaining thugs. A raider grabbed one of the unarmed travelers. Hiding behind his new shield, he shot Khayin. It hit and went clean through his left arm. The injured arm swung from the impact and Khayin used the momentum, taking a wild shot and putting a hole through the raider's head. The spray of gore covered the last raider before he decided to run. Kira Pulled him up high into the air. She let him dangle there a moment before she slammed him so hard into the ground that what was left of him barely looked human anymore.

The elation, the pure ecstasy of the moment filled Kira. The magic coursed through her veins; it buzzed and tingled all around her. The feeling she had felt back at Merlin's place when her magic had returned was almost a rebirth, an awakening of part of herself. What she felt when she unleashed her power, though, was like she could challenge the gods themselves.

The travelers in the caravan picked themselves up and started to climb into their wagon. The wagon, Kira noticed, looked very similar to the covered wagons of a caravan, except that it had no horses pulling it. The wheels were made of a combination of metal and rubber. The travelers paid them no mind. They gave no indication that Kira and Khayin were even there.

"Can we help you?" Khayin asked.

They ignored him and continued repacking their possessions.

Kira thought she'd try. "Are you going to be all right? Are any of you hurt?" Just saying that reminded her of her own injuries and her shoulder began to throb.

Again, they ignored them.

Khayin threw up his hands then winced from the pain in his arm. "Fine, we take bullets and bolts for you and you can't even throw out a thank you. Hell, I'd even settle for a 'Fuck you! We didn't need your help.'" He said the last part in a weird accent that Kira wasn't familiar with.

At that, one of the robed figures approached Khayin. Kira peeked in the hood and saw the most beautiful man she had ever seen. His skin was without blemish and his eyes were as blue/green as the sea. The man dropped a single gold coin into Khayin's hand and he walked away. The two of them just watched the caravan leave.

When the wagon was out of ear shot, Khayin turned to Kira. "Did you get a look at that face?" Khayin asked. Kira nodded. "No offense, you're hot, but that was the most beautiful woman I had ever seen."

"I know, I...wait. You saw a woman?" Kira asked confused.

"Yeah, why, what did you see?"

"A man."

Did he just say I was hot? As in, pretty?

They both just looked at each other. Khayin then inspected the gold coin in his hand, holding it up for Kira to see as well. On one side of the coin was a picture of a man with a trimmed beard. On the other side was an island with a strange symbol at its center and a row of symbols that followed the top curve of the coin. Kira snatched the gold from Khayin. She examined it more closely.

"Atlantis," was all she said.

"You can read that?"

"No, not really, I've seen this kind of coin before," she said with a tad bit of smugness.

"What do you know about Atlantis?" Khayin asked.

"Nothing much. I heard from traders that it's a paradise, but not easy to get to. And they are picky on who they let enter. Of course, this is all hearsay."

"Hmm...I've heard the same. I've never tried getting there." He shook his head. "Anyway."

Before they mounted their horses Khayin took a small round tin from a saddle bag. With a twist Khayin opened it. Inside was a milky paste-like substance.

"Smear this on your wounds. By the time we make camp they should be healed." Khayin explained. Kira took the tin and did what he instructed before handing it back. He applied some on his own injury and then mounted his horse.

****

They found an old run-down shack on the side of the road at dusk. No other buildings in the immediate area remained standing and by the look of the one that was, it didn't seem it was going to stand very much longer. They unpacked the things they would need for the night and left the rest on the horses. Kira drew a warding circle around the horses to alert them if anyone got too close. Khayin started a fire and they ate.

"That was pretty badass," Khayin said, handing Kira a cigarette. "I mean, I've seen plenty of people use magic, but what you did, and that control. It's like breathing to you, isn't it? Like second nature."

Kira took the cigarette. She was beaming. She was still riding the high. It had been several hours since, but she was still thrilled. "I was holding back," she managed to say.

"Well shit, remind me not to get on your bad side, Princess."

"You keep calling me that and you soon will," she said with a smile. Khayin laughed. She flexed her once-wounded shoulder. "That stuff worked great."

"Yeah, I got it off a traveling Alchemist. I don't need it much, because I tend to heal quickly on my own, but sometimes I use it to jumpstart the process."

"You mentioned your fast healing before. Magic?" she asked.

"No idea; it's just part of being me. I'm turning in early. The healing wore me out." He finished his cigarette and excused himself.

Kira sat by the fire a little longer. She looked at the stars. The moon was full and bright and the night was filled with silence. After a while she got up and entered the shack. Khayin was asleep. She stripped down to just her underwear and tank top and stood over him. She needed him right then. Khayin never zipped his bag, so she could open it without him knowing. She straddled him and his eyes jerked open. She immediately placed her index and middle fingers over his lips.

"I need this," she said plainly.

The magic still coursed through her. She could feel it tickle her skin. She moved Khayin's hands, encouraging him. He was reluctant and reached up to keep her away.

"Kira, I don't think we..."

She slapped his arm away and kissed him hard, cutting off his words. He resisted, but quickly gave in. Their tongues wrestled and their bodies entwined. Kira needed this. She was in control and all she cared about was that moment. There was no tomorrow. There was no yesterday. There was only that moment and she wanted it; she wanted him.

****

Kira was the first to awake. Khayin held her. They were both completely nude and their clothes were scattered around the shack. She thought about the night. She smiled and her heart fluttered. *What the fuck! No! I'm not falling for him. This can't happen. This isn't supposed to happen. It was just sex.* Kira got up with a sudden jerk and Khayin awoke.

"Is everything OK?" Khayin asked.

"No!" she snapped. She grabbed her clothes and marched outside.

Khayin appeared in the doorway, naked body welcoming the morning. His tattooed skin glistened in the dawn light. The tattoos were of patterns and symbols, no pictures. Scars from various wounds were faint but noticeable, and not at all marring.

"What..." he began.

"Shut up!" she barked, pulling up her pants. She spun around naked from the waist up. "Just shut up." The last part was almost a whisper, and tears were streaming down her face. She picked up her shirt and stormed off.

Chapter 14   The Seer

It had been two weeks of silence. Well, Khayin spoke, but Kira had remained quiet. Khayin was beside himself. *What the hell? She wanted sex. I even tried pushing her away. Fuck, I knew this was going to happen.* He tried confronting her, almost demanding a response, but all he got was a glare. He liked Kira and they had been getting along great, or so he thought. Now he was looking forward to just dropping her off with her sisters and leaving.

Their trip was uneventful. They managed to stay away from all known hot spots and they made good time. They were less than a week away from Panama and Khayin couldn't wait. The morning was like all the others and Khayin got up early for his run. When he got back, Kira was preparing breakfast. Khayin took a towel from his pack and wiped the sweat from his face.

He walked over to the area they made up for dining and reached to take a portion of what she had made. To his surprise she had already made him a plate. She handed it to him and their eyes met briefly, she turned away. They ate in silence, but Khayin was happy that she made a gesture.

Before they broke camp they saw a large traveling caravan headed their way. Khayin saw there was a rifle next to coach driver and the few people on horseback had little to no weapons at all. There were a dozen covered wagons, painted and draped in multiple colors. *Gypsies in Central America? Why not? They may steal some chips, but we should be safe.* Strange though it was,

Khayin was happy to see them. They continued to pack their things, but waited to greet the gypsies before they left.

The caravan stopped when they reached the small camp. A tall, lanky, athletic man in bright loose clothing jumped from the lead wagon and walked toward them. There was a ring on every finger and multiple earrings in both ears.

"Well met. The name is Fonso." He bowed. "I'm spokesman of our wandering tribe. We're a long way from home, exploring new lands and meeting new people."

"I'm Khayin and this here is my friend Kira." He held out his hand for a shake.

"Ah, yes the customary handshake, very good." He shook Khayin's hand. He turned his attention to Kira. "And you, lovely lady, a pleasure to meet you." He bowed again, but this time much more deeply. He took Kira's hand, which she allowed, and he kissed her knuckles.

Kira looked at Khayin then back to Fonso. She gave a slight nod and whispered, "Thank you."

"Oh, the pleasure's all mine," he said with a wide smile. "May I ask where you're headed? We've noticed you packing."

Khayin regarded him. Seems harmless enough. "Panama. We've been on the road for nearly three weeks."

"Oh my. On horseback? I can't imagine how your asses must feel." He laughed. "Please, let me welcome you as our honored guests." He gestured to the caravan behind him. "For we Romani are headed for the same destination. We'd welcome your stories and we shall entertain you with song and dance."

"We couldn't possible pay you." Khayin lied.

"Nonsense. Your company and stories will be payment enough, as long as you allow us to retell them." His smile never faded.

Khayin looked at Kira. She shrugged with a slight nod. "OK, Fonso. We'd be happy to tag along."

Though Khayin didn't think it was possible, Fonso's smile grew bigger. "Huzzah!" he yelled. And the caravan behind him mimicked him.

Several gypsies took their horses and tied them into the

caravan. A group of women around Kira's age led her to a wagon in the center of the train. Fonso offered Khayin the seat next him on the lead wagon. Khayin happily climbed aboard. With a snap of the reins the caravan was moving once again.

"So, Khayin, what's it you seek in Panama?" Fonso's eyes were transfixed to the road ahead. "If you don't mind me inquiring."

"Seeking an old acquaintance. We're searching for something and I've reason to believe he'll have answers." Khayin wanted to keep it vague, but truthful enough in hopes Fonso wouldn't pry.

"Is that what you do then?" he asked. "For a living."

"Kinda, I'm a Bounty Hunter." He could see Fonso physically tense up. *Had a run-in with hunters before?*

"I see." His voice never changed despite his apparent uneasiness.

Khayin smiled. "You needn't worry about me. I've never had any trouble with the Romani, always passed on jobs for your people. I've even warned a few Romani caravans to steer clear of some towns, if you know what I mean," Khayin said to put him at ease.

"I appreciate that, my friend." He gave Khayin a smile and a nod.

****

Kira sat on a pile of pillows in an overly decorated wagon. Paintings, portraits, silks and linens hung on all four walls. She felt as though she were sitting on a cloud. It felt so nice that she almost fell asleep. The other girls asked her a ton of questions though, so sleep wasn't an option. She spent the whole day's trip relaying stories of how she and Khayin had met and their travels together thus far. The Romani girls kept inquiring about Khayin and her relationship with him. She started to feel bad for the way she had been treating him. *Why am I treating him like this? I keep getting these emotional feelings for him. It was just sex, why do I feel anything?* She was mad at herself.

The conversation finally ended when the caravan decided to camp for the evening. The gypsies wouldn't allow Khayin or Kira to help with anything. They refused any and all liquor and food Khayin offered, instead offering their own for the two of them to partake as much as they liked. It was the best meal she had had since leaving the Barragan's farm.

Dinner ended and was promptly followed by song and dance. Khayin showed no shame and danced when a couple of young ladies pulled him into the circle around the fire. The music was beautiful and the dancing was mesmerizing. Two more girls tried pulling Kira into the dance. She fought it at first, but the girls wouldn't take no for an answer and she eventually relented.

The Romani moved in an almost ritualistic fashion. They were hypnotic. Their skin glistened with perspiration from the heat of the fire. Some dancers shed their clothing. The music was heavy with drums. The guitar provided the rhythm and the violin was fast and beautiful.

Kira danced. She would catch glimpses of Khayin with other girls. The Romani girls danced very close with him and touched him, which made her feel a twisting in her stomach. She would quickly look away. She lost herself in the music, moving and swaying to the rhythm. Kira allowed her magic to swell within her. She became one with the song, dancing with both and women. Memories of her sisters flooded her mind. She missed home, but she was enraptured in the moment.

The music slowed and the other dancers surreptitiously moved Kira and Khayin closer. The dance moved slow and deliberate. They both were caught in the magic of music before they realized they were dancing with each other.

They both stopped and looked into each other's eyes. Khayin opened his mouth, but before he could speak Kira turned and walked away. *I'm not ready. What is holding me back? I need to figure this out. I need to talk to him.* She looked back to him and caught his gaze, snapping her head back and quietly strolling back to the wagon. An elderly woman approached Kira before she could fully retreat to her bed.

"Young one, may I have a word?" There was something familiar about her. Kira felt that she knew her somehow. The old gypsy was dressed in layers of fine fabrics, most of which were silks of different colors. She wore a head-covering made of silk as well. Beads and metal charms hung from her waist and hair. Kira guessed that the woman had to be pushing 100 years of age. She looked frail, but seemed to get along on her own just fine.

"Sure," she said.

Kira followed the old woman to a different wagon. It looked older than the rest. The walls had carved pictorials of wooded landscapes with a cabin that looked like it stood on legs. The carving was also beautifully painted. The wagon had a couple of windows with the curtains drawn. The old woman took the stairs one at a time. She opened the door and stepped in, beckoning for Kira to follow her.

"Come in, come in, I'm not going to bite, I promise." Her voice was inviting, clear and melodic. She smiled a crooked tooth smile.

It was in the light when Kira noticed the woman's face. Simply put, she was ugly, though Kira would never say it. Her nose was too big and her eyes too small. Warts and a large discolored birthmark marred her visage as well. Kira cleared the threshold and entered the wagon. The inside was much more lavish than the one she rode in. Pillows and silks surrounded her, with no furniture to speak of save a rocking chair in the far corner. The woman motioned for Kira to relax on the pillows in front of the chair.

The woman sat in her chair. "May I see your hands, child?"

A reading? I'm coming in here for a reading? Maybe I'll learn something.

Kira turned her hands palms up and displayed them in front of her. The gypsy woman firmly held both of Kira's hands and studied her palms. She then looked her straight in the eyes. They locked gazes for a long time. The gypsy looked back down to Kira's palms and then dropped her hands.

"You carry a lot of weight, child." She sighed. "Much more than you can bear."

"I'm lost. I'm trying to find my home, to get back to my family." Tears started to well up. She wiped her eyes with the back of her hands.

"I see that, too." The woman rocked. She pulled out a small

rolled cigarette and she lit it with nothing. It literally lit itself. The smoke from the cigarette smelled funny. Definitely not cigarette smoke, it gave off more of a sweet skunky smell. "But that is not what I'm talking about."

Kira winced. *What does she see?* She felt exposed and she didn't like it. "I don't remember how or when I got lost. I have no memories of it, not even vague flashes."

"What are you hiding from, child?" The old woman probed. "Something happened to you when you were young. What happened?"

She couldn't have seen that. No, I don't want to remember.
"Please, I don't want to relive that," she pleaded.

"You will never see your full potential if you do not. You must face that demon. You must own it. Tell me. You are safe here." She gently rocked in her chair.

Kira started to feel euphoric. The smoke in the wagon was effecting her. She wasn't entirely sure if it was magic or just an herbal hallucinogen. "When I was a girl of sixteen I had a friend. It was a slave boy of the same age. We would secretly play out of sight of my mother and sisters, or so I thought." Tears began to flow and Kira didn't bother to wipe them. "We drew close, as close as kids could get. I truly believe I loved him and him me." She sniffled. "I would spend every spare minute of free time I had with him. He was my best friend. We would talk for hours. I felt most happy when I was with him. I didn't care that he was a slave and he didn't care that I was the Crone's daughter." She looked up at the old gypsy through wells of tears. "We made plans to escape together, because we knew that what we had was forbidden. Men were tools, they weren't lovers. My tribe would never condone what we had. We would never be accepted. We had to run away; it was our only hope."

She paused to choke down the lump that was forming in her throat. It was difficult to talk. She drew her knees to her chest and sat in a fetal position. She started to rock slightly.

"The night we planned our escape everything seemed to go smoothly. Looking back on it now I would say it went too smooth, but I was young and in love, blind to everything but him." She paused to wipe away some snot that ran from her nose. "There was a path in the back woods that I was sure I was the only one who knew about. We were supposed to meet there. Only when I got there..."

There was a long silence. The old lady just smoked her short cigarette and waited patiently. Kira looked at her, not wanting to go on. Her stomach was in knots, her muscles tense, and her heart raced.

"He was there...but so was my sister Brianna and the Crone, my mother." She let out a whimper, trying to hold back an all-out wail. "His hands were tied behind his back and he was on his knees. Brianna held a dagger. They both glared at me. As soon as Brianna saw me she hit him in the back of the neck hard. I could hear him cry out from the pain. I was in a panic. My mind raced, trying to find some way out of it. But there wasn't any and they knew it."

The memory hurt and it took every ounce of her will not to completely break down. She grabbed a pillow and hugged it tightly, rocking all the while. "The Crone beckoned me forth. I had to obey. Part of me said to run, but the part that was in love insisted I stay. I approached her. She was the leader of the tribe, so to disobey could be fatal, daughter or not. I stood a few feet from her. She looked at me, her face completely neutral. She held her hand out to Brianna who handed her the dagger, and then she handed it to me. I hesitated, which awarded me a sharp smack across my face. I knew that was nothing compared to what would happen if I didn't take the knife."

The old woman offered Kira a glass of water that suddenly appeared in her hand. Kira didn't inquire, but took it and drank. "The Crone looked at me as I held the dagger and asked, 'Who is this boy to you?' I knew I couldn't lie; she would see right through it. She knew everything. 'I love him,' I said. She slapped me hard. I fell and hit the ground. Brianna laughed. She asked again, 'Who is this boy to you?' I was weak. I should've stood up to her, but...I didn't. I told her, 'He's a slave.' I stood up and she smiled. 'Good,' she said. 'And what do we do to runaway slaves?' I pleaded with her, but she hit me again, harder. I remember tasting blood.

Brianna giggled. 'Don't make me ask again, Kira'Tal. The punishment for your disobedience could result in the forfeiture of your life, despite being my daughter,' she warned. 'We kill them, zero tolerance.' I replied." She took another drink. The tears still flowed and it was difficult to swallow.

"Brianna was ecstatic and the Crone was stoic. 'Good,' the Crone said, 'we caught him trying to escape and you will carry out the sentence.'" Kira was crying uncontrollably. "No, no more please."

The old gypsy woman just rocked. "What was his name, Kira'Tal?"

"Wh...what?"

"His name. What was his name?" she repeated.

"No."

"His name, child. What was his name?" Her voice was calm.

"NO!" she yelled. "Enough! I've had enough." She stood up and threw the glass of water and it shattered against the far wall. She wailed.

"Face your demons, Kira'Tal. What was his name?" she persisted.

She turned to face the old woman. Her face red and wet with tears. "They made me kill Quinn. I had no choice. They made me. I killed him. I killed my only friend. I killed my love. Fuck! Are you happy? And my sister laughed the whole time. I slit his throat. His blood ran and covered me as I held him. I watched him die. I saw the look of betrayal in his eyes. I killed him. He did nothing wrong and I murdered him."

Chapter 15   The Gift

The silk was smooth and the pillows made her feel as if she were sleeping suspended in mid-air. Kira had cried herself to sleep. She was surprised about the total recall. Whatever the old gypsy was smoking had filled the entirety of the wagon. It must have induced a trance. The emotions were real. She felt as though she was there all over again. Oh, how she had hated her mother and sister after that. She never truly forgave them, but she did bury the incident or she would have never been able to live with them.

Shit! Khayin. No wonder I treated him like dirt. The feelings I once felt for Quinn, I...

Nope, she wasn't going to finish that thought. Too fresh. She stretched. She smelled...bacon. Kira slowly opened her eyes. The old woman sat in her rocker, hand sewing a scarf made of a dark red silk. Kira noticed that the color closely matched her hair. *How long was I out?*

"You slept through the night, child," the gypsy answered.

Did she hear my thoughts?

"Shh...Don't tell anyone. They believe me a feeble old lady." She chuckled. "Come, eat. I have food for you. You slept through breakfast."

Kira crept over to a short table next to the stack of pillows where she lay. There was fresh fruit, bacon, eggs, and grilled buttered bread. She grabbed the tall glass of squeezed orange juice first, then started in on the bacon. There was silence while she ate.

When she finished Kira looked at the old woman who was still sewing charms and lace onto the red scarf. "May I ask your name?"

"Yes you may. Which one would you like, child?" the gypsy responded, never looking up from her work.

"You have more than one?"

"Oh yes, I have gone by many. Some I have been given and some I have taken, much like that dragon your sisters are so fond of." She rocked a steady rhythm.

That threw her. *What does she know? How much does she know?*

"I know very little, I am afraid. Of your sisters and your culture, I mean. That dragon on the other hand. I know her very well, but that is not a story for me to tell." Her rocking stopped for a brief moment as if she needed all her concentration for something, then she started again like she had never stopped. "I have gone by Baba, or Jezibaba. Some have called me Gorska, Gvozdenzuba, or Holda, but the caravan calls me Muma, I think that would suffice."

"Muma Padurii," Kira whispered. "I've heard...stories."

"If we were being formal, yes, but please, do not get caught up in names, child. You have some things to work through. You need to decide who you are." Kira looked at Muma and their gazes locked. "Are you going to be that sixteen-year-old girl who followed her heart, or are you going to be the girl that slit her first love's throat? Whose life are you to live?"

Kira looked away. She almost felt embarrassed. This woman knew her too well. She had so many questions, but somehow she knew the only reason they spoke so openly was that Muma meant to help guide her.

"I thank you, Muma Padurii," Kira said with a deep bow while kneeling.

"Oh, for heaven's sake, child. Get up." She started to rock more feverously. "I am just an old gypsy."

Kira straightened and stood up. She still wore the same clothes she had the night before. She turned to clean up her breakfast, only to find that it was no longer there. Her gaze fell on

Muma. The old woman held out the scarf to her.

"For you." Kira showed a look of surprise. "Now do not be so surprised. You knew I would give this to you when you noticed its color." Kira bowed once again. "Get. You are embarrassing yourself."

****

Khayin helped the gypsies pack up. The sun peeked out over the horizon when everything and everyone was ready to leave. The plan was for the caravan to head to Panama without stopping. They were only a few days out and the gypsies had a performance scheduled in the city at the end of the week. Khayin didn't argue. He wasn't entirely sure what bug had crawled up Kira's ass, but he was looking forward to dropping her off. All his hopes rested on Tippy. *Too bad, I was really beginning to like her.*

He saw Kira leave the old gypsy Muma's wagon. He had asked around. From the stories he had gathered about the old woman, it hadn't taken long for him to figure out who she was. With her traveling with the gypsies it was no wonder how they had survived their travels unscathed. He just hoped Muma was in one of her better moods.

Kira seemed fine and she even nodded when she spotted him. He nodded back. Kira walked to a group of women, helped with whatever they needed and then entered their wagon, but not before looking back to catch Khayin's gaze again. *Something happened in there.*

The way was long and the roads were uneven and rocky at their best. Khayin would sometimes ride shotgun with Fonso, though Khayin kept calling it 'Wookiee' and not 'Shotgun,' and no one knew what he was talking about. This was also about the time that Khayin's falcon, Millennium, returned. Khayin could sense that Millennium liked it when he teleported on occasion; it gave the bird of prey freedom to hunt and play when he wanted.

After greeting Khayin, Millennium flew over to the wagon Kira was in and rested on top. The rest of the trip remained as peaceful as it could be. The caravan pulled into Panama just before dusk on the fifth day after Khayin and Kira had joined them. The gypsies stopped and Khayin and Kira bid their farewells. They were given more food than they could've possibly eaten and more wine than...well, Khayin didn't mind the wine. Then the pair set off to find lodging for the night. They would search for Tippy in the morning.

The city was about as mag-technologically advanced as Mexico City, which was to say not much at all. There were some buildings with magical energy lighting them up, but for the most part it was old school third world. That didn't mean the city was dead. On the contrary, it was quite alive. The city was a shipping port and it was the central hub for imports and exports for all the surrounding cities and towns.

The wizards that operated here were mainly Spellcasters and Artificers. There was only one Tech Wizard here and he kept most of his magic to himself. The Spellcasters were used on the ships, to help protect against pirates, though their services were very expensive. Ship battles with wizards tended to last a very long time. They would cast incantations to protect the hull from cannonball fire and spells. The ships would just lob cannonballs back and forth until they ran out of cannonballs or wizards ran out of spells. And Artificers, well who doesn't like magical weapons and items?

Khayin and Kira found a hotel near the center of the city. Hotel Panama--the hotel never changed the name. They checked their horses in a nearby stable that once was a parking structure and they entered the hotel. They were greeted by a bellhop who was more than eager to get their bags. Together with the bellhop they went to the counter to get a room.

"We'd like a couple of rooms," Khayin explained.

The clerk, a young man wearing a vest over a tailored shirt checked the registry and looked up with a frown. The frown did his face no favors. His face was full of pock marks and other blemishes. "I'm sorry, sir, we only have one room available. With the gypsy caravan in town we are all booked. The room has double beds." He said the last part with a smile.

Khayin looked at Kira thoughtfully. She gazed back and gave

him a nod and shrug. "We'll take it." Khayin reached for his pouch of chips.

"How many nights will you be staying with us, sir?"

"How long are the gypsies in town?" Khayin asked.

"Through the weekend, sir." He said through a toothy grin.

"I'll pay through the weekend then." He opened his pouch. "If we need more time, how much notice do you need for me to extend it?"

"Well, considering most of our guests are leaving when the caravan does and we don't have very many bookings after, you can let us know as late as Saturday evening."

"Can you write that down in your book, just in case you aren't the one at the desk?" Khayin winked at him.

"Why certainly, sir." The clerk made a notation in the registry. "That will be one-hundred fifty chips."

Khayin raised an eyebrow, but didn't argue. He counted out the chips and handed them to the clerk. He closed the pouch and tied it to his belt. He looked at Kira and rolled his eyes. She grinned. The clerk finished writing in his book and he turned around and grabbed the room key.

"Here you are, sir. Room 1138," he said with a big smile.

"Are you shittin' me?" Khayin was half surprised and half amused.

"Something wrong, sir?" The clerk looked concerned.

"No, no, nothing wrong. Thanks." Khayin took the key and walked away shaking his head in amusement.

Kira looked at Khayin. "Something wrong with the room?"

"No, it's nothing." *Just another movie reference you wouldn't understand.*

The room was clean. That was all Khayin really cared about, that and beds. He lit a couple of lamps and plopped down on the sofa. He let his head fall back to rest on the back of the couch. Kira dropped her bags at the foot of one of the beds and took a seat in a cushioned chair across from Khayin. He needed to talk to her and he hoped she was ready to listen.

"Kira." He kept looking at the ceiling. He thought by using her actual name and not one of his nicknames for her, she would know he was serious. "I'm assuming you are going through some shit and I'm not going to pretend what that may be." He sighed, and Kira remained quiet. "Look, you're almost home, so this may be a moot point. You're a bad-ass. You don't take no shit, you can hold your own in a fight, and you aren't afraid to stand up for yourself. I've got a lot of respect for you."

"Khayin..."

"No, let me finish. I've got no idea what happened three weeks ago and frankly a part of me is going to say good riddance when we find your home." He lowered his gaze to meet hers. "But for some real annoying reason I've no clue on, I can't leave our relationship like this. I don't have many 'friends'. I just act like I do. I've got my own personal demons and I tend to push people away and only a few very persistent individuals have stuck around long enough to actually befriend me, but more importantly, me to them. You've worked your way in a hella lot faster than anyone, and that is saying somethin'."

Khayin waited till her eyes fell on him and they locked gazes. "Here's the deal. Tell me to fuck off--I won't ask why--and I'll still get you home. Or..." He paused, studying her a bit. His heart fluttered and his skin felt tingly. "There's a saying 'shit or get off the pot'." He smiled and he hoped he didn't offend her.

"Khayin." She waited a long moment and exhaled audibly. "Thank you." He could tell that that wasn't easy for her to say. "Muma made me face my past and she made me realize I have a choice to make. I'm not ready to tell you what happened in her wagon, but," she breathed in deep and exhaled. "Look, that night, it...what we did, it...it meant more to me than I expected. Feelings I haven't felt for a...I freaked out. It wasn't your fault. I'm sorry." He looked deep into her pale blue eyes. "I don't know what will happen if or when we find my home. I still don't know why I ended up with that Mexican bounty hunter to begin with. For all I know I was exiled." She bit her lower lip. "You have been more than kind to me, and after all the shit we've been through I hope I can call you a friend."

She got up from her chair, walked over to Khayin, grabbed his hand and pulled him up for an embrace. It was a nice hug that lasted a couple of minutes.

"Let's get some sleep. I have a feeling we are going to need a full night's rest," Khayin said. "And thank you for your honesty."

Chapter 16   The Interrogator

Chicago was considered the most high-tech in all of the Americas. The whole city ran on magically infused generators, which provided a faux electricity. It was magic that powered everything, but to the layman it was referred to as electricity. Lights, heat, and just about anything else that needed power to work just needed to be plugged in and directly linked to an infused generator. It took nearly two centuries and a whole lot of chips to achieve what Chi-Town had accomplished.

Motorized vehicles rode the streets, though not as many as before the Cataclysm. It was a rare Tech Wizard who specialized in cars. It was dirty work, but it paid very well. Most couldn't afford to keep one on the road. The mechanical parts worked fine, but anything electrical needed that wizard touch. Also with no oil refineries, Tech Wizards had to come up with an entirely different kind of fuel.

Joshua Dorne woke early. He loved the mornings. He had an early workout and a hearty breakfast. He kissed his wife and baby goodbye and headed off to work. It was a beautiful day. Dorne walked, as he lived only a few blocks from the Nueden Corporation Building where he worked for the security division. The Chief was his boss and he headed up security while Dorne was second in command and handled field operations, though he never personally went into the field.

The Nueden building was only two stories tall, but had many

sub-floors. Dorne entered the building and gave a polite smile and wave to the security desk just inside. He took the stairs down to sub-floor thirteen. Dorne nodded a greeting to the security guard just outside the door and he entered the lobby. A pretty, young woman sat behind the reception desk. She smiled when she saw him. He liked that. He never got that kind of attention when he was younger. He wouldn't have even gotten the time of day from a girl like her.

"Good morning, Susan. How is my favorite secretary today?" he said warmly.

She pouted. "I'm your only secretary, Mr. Dorne."

"Because God broke the mold after he made you." Dorne poured on the charm. Susan blushed. "How's our guest?"

"Not a peep," she said in a chipper tone.

"Excellent." Dorne knew she wouldn't have heard anything anyway. Their guest rooms were all soundproofed. "I'll be entertaining our guest all morning so please see to it that I am not disturbed."

"Yes, sir," she said with a flimsy, inaccurate salute that he adored.

Dorne walked down a long hall and entered the door at its end. It opened to another hall with several doors running alongside both walls. He followed the hall until he found the door he needed, unlocking the three locks and entering. Dorne stood in a small cubicle-like lobby, only big enough to fit two people standing side-by-side. The door in front of him was solid metal filled with a sound-suppressing foam. Glued onto the other side of the door was more soundproofing foam. All four walls and the ceiling were covered in the same foam.

In the center of the room in a chair sat a woman, badly beaten. She had once been beautiful, but that had never stopped Dorne before. She was tied to the chair with zip ties and the chair was fastened to the floor. On the far wall was a table with many tools and surgical instruments ceremoniously displayed. Dorne approached the woman.

"Good morning, Maria. How are we feeling today?" Dorne said, all smiles. He could feel his excitement grow. Just the thought of what he planned to do aroused him.

Maria's long black hair hung in her face as she looked at the floor. She said nothing. She never said anything. Maria was a hard one to break. He had gotten Jesus to talk, but the old bartender hadn't really known anything of worth. Dorne had a feeling that Maria knew something.

"The pain will end when you tell me what I need to know. It's really that simple." She remained silent. He exhaled loudly. "Fine. I only have you until lunch today and if you're smart, you'll talk, because the Boss wants to have a chat with you if I'm unsuccessful."

She perked up and looked at him. "Your Chief don't scare me, pendejo." She spat at his feet.

Dorne smiled. "My, what a beautiful voice, I can see why he likes you." He turned away and walked toward the table as a small shiver ran up his spine. "But I'm not referring to the Chief. I'm talking about the boss's boss. The one in charge of the corporation. I guarantee you, you will not like her, especially that pet of hers. No, you are much better off talking to me."

Dorne stopped at the table and examined his toys. He caressed them, gently and softly with his fingertips. He picked up a speculum, a scalpel, and a pair of forceps. "I think we are going to try something different today."

****

Dorne stood in the waiting room of Chief Rantz's office. Elizabeth sat behind her desk doing paperwork. She looked at him and he smiled with a wink. An alarm buzzed on her desk.

"The Chief will see you now, Mr. Dorne," she said politely.

"Thank you, Elizabeth." He marched right into the office, closing the door behind him.

"Well?" the Chief asked as soon as the door shut.

He took a deep breath. "I am afraid all I was able to extract before her untimely demise was a name," he reported. There was a long pause while Dorne waited for the Chief to speak.

"Do I have to beat it out of you?" he barked. Lawrence Rantz had a full beard and wore a military uniform. Dorne never understood why. He couldn't remember the last war, or Chicago ever having an army.

Dorne tried to stay calm. He hated Chief Rantz and the man scared him. He could go off suddenly and Dorne would become part of the wall decorations. He sucked in his gut and stood tall.

"Codex," he said.

"What?" the Chief asked.

"Codex, sir. That's all she knew."

"Are you sure?" he huffed.

"Yes, sir. I am quite sure. She was telling me all kinds of personal stories at the end." He was proud of himself.

"Hmph! We already questioned this...Codex."

"And we got nothing." Dorne reminded him.

"Let's send a squad to Vegas this time. Maybe she'll listen to brute force." Chief Rantz started to pace.

Dorne hated to question the Chief's tactics, but he knew a direct approach on Codex would be bad. He tried to suppress his body shivers. "Sir, is that wise? All reports suggest that she is a quite formidable wizard. As powerful, if not more so, than the Boss herself."

"What do you suggest, Dorne?"

Dorne was in shock. *He's asking my advice?* "Isn't the Boss already involved, sir?"

"Yes, but she must remain behind the scenes for the time being." Rantz played with his beard.

"We can send some battlemages," he suggested. "Don't go after this Codex directly. We'll do some recon; hit the people close to her."

"I will run this by the Boss, but I like the way you think, Dorne." A smile stretched across his face. "I think you should lead this expedition."

Dorne nearly choked on his own saliva. "R-really, sir?" He wasn't thrilled with the idea. The field was definitely out of his comfort zone.

"Yes. I think the field experience will do you good. You need to see our battlemages in action. And it'll be more effective to issue commands and make quick decisions." Chief Rantz took a seat. "And don't worry, we'll hire some more of those Black Tempest Mercenaries. They were highly effective on that island."

"I..." Dorne began.

"Look at it like a promotion, Dorne. You succeed at this and we'll have a serious talk about your future when you return." Something on his desk caught his attention and he took his eyes off Dorne. "You may leave. We'll talk soon about the details on this mission."

"Yes, sir," Dorne said with hesitation, then he turned and left.

Chapter 17   The Ogre

Panama's a shit hole. Khayin had never liked it much there. The city attracted all kinds of scum and even with all the legitimate business in the big city it didn't stop the pirates from making port. They even had their own bar, One-Eyed Pete's. The morning was overcast. The air smelled of rain and the streets were busy with traveling Alchemists and Artificers setting up shop. The gypsies brought in a crowd.

Tippy's office was just off the port. Tippy was a water faerie and he pretty much ran the port in Panama. Most people, and probably everyone in Panama, didn't know Tippy was a faerie, which Khayin found hard to believe. Tippy was anything but human. And one would think that the name Tippy would set off some red flags. It surprised Khayin that with the return of magic people could be still so ignorant.

Khayin definitely felt better about Kira, but he was conflicted. Yeah, he was attracted to her, but it would only end in disaster if they were ever to give it a shot. He was happy to have met her and learn some about a culture he had never encountered before and that had only lived in myth. It amazed him there were still things in this world that could surprise him.

They left the hotel after having a small breakfast in their room. The lobby was full and they felt like fish swimming upstream. They made their way toward the port side of the city. Khayin decided it was best to walk and leave their horses in the stable. He sent Millennium ahead to scout their path. He wanted to avoid pirates or any other criminals preying on the tourists. In a city like Panama they prowled the streets at all hours.

They were stopped briefly when a tiny beggar boy tried stealing Kira's new scarf. His little hand grabbed the dangling corner of cloth, but he came to a jerking halt when he realized the scarf was tied around her waist. The boy wasn't fast enough to escape Kira's grasping hands.

"You little shit." She seethed.

She let go and Pulled him off the ground about a foot. The boy's eyes went wide, and his head darted from side to side as he started to tremble. Khayin had walked a few feet away before he noticed the confrontation. He hurried back.

"You thought you'd steal from me?" Kira was turning red.

"I...I'm...sorry...miss," he barely uttered. "I...just, just...wan' to eat."

"Kira," Khayin whispered in her ear. "Let him go. Look around." He gestured with his eyes. "There are homeless everywhere. Starving kids too. He's only trying to get by."

She looked at Khayin and her eyes began to soften. Khayin reached into his chip bag to produce some chips, but as soon as Kira let the boy down he ran off and got lost in the crowd. He replaced the currency and retied the bag to his belt. Kira's face went from anger to sorrow within seconds.

"I'm sorry, I didn't know." She looked at Khayin.

"How could you have?" He shrugged. "Don't worry about it."

With the help of Millennium they made it the rest of the way to the port without incident. The shipping yard was large and the last time Khayin was there Tippy had set up shop in a warehouse that he had constructed out of wood. Khayin couldn't help but admire the ships. Schooners, frigates, brigantines, and a Man-of-War took up every last inch of the harbor. He noticed Kira's wide eyes as well.

"I was a sailor for a while," Khayin said.

Kira's mouth fell slightly open. "Really? I can't see you as one. You seem to love the dry land too much. You're good with horses and you get queasy every time you teleport anywhere. I figured you had a motion sickness thing going on."

"Look at you, being all observant," he said with a smile. "Actually, that's got more to do with magic than motion." He looked out over the water. "It's quite freeing out there."

They slowly approached a fenced in area with a guard post. Khayin walked straight to the post like a man with a purpose. The guard was a head taller than Khayin. He was large. Muscles bulged in an inhuman display and he didn't look happy.

"Who you?" The man said with his massive arms crossed over his chest.

"I Khayin, her Kira." Khayin spoke slow and deliberate as if he were talking to a child.

"You not funny." He pointed a kielbasa sized finger at him.

"And you not very intelligent, but I bet you do your job well." It was hard for him to stop mocking the poor guy. Kira took a step back.

"You leave now. Drokk don't like you." His arms went back in their crossed position.

"Well, it's a good thing I'm not here to impress Drokk." Khayin shifted back to his usual tone. "I'm here to see Tippy."

"Tippy no want to see you," the guard replied.

Khayin sighed. "Tell Tippy that Khayin is here to see him. Go, I can wait." Khayin shooed him with his hand. The guard just stared at him. Khayin shooed him with a little more authority.

The big guy's large shoulders slumped. "You wait here." And he left.

"What was that about?" Kira asked.

"Faerie enforcer, an ogre in a piss-poor human guise to be more precise."

The wait wasn't too long. The ogre returned about fifteen minutes later. He wore a big grin. "Tippy said he don't know you and to tell that bounty hunter to fuck off." He was obviously proud of himself.

Khayin sighed again. He looked at Kira and shrugged. Faster than even Kira thought was possible, Khayin pulled a kukri from his belt and placed its sharp curved edge on the ogre's crotch. The ogre let out a small yelp that was almost inaudible.

"Here's how this is going to play out. You're going to let us walk past and I won't have to cut off your..." He twitched his blade.

"Drokk let you walk pass." The ogre stepped aside.

When they were a few yards away Kira said, "He fell for that? He's not very tough."

"Most males aren't when you threaten their manhood." He smiled. "But I'm also pretty sure that Tippy told him more about me than he let on."

Khayin saw no more guards between the gate and the warehouse. Apparently Tippy thought the ogre was enough. Containers scattered the yard and the smell of salt water seemed thickest there. The warehouse itself was enormous and appeared, from a distance, to be in good repair. A pair of bay doors stood ajar. Khayin and Kira entered there.

It was a two-story building. The warehouse was filled with clutter. Khayin couldn't see any rhyme or reason of how things were organized. He couldn't even tell what was stocked. Everything was in boxes. Wood boxes, cardboard boxes, and plastic boxes all were haphazardly placed around them. In other words, chaos. *Faeries.* He shook his head.

Tippy made his home on the main floor. He had engineered a small canal that connected to the ocean, making him an impressive force to reckon with. With a direct link to water he'd have access to all his faerie magicks. Faeries' control over nature was uncanny and many a wizard tried tapping into that magic, with or without faerie help. Faerie folk didn't cast conventional magic. Everything they did was related to the element they were part of. The kicker was that if a faerie died, that element was hurt. Woodland faerie died, trees died. Water faerie died, and rivers or lakes receded or dried up.

There were several pixies flying around. Khayin couldn't be sure on the exact count. In one corner of the room were couches and chairs. A table with assorted foods sat in the middle of them. Three other sprites relaxed on a sofa. A young woman sat on another couch. Khayin recognized her immediately-- Rosa. He couldn't worry about that; he had other things to do first.

A geyser sprung from the canal in the middle of the room. It shot straight up and hit the ceiling, effectively making it rain. A spout of water shot out from the geyser and directly at Khayin. It hit him square in the chest, knocking him down several feet from where he once stood. The water kept coming, pinning him to the floor. Other than making him wet and annoyed it did no other harm. Kira reacted. She Pulled at the geyser, the water exploded and dispersed everywhere.

A figure of a boyish man stood on the water. He wore nothing. He stood before them in all his naked glory. His hands were balled up into fists and resting on his hips. His face wore a scowl as he stared at Khayin. He raised a hand to point at Khayin, when he finally took notice of Kira.

"Yous!" Tippy jabbed a finger toward Kira. "What're yous doing here? My's part is done. I's don't owe you anything. I's done."

Her eyes and tattoos were aglow and her stance indicated that she was ready for whatever else Tippy may throw at them. Kira's face squinched up in confusion. She glanced at Khayin who was getting back up to his feet. He reflexively brushed himself off as if that would dry his clothes. He looked at Kira and to Tippy. The fairy now pointed at Kira.

"I's out. I's told that boss lady I's done." He screeched. "Go! Gooo!"

Khayin looked back to Kira. "Let me handle this. You obviously freak him out." She nodded and shrugged.

"Tippy, buddy, pal, it's been awhile. You've done well for yourself." He gestured to the room around him.

Tippy crossed his arms in front of his chest, he also shifted his weight to one foot taking a more relaxed posture. "Khayin." Tippy's eyes kept darting from Khayin to Kira and back. "Why are yous here and with that witch? Yous don't travel with partners and she don't look like a bounty."

"That's because she isn't. This is Kira, Tippy." Khayin walked over to her and put his hand on her shoulder. "She is a friend and we need your help."

"Ha!" Tippy busted out in a loud laugh. "Yous don't have friends, Khayin."

"I have you and Codex." The faerie tilted his head in thought. "And now I have Kira. I only make friends with the most powerful people. That is why I have so few."

"Hmm...Maybe I's believe yous." Tippy fully relaxed and dropped his arms to his sides uncurling his fists. "What do yous need with me?"

"Kira is lost and we are trying to find her home. I was hoping you might know where that may be." Khayin side hugged Kira. She looked at him, but didn't flinch.

"What does she need there?" he asked, rubbing his chin.

What kind of question is that? "It's her home, Tippy."

"I's know, but there is nothing there now."

"What do you mean there's nothing there?" Kira fumed. Khayin could feel her tense up.

Khayin leaned in close and whispered in her ear. "Careful, we don't want a fight." She nodded slowly.

"Well, if the rumors are true, there is nothing there," Tippy repeated.

"That doesn't answer her question, Tippy. Did the island disappear? Did the people leave? What happened?" Khayin started to get a little frustrated.

"There was a war. No more witches. They's are all dead, except your girlfriend there, of course."

Kira grabbed Khayin's bicep in a vice like grip. Her eyes were wide. He could see the start of tears. He placed his hand over hers and gave her a slight nod. He looked back to Tippy.

"Look, Tippy, can you help us or not?" Khayin asked impatiently.

"I's can help yous, but yous don't need directions, I's can send yous there." He put his fists back to his sides and pushed out his chest.

"I want those directions anyway," Khayin said. "And the port."

"I's can, for a price," he said smugly.

"Of course, Tippy." Khayin reached for his chip purse and started to fish out some chips.

"Five thousand chips," Tippy said proudly.

"That's outrageous, you little thief." It was Khayin's turn to get angry.

"That's my's price, take it or leave it."

Khayin seethed. He put his money purse away. Kira elbowed him. Khayin just shook his head. He reached into a pocket and pulled out the gold coin they received from the Atlantean. He flipped to Tippy who deftly caught it and examined it.

"Where'd yous get this?"

"That's not important. It's yours on three conditions."

"What? Name it," he said never looking from the coin.

"One, you give us safe passage to the island."

"Done. Next?"

"Two; give us directions so that we don't have to come see you if we ever need to get there again."

"Done. And the last one?"

"The last one I will name at a later date."

Tippy looked up from the coin and stared at Khayin. Khayin didn't flinch. "Done." The faerie waved a hand at a female sprite sitting on a couch out of the line of sight. "Go grab that map in the top right top drawer of my's desk." The sprite did as instructed. A minute later she returned holding a rolled-up map. "Give it to our friend Khayin."

The sprite walked over to Khayin and handed him the map. She was small and beautiful, but she reminded him too much of a child. She didn't let go right away and they locked eyes. She bit her lower lip and looked him over with a lustful purpose. Khayin nodded and yanked at the map hard to free it from her hand. She stood there a moment longer before returning to her seat. *Faeries.* Khayin shook his head.

"Step into the water if yous are satisfied," Tippy said.

Khayin unrolled the map and examined it. The map displayed Central America. He found Panama, but nothing stood out in the Atlantic so he checked the Pacific. There, about 25 miles off shore, was an island circled and titled, in childlike writing, 'really, really, really, bad witches.'

"Everything OK?" Tippy asked.

"Yep." Khayin and Kira stepped into the shallow water of the canal. Tippy jolted to attention and spun around several times in place. He hooted and hollered and just when Khayin thought Tippy might fall over from dizziness, Tippy stopped, bowed, clapped his hands once and they were gone.

Chapter 18   The Island

    The water was cool, refreshing, and not too cold. They were in up to mid-calf. Khayin doubled over and nearly lost his breakfast. Kira felt badly for him, but she couldn't help but smile. They stood on the east shore of the island. There was no port. The island wasn't easily accessible and the witches wanted it that way.

    Kira turned around and looked out over the Pacific. She saw ship masts and parts of hulls breaking the water's surface. The beach was littered with the lifeless bodies of both witches and sailors. She was grateful that she didn't recognized any of her sisters, only witches from different tribes. Seems like the faerie was right. What happened here?

    They proceeded inland. The tall trees loomed over them. The trees stood over 400 feet, the branches providing a canopy that blocked out the sun and cast the entire island in a deep shadow. Nothing along their trek to Kira's village indicated that any kind of fighting had taken place. The forest was silent. No birds sang. No squirrels skittered. No wildlife at all stirred. Something didn't feel right, and she was nervous.

    "What's going on, Kira?" Khayin broke the silence first.

    "I don't know. Seems like everything, but the trees, is dead." She had a bad feeling. She started to sweat and her heart beat slightly faster.

    "Were those your sisters on the beach?" He sounded concerned.

"No, other tribes." She moved more quickly. She was anxious and worried. "We're close. It's just over this hill," she said as she ran up the incline.

Khayin followed behind. The hill rested at the east side of the settlement. She could see the tall structure that had been her home as a child. The domain of the Crone, it was the tallest building in the village. *It's still standing. Good sign, right? I'm talking to myself.*

"That building ahead was my home. It's still standing. That's a good sign, right?" She asked Khayin. She was beginning to feel hope.

"Yeah, let's hope so." He didn't sound convinced.

Kira reached the top of the hill and all hope was lost. Before her were her sisters. They were scattered and lying dead all around the village. She fell to her knees as she saw with her eyes what her heart had already told her. Among her sister's bodies were the bodies of those who had attacked. She saw no insignia to identify who they were, but she did see a couple of Battlemages, the kind that she and Khayin had run into in Vegas. It took every bit of will to keep her from crying out in rage and anguish. The hairs on the back of her neck raised. Her skin became hot and started to turn pink with the heat.

The scene was gruesome but the smell was worse. Rotting corpses and human feces permeated the air. People didn't simply lie dead; corpses were burnt, some with the flesh melted to the bone. Bodies were torn in half, missing heads and other limbs. Some were disemboweled or had holes in the chest where their hearts had been torn from them. Kira's emotions were at war with each other. She didn't know if she wanted to be mad or sad, so she settled for both.

"Kira," Khayin said.

She whipped around to find him standing behind her only a few feet away. Her eyes were pooled with tears. Magic coursed through her veins and her tattoos started to radiate. Her heart pounded in her chest; it felt like it would explode and a part of her wished it would.

In the softest voice she was capable of at that moment she

said, "Khayin, not right now." He nodded. "I need to be alone. I'm going to search my house. Can you search around to see who might have been behind this and why?"

"Of course."

"Thank you." She spun on her heel and headed to the domain of the Crone.

****

Khayin wandered the village. The various homes were made of wood, like log cabins. He tried to be as respectful as he could around the bodies he recognized as being her sisters. The homes were damaged beyond any repair. Some were burnt, while others were crushed. Magic had definitely been used in the fight. The sheer amount of corpses on both sides made it hard to tell who had actually won, if what had happened here could be called a victory by anyone at all.

He felt disgusted by so much violence. He found it ironic, as he himself had no qualms for killing people he felt deserved it, but as he walked past bodies of children a wave of sorrow washed over him. There was no excuse to kill a child. Everywhere he looked he saw the same. He could only imagine what Kira was going through.

The west side of the village housed the slaves, though the term "housed" could be used only loosely. It was more a scattering of mud huts with straw roofs. Khayin even saw some tents. The pen was surrounded by large sharp wooden spikes crisscrossed as a fence. There were even more dead scattered in the slave pen. Men and boys, slaughtered, like fish in a barrel. They had had no chance. Whoever had attacked the sisters didn't want to leave any witnesses behind.

Khayin wished he had Millennium, but he doubted they'd be there long enough. He had directed the bird to stay with the gypsies to keep an eye on Muma. He knew what she was and he didn't entirely trust her. With no Millennium, he'd have to rely on his own senses.

He got his first clue when he saw a familiar black Lycra suit among the bodies of the dead. Battlemage. This has got to be the work of the same people from Chicago, but what do they want with these witches? He searched the body and found nothing of use.

Khayin stood just outside the slave pen. He thought it was messed up that people still had slaves, but slaves or not, it didn't call for the massacre that had befallen the witches. Khayin made a decision.

This can't go unpunished. These bastards are going to pay.

He saw a flicker. Then nothing. Khayin readied a pistol. He saw it again before it came into full view in front of him. The Battlemage swiped at him with a clawed hand and missed. Khayin's reflexes were faster. His blood ran warm and his breathing became more rapid. The mage flickered out of sight. Khayin sensed the mage behind him before it could strike, and he spun and fired. His eyes saw nothing, but the bullet hit true. The spray of blood appeared first, then the mage. The mage flickered out again.

How did they find us?

Khayin felt four razor claws open up his back. The blood began to run immediately; the cuts were deep. He stiffened. The adrenaline numbed the pain, but he still felt it. Khayin waited and listened. He saw the flicker out of the corner of his eye, so rolled to his left, putting distance between him and where his instincts said his opponent was. He pulled the trigger, the shot loud. The battlemage stood with his hand outstretched, as if he had been going to cast a spell before Khayin put a bullet through his head.

Khayin didn't have time to celebrate his victory before the ground shook. Doors flew off their hinges and the roofs of cabins flew straight into the air. A tree uprooted and demolished a house. A large boulder rose and leveled a home on the other side of the village. Chaos erupted. Khayin didn't feel any change in weather, but he felt powerful magic in the air. Then suddenly debris of all sizes whirled and started launching itself haphazardly.

Khayin had no defense for the onslaught. He quickly dismissed hiding behind anything and instead tried to outrun it. Before he could get clear of the storm he was lifted high in the air. His body was slammed into the slaves' pen fence. He felt himself

The Malevolent Witch

being impaled through the back. Blood sprayed from his chest. He looked down to see a wooden spike pierce through him. There was excruciating pain, then everything went black.

****

After watching Khayin begin his search, Kira entered the large house. She first saw the stairs where she and her sister used play, in ruins. Wood from the broken stairs lay in piles all over the floor. She saw several bodies, none of which were her mother or sister Brianna. Everything was surreal, like she was an outsider in a stranger's home. As Kira moved aside a broken chair and caught a glimpse of her initials carved on its back, she felt a sudden wave of guilt wash over her. Half-burnt tapestries lay crumpled on the floor beneath where they once hung. She moved to the audience chamber where the Crone had always held court. She and her sister had never been permitted in that room and she remembered the day when she was finally allowed entry and her sister was not. It was that day that she saw the hatred boiling in her sister's eyes. The room looked as much destroyed as the other. The Crone's throne still sat on its pedestal, while behind the throne lay a large broken ritual table.

She sensed it before she saw it. The magic in the air became alive. In front of the ceremonial table a Battlemage flickered into view. A gout of flame shot from the mage's hands, Kira dodged to the side. She channeled her magic and Pulled the mage across the room. It was a reaction; she didn't have time to choose the path. The mage landed amongst some debris. Kira's breathing quickened.

She readied herself, making sure her hands and eyesight were clear. The magic energy coursed through her. Her tattoos began to glow. The beating of her heart became loud and fast. She scanned the room and lost sight of the mage. Goddess, these things are annoying. She felt the surge of magic before she felt the pain. The Battlemage flickered back into sight to grab her arm with a white hot hand. She ignored the pain and grabbed its forearm. She Pulled and the mage launched into the air. Kira held it there suspended. She reached deep within herself and Pulled at the body in separate directions, like two opposing forces playing a game of tug-of-war. She could hear bones snap and flesh tear, until finally the body was torn in two. Blood sprayed into a red cloud of mist as the remains fell to the floor.

She knelt to steady her breathing and extend her awareness for any more mages that might be lurking. When she felt satisfied she searched the rest of the room. It was then that she spotted her. Lying on the floor, half-covered by the table, was her mother, the Crone. She had no real love for her mother, but it was still her mother. She held back her grief. The battle had happened almost two months ago, she guessed, but the body looked as if it had just died. Blood spilled from her mother's mouth. Kira didn't find any outward injuries to give her any insight on what may have happened. Magic? During her inspection she found a wooden puzzle box under the folds of the Crone's robes. Kira recognized it as her own right away. It was a gift given to her by her mother.

When she opened the box, a small blood red crystal fell into her hand. As soon as the crystal touched her skin a translucent image of her mother stood in front of her, startling her.

"My daughter, I pray to our Dragon-Mother you find this." Kira's eyes started to well up, but she fought it back. She had no idea how long it had been since she had heard her mother's voice, but it wasn't until now that she found how much she missed it. Not her mother so much, but home.

"We have been betrayed," her mother continued. "Your sister Brianna conspired against us for promises of power. She framed you for killing our Sister-Mother Helga; I know that now. I only hope you can forgive me for not believing you." Rage filled Kira.

Sister-Mother Helga...dead, why can't I remember?

"I was convinced of your guilt when you escaped. Your sister had set bounty hunters after you and gave them the means to subdue you. I only learned this recently when Brianna confessed over my dying body. I am so sorry, my daughter."

A single tear trickled down Kira's face. She squeezed the crystal so hard it cut her palm. and blood started to drip to the floor. Anger, grief, and the pain from the cut on her hand swirled around in her head. She wanted to lash out. She needed to destroy something. If she couldn't break her sister's face she needed to break something else.

"A land called Chicago is where she went. She allied with someone called 'Mother' there. You must stop her. You must kill your sister."

With pleasure, Mother.

Her magic lashed out. Anything that wasn't nailed down flew in a whirlwind. Soon her power picked up momentum and started to rip things off walls and out of the ground. She could hear the destruction even outside. Kira sat in the eye of her own telekinetic storm.

"Seek the Dragon-Mother; seek Lilith. Your sister couldn't get to her. You're our future now, daughter. Know that I've always..., but I was always the Crone first." The image shimmered and flickered. "One last thing," the voice and image started to fade. "There is one...who can help you, you...will need...him...Lilith knows. His...name...is..." The Crone died.

"No, no, no, no, no, no!" Each 'no' increased in volume until she was screaming.

The roof of her home tore free and hit a nearby tree. The walls of the building exploded out, leaving Kira and her mom's body exposed to the chaos outside. A large tree of 300 feet ripped free from the ground and hit a cluster of trees with such force that they exploded into splinters. Kira held her mother's limp form as she rocked, her tears now a steady flow. She rocked and cried until she calmed enough for the storm she had created to stop.

Kira gently laid her mother down. She got up and wiped her tears and snot on the sleeve of her shirt. She rubbed her swollen eyes. *I must find Khayin.*

The village around her was flattened and a panic started to rise within her. *I hope Khayin got clear of this.* She searched, but there was so much debris. She heard a faint ringing, or beeping. It sounded similar to the tones the buttons made on Khayin's communicator that he used to talk to Codex.

She followed the sound. The closer she got to the slave pen, the louder the noise became. Kira stopped when the sound was loud enough to pinpoint its location. She Pulled and removed the wood from the nearby homes and trees away from the melodic tone. Her heart wrenched.

No! What have I done? Goddess no!

Khayin was impaled by the fence and his blood covered the front of him. New tears flowed. Kira Pulled him off the spike and laid him on the ground. His pocket was ringing.

"No! Not you too! Fuck! What have I done? What have I done? I'm sorry, I'm so, so, sorry. Shit! Goddess no!" She wailed.

His pocket rang.

It's got to be Codex. What do I say? Shit! Fuck!

Kira reached into Khayin's ringing pocket and freed the communicator. She flipped it open and hit the talk button. She concentrated on breathing and calmed herself.

"Hey, Snuggly Bear. What took you so long? You hookin' up with that foxy witch? You need to go for that honey or I will. You two would be great together."

"Codex," Kira whimpered.

"You could be like Batman and a really hot Robin, though you two look nothing like those two, but still. I called to check in and give you an update of what I found out. Sorry it took so long, I am soooo swamped and Tao has been demanding more attention, which I only allow her to do. It is kinda sexy letting her be all alpha."

"Codex," she said a bit more loudly.

"Those Chicago punks have been asking around about you and your girl. Oh, I should be a bit more respectful. My mother tells me I can be so disrespectful sometimes and I told her I would work on that. Like whatever. How is Kira anyway, I hope you are being a gentleman. Why do men find it so difficult to be gentlemen? They all demand respect, then they treat women like meat, but I know you wouldn't do that. I..."

"CODEX!" Kira screamed.

"Kira, darling, why are you answering the phone? Where is Khayin?"

"I killed him," she sobbed.

Chapter 19 The Calling

Kira started to hyperventilate. The events over the last few days were overwhelming, the total recall of the death of Quinn her first love and now Khayin. The slaughter of her entire tribe, oddly became second to the death of Khayin. She felt strongly for him, but really hadn't realized it until she saw his lifeless form. She wanted to meditate, but she had Codex on the communicator.

"Whoa! OK. What happened? No never-mind. If it was intentional you wouldn't have picked up the phone. OK, don't panic." Codex tried to calm her.

"Don't panic? I killed him. My only friend in the fucking world and I killed him," she shouted.

"Breathe, Kira," Codex said with a soothing voice.

There was silence for a minute. "I killed him," she whimpered. Her voice was so low it could barely be called a whisper.

"OK," Codex began, "Kira, I need you to listen to me." Kira said nothing. "Good. Now I can help you, but you have to trust me. Can you do that?"

"Yes," she whispered and nodded.

"Good. What actually killed him?"

"What?! Why does that matter? I..." Kira was in shock.

"Kira!" Codex snapped. "You said you'd trust me."

Kira sniffled. "He was impaled by a wooden stake."

"How large was the stake? Did it pierce his heart? Or is the heart completely gone?"

Kira was aghast. "Codex!"

"Kira," her voice was smooth as silk.

"Sorry," she replied. "The stake was about three inches in diameter. Without digging around in his chest," *please don't ask me to do that,* "I can't say for certain, but at the angle of the stake and where it exited I'd say there was some left. Does it matter?"

"A little, just on how long it will take." Codex said.

"How long what will take?" Kira asked in confusion.

"How long it will take for him to resurrect."

"Resurrect? On his own? How is that possible?" She was even more confused. "My sister Brianna was the only one of us in over a century that was blessed with that gift, but she wouldn't have been able to do it to herself. She could only bring others back from death. How is this possible?"

"Very good questions, darling. I'm going to let Khayin answer those." Kira's mind was a whirlwind of thoughts and questions. "I do ask one tiny favor from you, darling, and I'd hate to do this to you, but there's only one answer I'll accept."

"OK," Kira said with hesitancy.

"Can you keep a secret?" Codex asked.

"Yes."

"Keep this one. You are among a very short list of people who know this about Khayin. A vindictive god once sealed him in a tomb for years without food and water. He died and came back many times over before he freed himself. There are worse things than death and Khayin has made more than a few enemies in his life."

"But, how? How does he resurrect?" Kira was fascinated, which made for an odd pairing with the grief.

"He's cursed," Codex said plainly.

"Cursed? Who cursed him?"

Codex sighed. "Khayin is very old. And these are things I'm sure he'll be happy to fill you in on, but right now is not good. The juice on that phone isn't going to last and I still need to talk to him. Also, it needs to get the two of you back here. I'm going to have to say goodbye for now, OK?"

"OK," Kira said.

"Kira?"

"Yeah."

"It wasn't your fault. Shit happens. He'll understand." Kira could tell Codex was trying to reassure her.

"OK."

"Khayin will probably be out for an hour or so, give or take. If you have to go do something, don't feel bad leaving him. He'll be fine. Just leave the phone on him. I'm usually the first person he calls when he wakes after dying. I've got to go."

"Bye, Codex."

"I'll see you soon, darling." The line went dead.

Kira placed the phone onto Khayin's stomach. She stroked his arm gently and then she rose. Tears and soot smeared her face. She wiped her nose with the bottom of her shirt, took one last look at her friend and marched off into the woods.

The cave to the Dragon-Mother wasn't far and she ran into more than a few dead. *Seems my sisters tried to stop Brianna.* The cave's mouth was a clutter of corpses. It took effort to tiptoe around them. The causes of death seemed to be more of the same she had seen back in the village: burnt, mutilated, and some just shot from bow, dart or bullet.

The bodies became fewer the further into the cave she went. She bent down and plucked a torch from a corpse and lit it with a little firestarter cantrip. The torch lit up in a bright blue flame illuminating the cavern. She got a sense of deja vu. Kira hadn't been here since her Gnoxel and back then she was dropped into a random cave in the dark. The familiarity didn't stop the tinge of fear that crept up her spine.

The cave was more linear than she remembered. *Is the Dragon-Mother leading me? What did mother call her? Lilith?* The path led her to a chamber, and she realized she remembered this from her Gnoxel. The high ceiling had the same luminescence from the moss and plant life. She heard the faint sound of dripping water and an old musty smell. She walked further in.

The blue flame of the torch revealed more of the cavern than she had seen on her last visit. On the far side she saw a pool of a black tar-like substance. The pool started to bubble before something began to emerge. First a human head rose from the depths, as shoulders followed, and then a female torso, until the whole being was hovering above the pool. The inky, black liquid dripped from the naked form of a woman. Her eyes opened.

The glowing yellow eyes stared straight through Kira. She recognized those eyes. The woman remained silent and the two of them kept their gazes fixed. Kira was nervous. She felt the tiny hairs on her arms rise. She could feel the power radiating off this woman. This was Lilith, the Dragon-Mother.

"Kira'Tal," the voices purred. "Have you come to subdue me, or are you here to sate mine hunger?"

"I know your name," she said confidently ignoring the question.

"I've had many, of which do you speak?"

"Lilith."

"Ah, yes." She paused, as if in some deep thought. "Are you the last?"

That stung. Am I really the last?

"You truly are, daught'r of the dragon." The voices were soft. "The unforeseen has happened."

"And you did nothing. You hid in your hole and ignored the slaughter of my sisters? What kind of monster are you? You let your followers meet their end. Why?" Kira was angry and that fueled her courage.

"My time is done. Yours is anon. You will lead thy sisters to a new age." Lilith floated to the ground before the pool and touched softly down. Her slick body glistened in the torch light.

"Didn't you hear me? Everyone is dead. You said it yourself. There is no one to lead anywhere." *What world is this thing on?*

The Dragon-Mother was silent for a while. "Recent events have changed the fortunes. What lies ahead is yours to forge."

This isn't making sense. Why would mother send me here? This being is so far gone, I don't even think she knows what plane she is on.

"The Fates have decid'd. Thy sisters have outlived their usefulness. You will choose a new path. What will you choose?"

"I don't understand. What do you mean?" Kira was nearly

pleading.

"This is a new age. The old gods have returned to find their people scattered and worshiping new gods. Thy sister Brianna aligned herself with these old gods for power at the cost of her people. You have prevented that from coming to fruition," she explained.

"How did I stop it? What am I supposed to do?"

"You are alive. The deal she struck requires you dead. You can run, or you can face her. The choice is yours. How shall you choose?"

"I can't run." Her words were spoken to the floor.

"Then come. Wade in my pool. Wade in the blood of chaos and be born anew; be born the Dragon-Mother." Lilith waded into the pool. She stopped in the middle and turned to face Kira.

"One last bit of counsel. The one you travel with. He is crucial to thy success. You need to convince him," Lilith said.

"Khayin? What do you know of him?" *Maybe I can get answers from her?*

"He is old. He has the means to kill gods. He will be invaluable."

"But, what do you know about him?" She wanted answers.

"Enough to know you can trust him and he has nay love for the gods. The rest you will have to find out on thy own. Now come."

Lilith raised a hand, the nail on her index finger grew into a talon and she slit her own throat. Her blood flowed freely like a rushing river. Kira gasped, watching in horror as the life drained from Lilith and into the pool. She felt Lilith's magic pour from her veins and merge with the black liquid in the basin.

By the goddess what just happened? She called me the Dragon-Mother and killed herself. I don't understand.

"Come," came the voices of Lilith in her mind.

She hesitated, not entirely sure what to do. *Am I to become the Dragon-Mother? This doesn't make any sense.*

"Come," came the voices again, but this time she didn't hear Lilith. She heard the voices of her ancestors.

Kira stripped her clothing. She stepped into the pool and

completely submerged herself. She heard voices, many voices. Too many to count. Too many to understand. Her blood began to run hot. The magic pumped through her veins. She could feel it course through her, revitalizing and consuming her. The power was almost too much, and she felt as if she were going to lose control. Her ancestors pulled and tugged, trying to drag her further in. She could feel hands groping, nails biting into her flesh. This was the test of the Crone she realized, but something more, much more. These weren't just souls of initiates, they were powerful souls. Souls that would have become the Crone. She started to panic, trying frantically to swim to the surface of the pool; she tried to break free from the grasping hands.

Is this what Lilith did? Does she consume all of our unworthy? Will she consume me? No! This will not happen to me.

She stopped her struggle, calmed her breathing and meditated. She was stronger than the magic. She was the Crone. She was the Dragon-Mother. She would prevail. She realized in that moment that the magic wasn't trying to subdue her, but strengthen her. Her ancestors had accepted her. The energy and power was bright, a display of colors and of none. It was loud, as if all the creatures of the island cried out at once, and it felt cold and hot at the same time, but Kira remained in control.

Kira awoke lying in the fetal position naked and clean at the bottom of a dried basin. Her breathing was slow and her skin tingled with magic. She could hear her ancestors in the depths of her mind. Kira sensed the whole of the island, and felt as the animals slowly returned to their homes. She could sense no other human life, not even Khayin. She should have been overwhelmed from her new sensations, but she was somehow content.

She climbed out of the basin and redressed. Kira could see clearly now, like a dozen torches lit the cavern. She noticed a nook in the far wall, and closer examination revealed another room. A real room. It was totally furnished, as if it was in a wealthy nobleman's home. She stepped inside.

In the room's center was a circular bed. On three of the four walls hung elaborate tapestries with images of wars, dragons, and humanoid beings with wings. Half of the winged people had wings of feather while the other half looked like a bat's. The fourth wall had a mural that depicted a garden. It was the most beautiful garden she had ever seen. Two people, a man and a woman, stood in the garden next to a large tree that seemed to be the focal point of the mural. She stood entranced. It took her a few moments to pull herself away.

She walked around the room and found a door behind one of the tapestries. In the second room were several tables. Each table had a different set of tools--tools for all known magical talents. On one wall she saw a large book case. She looked over the books and found that most were books of history and lore. Others she found were old journals of Lilith's.

In a display case next to the book shelves was a large opened book. The pages were yellowing with age and the text was written in a language she didn't understand. Khayin's glasses would help right about now. She opened the case. She was half afraid that exposure to the air may cause the book to fall apart, but the other half was too excited to care. To her amazement the book did not disintegrate; in fact it looked and felt very sturdy. She picked it up. The cover was made from some sort of skin, of what she wasn't entirely sure and part of her didn't really want to find out. With the book in her hands the script became legible. She started to read.

This is Lilith's grimoire.

Chapter 20   The Curse

Nothingness. A void. Complete utter darkness. Silence. Khayin couldn't even hear his own breathing. Was he breathing? It was disorienting, floating in the emptiness, no up or down. If he were alive he'd be vomiting from the dizzying sensation. But no, Khayin was dead, again. The curse. An event to relive again and again, only to forget upon resurrection, for eternity. No way to grow numb.

A room slowly took shape around him. He awoke and was tied tightly to a chair. Khayin's weary eyes took stock of the room he found himself in. There was only one large room with cloth that partially segregated a bed. He sat facing the bed. There was a ladder that led to a small loft. In the corner was a stove and table. Fruits and vegetables hung from the ceiling. Chests rested at the foot of the bed and under the shuttered window. The room was sparsely decorated. Two paintings hung from the walls, one depicting the landscape and the other of his family--he, his wife and their daughter.

Shock and panic overrode him when he finally realized he was in his own home. He fidgeted, trying to get his hands free. That was when he realized his feet were tied to the chair as well. He began to sweat. There was a rag or something in his mouth, and he tasted blood. His muscles tensed and he began to shake. *What is happening?* He struggled, and with more tugging at the ropes around his hands, pain shot through his arms. The ropes dug deep and started to tear and burn away flesh. He screamed, but it only sounded like a whimper.

Khayin smelled rosemary and sage. His wife Rebekah loved the scent. There were candles aflame, illuminating the shuttered home. Rebekah and Adelaide were at the market; Khayin was alone. He had been attacked in the garden, but by whom? With a swift blow to the head, he was out before he could see his attackers. The front door of his home crashed open, a flood of blinding sunlight assaulting his eyes. A group of men entered, all armed with clubs and knives made of wood and bone.

There were six that he could see and a seventh that stayed in the shadows and out of full view. Their clothes were dirty and their faces haggard. One had a scar across his left cheek. They rooted through the kitchen and began to pour themselves mugs of his mead. A few sat around his table. They were waiting. Waiting for his family to return.

Panic rose again. He twisted and pulled against his bonds, only to result in making him bleed even more. He ignored the pain as his adrenaline started to pump through him. A short stocky man approached him and hit him hard in the nose. Blood flowed immediately, and Khayin stopped struggling.

The door opened again and Rebekah was the first to walk through. The large man with the scar violently grabbed her arm. She yelped in pain as Scar dragged her to the bed. Her struggles only made it worse. She tried to pull herself free, ripping the sleeve of her dress in the process. That's when she caught Khayin's eyes. They were pleading with him. She opened her mouth to speak, only to be slapped hard across the mouth. She cried out and fell onto the bed; blood trickled from her lips. Her eyes only briefly left Khayin as she recoiled from the blow.

Adelaide ran into the house closely behind her mother, her blonde pigtails bouncing. "Mommy!" she cried. She was eight and their only child.

The stocky man blocked Adelaide before she could reach her mother. The little girl screeched when she saw Khayin, her tiny hands covered her mouth. The stranger knelt down and tried to grab the girl, but she wiggled free and ran for Khayin.

"Papa!" she cried. She almost made it to Khayin, but was intercepted by the stocky man who moved faster than what Khayin would have imagined. Khayin tugged again, drawing more blood and pain.

"Adelaide!" Rebekah screamed. "Leave my baby alone." She sat up to get off the bed and was slapped again. Her moans on top of Adelaide's cries were too much for Khayin to bear.

He struggled in his chair, trying to pull his arms free. The bonds just seemed to get tighter. Scar leaned in over Rebekah, tearing her dress and exposing her breasts. He lifted her skirt. She barely moved, nearly unconscious from the last blow. Khayin could see her breathing had slowed. His heart pounded and his stomach churned for what he dreaded was about to happen. Scar loosened his breeches and let them drop to the floor. Khayin closed his eyes.

A burst of pain exploded onto Khayin's face. His eyes shot open. Before the tears blurred his vision he saw that he was eye to eye with a man who had a perfectly trimmed beard. He was much cleaner than the others. The man in the shadows.

Khayin tried to kick out, but his legs were tied. He tried to scream, but only produced a muffled whimper. He rocked his chair in hopes to fall over, thus breaking the chair and freeing him. Another man got behind him and grabbed Khayin in his big burly arms. His grip was hard, stopping Khayin's struggle and steadying the chair.

"You will watch." Trim Beard's voice was low and he spoke with a cadence. "You will watch or your daughter is next."

The look in his eyes told Khayin that he wasn't lying. Khayin's chair was positioned perfectly for the brutal show. He watched as his wife was repeatedly raped. Each man took his turn. No perversion was neglected; they were like animals in the wild showing their dominance. Rebekah didn't cry out, she just laid there limp and devoid of emotion. Khayin wasn't sure if she was dead or simply unconscious. Khayin was horrified and he felt sick. His stomach twisted.

The rape seemed to last for hours and Adelaide's howling felt like daggers in his ears. Scar crawled onto the bed and pulled

The Malevolent Witch

Rebekah's listless form up toward the head. Khayin could see her chest rise and fall, but she didn't move otherwise. Scar held her and put a stone knife to her throat. Khayin heard an interruption in his daughter's wailing.

He saw Adelaide get partially dragged and partially carried to the bed by her arm. Bruises started to form under the man's grip. Her eyes burned with rage. She threw punches, kicks and even tried to bite her captor. Adelaide was thrown onto the bed at her mother's feet. She was then held down by a couple of the bandits.

"Papa, please!" she cried. Tears ran down her face, eyes pleading.

Khayin was wide-eyed and he shook his head wildly. He tried to scream, but nothing got past that damn rag in his mouth. *They said they would leave her alone if I watched.* Trim Beard approached Khayin.

"Now it's my turn." He looked at Khayin's wife, then back to Khayin. "Your woman is a bit too old for my taste." Khayin tried to protest, again yelling through the rag. "Oh, you will watch this too or your wife will die." The man grinned.

"Watch," said a gruff gravelly voice that came from the man holding him. "She may enjoy it." He heard him laugh.

Trim Beard tore Adelaide's clothes leaving her totally exposed. He dropped his breeches. There was screaming, a screaming Khayin had never heard before. It was unnerving, and terrifying, and then everything suddenly went quiet. Khayin could still hear her cries tearing at his mind. Adelaide laid still, like a corpse. Her eyes were closed and there was blood, too much blood.

Trim Beard pulled up his pants and faced Khayin. "My name is Molek. I want you to remember me. I own these lands now and I own you. Nothing you possess is yours, it all belongs to me."

Khayin stared at the man. He memorized that face, as he did every man in the room. His blood ran hot. Rage filled him. He hated this Molek. *I'm going to kill you and everything you love.*

"I see that anger, that...hate. Good. Remember what happened here today. Never cross me." He spat in Khayin's face and left.

Khayin rocked his chair till it fell. His head hit a nearby table and knocked a lit candle off. The tiny flame landed onto a pile of furs which quickly went ablaze. The impact broke the chair, but his bonds were still very tight. It took several minutes before he freed his hands. It would have taken several more if it weren't for all the blood.

The home filled with smoke and it was hard to see. Adrenaline pumped through his veins. His heart beat rapidly and his breaths were shallow. Khayin grabbed Adelaide first and ran out. He laid her on a cart and darted back into the burning house. The bed was aflame. Rebekah was screaming, and half her body was burning. It was hard to breathe. Khayin beat the flames with a towel he found on the table and carried his wife out. He placed her on the cart next to his daughter.

Adelaide was dead. Khayin didn't have the heart to examine her. There was a lot of blood and bruising. Her tiny frame couldn't take the abuse. He touched her face and brushed a golden lock to the side. Khayin could feel the ache of his ravaged heart.

Rebekah would sustain permanent injuries from both the attack and the fire. Her entire left side would be scarred from the fire and she would forever be with a limp.

The scene faded and was black for several minutes. There was blinking and fluttering of light. In the distance Khayin could see a body hanged from the neck. He walked closer. The image before him looked as if he were looking through a window. He saw Rebekah as she hung from the rafters of their home, then everything faded to nothingness.

****

Khayin awoke.

Chapter 21 The Coin

There was a gasp, a large intake of air, a convulsion, then Khayin sat up. Something fell and bounced off his leg and into the dirt. He looked down and saw his phone. *Codex. I need to call Codex.* Khayin picked up the phone. "Huh, how'd this get here?" He hit the send button and Codex picked up immediately.

"So, you died," she said in a little sing-song.

"Yeah. Wait, how'd you know?"

"Kira found you." She went straight to the point. Khayin liked that.

"Shit! What happened? Did she call you?"

"No, I called to update you, Snuggly Bear, but you were dead, so Kira answered. As to what happened, I'm not entirely sure. You'll have to ask Kira, but she seems to think she killed you, so go easy on her. She likes you and I don't want you to muck things up like you usually do. You two can make a good team. I know, I know, you work alone." She said the last part in her best Khayin imitation. "But that is bullshit and you know it. She was really shaken up about it, which shows she cares. And that is not a bad thing. Having someone watching your back would be good for you. Maybe then you'd die less often and you'd not rely on me so much. I can't be your mom. I don't think Kira would want to be your mom either, but you know what I mean." She finally took a breath. "You know what I mean, right?"

"Yes, I know what you mean." Khayin sighed. "Codex..." he

hesitated.

"What is it, Snuggly Bear?" The inflection in her voice changed to a more sympathetic tone.

"I don't know how this is possible. I don't usually see anything while I'm regenerating. It's like waking from sleep and not remembering your dreams, but..." He was trying to gather his thoughts, trying to focus on an image that wasn't there before he died.

"What is it? You remember something?"

"Yeah, I've got a flitting image of a man. I think I recognize him, like I knew him." He strained to keep the image in his mind's eye.

"You think you knew him? From when?"

"I don't know, but I think I remember where I saw that face recently. I'll have to get back to you later on this." Khayin toyed with the bloody hole in his shirt while his mind shifted back to the problems at hand. "So, Chicago?"

"Yeah, right." Codex began. "The Nueden Corporation runs the city. And they have their own specialized security force, which is run by Chief Lawrence Rantz. And directly under him is a guy named Joshua Dorne. Dorne is the guy who sent that Battlemage after you. Seems he is the man in charge of all field operations. He is a sick individual. He tortures and kills whomever to get what he wants, a real nice guy. What they want with our Kira, I have no idea," she said in a casual pace.

"Maybe Kira found something. I should go check on her," Khayin said.

"No, stay put. Let her find you. She's had a rough day, and it would be better if she came to you. The last thing she needs is zombie Khayin sneaking up behind her."

"I should've never taken you to that movie."

"Night of the Living Dead was a great movie." He could hear her smile. "Anyway, get back here as soon as you can; something is going down. And I think it has to do with our friend Kira."

"I need to get back to Panama before that. Is there any way you can get me there fast?" he asked.

"Dial 507 on the phone and send, but, Snuggly Bear, I'm not

sure if there will be enough energy in that phone to get you here if you go there first. You know that only the mage that created it can charge it?" He could hear the concern in her voice.

"Yep, don't worry, I'm sure we'll figure out something."

"OK, I'll trust you, but don't dilly. Things are getting a little tense here." The line went dead.

Khayin closed the phone and looked up to see Kira. She looked...different. Her tattoos seemed to move. No, they did move. They not only crawled over her skin, but they changed shape as well, from tribal to symbols to numbers and some language Khayin didn't seem to recognize. As he studied her face more closely he could swear the tattoos reflected her mood as well. The blue of her eyes were brighter and took on a more aqua color. Those eyes bore holes into Khayin.

They both stood silent and motionless. He didn't know what to say. He didn't want to make the situation any weirder. Kira approached him. He didn't move. He began to sweat and felt a flash of warmth in his face. She poked him in the bicep. He just looked in her eyes. There were tears, small ones, but definitely tears. She poked harder, and then the poke turned into a hit in the arm. He still didn't flinch. There were a few more tears. She cocked her arm back to swing again, but she turned it into a hug. Her arms wrapped around him fully, and while he tried to return the hug, his arms were pinned.

"I'm so sorry." Her tears flowed. Her face was buried in his chest.

Khayin reciprocated the hug, forcing her arms to rise to almost around his neck. "It's fine, really." He smiled and held her.

She stepped away and turned her back to wipe her tears. "Everything I know and love is dead, then to see you..."

"It's OK," Khayin tried to assure her.

"The thought of..." she began.

"Really, Kira. I'm fine. When we get some time we should talk. I think I should probably explain some things." He smiled as she turned to face him again. "You know, since we are going to be working together a little while longer."

"So, we need to go back to Panama?" she asked, completely

changing the subject.

Khayin just stared at her. Kira had successfully burrowed her way into his head and heart and he wasn't too sure how he felt about it.

"Are you OK? You're staring." Her left eyebrow was raised.

Khayin shook his head. "Yeah, yeah. I'm fine." And that flash of warmth returned to his face.

"Panama?"

"Right, Panama. We have that bounty, remember?"

"Right, the one Mrs. Barragan gave us." She paused in thought. "Her daughter."

"Correct, I also have this image floating around in my head ever since I woke." His thoughts ran wild. He was trying to focus.

"An image?"

"A man's face. He is important somehow, someone I haven't seen in a very long time until the other day." It was hard to keep the face at the forefront of his mind.

"You saw him?"

"Kinda, I think it was the face on the coin from Atlantis. I've got to take another look at that coin." He walked toward Kira and placed his hands on her shoulders. "We good?"

She looked into his eyes. "You're my only friend, Khayin. Of course we are."

"Good. Let's go visit Tippy. I've got a few favors to ask of him. Then we'll check in with Codex. I've got a feeling we're going to be kicking some Chi-Town ass." He winked at her. She smiled.

Khayin pulled the phone from his pocket and flipped it open. He grabbed Kira's hand and dialed 507. He looked at Kira and hit send. The teleport dumped them in the heart of the city. Khayin vomited. His body was weakened from the resurrection and the queasiness he normally got from a port made for a bad combination.

"Give me a second," he coughed.

"Take your time, gorjcha." He could hear the smirk.

After he coughed up the last of the bile, he must have looked the spectacle. He still wore the bloody clothes he had died in. He straightened up and walked down the street, ignoring the onlookers. He led them to Hotel Panama first. They went to their room and packed their things.

"Just take what you think you'll need. We'll have to leave the horses behind again." Khayin rummaged through one of the saddlebags. He had to change his clothes.

"How many horses do you go through?" Kira asked.

Khayin chuckled. "Too many, but this is a special circumstance. I usually don't go through this many so close together."

Kira flung her bags over her shoulder. "Ready."

"OK, I'll pack what we won't need in this other bag and we'll take it with us. I think I'll just leave it with the hotel clerk." He finished packing the last bag and they left.

Khayin walked to the front desk and slapped the room key on the counter, giving the clerk a little startle. The clerk quickly regained his composure and he smiled.

"We're checking out," Khayin said.

"Of course, sir." He took the room key and looked up the room in the registry. "And how was your visit? I hope everything was to your satisfaction?"

"Yes, everything was fine." Khayin looked at Kira, then back to the clerk. "Do you have some paper and a permanent marker?"

"One moment, sir." The clerk disappeared into another room and brought out a couple sheets of paper and a handful of markers and handed them to Khayin. "Is there anything else that I can do for you?"

"Nope, and thanks. You can keep the rest of the payment for the room, and you can have this." Khayin lifted the saddlebags of extras and laid it on the counter. "Extra clothes and stuff we don't need. Give it to the homeless, sell it, toss it, I don't care." He examined the paper and smiled. Excellent. This'll do nicely.

"Uh, thank you, sir?" The clerk sounded a little unsure, but he picked up the bag and placed it behind the counter.

"Don't mention it. Are we good?"

"Ah yes, sir," the clerk responded and nodded.

"Good," Khayin said as he turned away.

Khayin walked to a table in the foyer and started to write and draw on the paper. Kira hovered over his shoulder watching. When he was done he examined his work and smiled. He tucked the page away in his inside vest pocket and they left the hotel, walking down the street toward the shipping port. The street was alive with vendors and gypsy performers, but Khayin didn't stop to browse or gawk.

"Where is the bounty? What's her name? Rosa?" Kira asked.

"Yeah, I believe I spotted her with Tippy."

"Really?"

"There was a human woman in his office, or throne room, or whatever he calls it. The only human aside from us anyway. Kinda looked like the picture too. Not sure why she's with Tippy." Khayin explained.

"How are you going to sneak a peek at that coin, get him to teleport us and get Rosa?" she asked.

"I've got a card up my sleeve." He winked at her.

"A what?" She looked at him, head cocked to the side.

"It's a card player term."

"Card player. Is that some kind of game?"

"Yes, like poker." He smiled, pleased that she understood.

"Oh, you mean the game where you won me?"

"Yes. Er...no. I mean yes, but it wasn't like that." Khayin was flustered.

"Relax, gorjcha. I know." She smiled and Khayin recognized that she had just made a joke. He smiled too.

They approached the guard post at the shipping yards. The same ogre guard stood watch. He tensed when he saw Khayin and Kira, shifting his weight from one foot to the other. Khayin grinned at the large oaf's nervous display.

Khayin looked at Kira and whispered, "Seems I made an impression last time." She smiled.

The ogre opened the gate and waved them in. Khayin flashed him his pearly whites and passed through. They walked through the yard to the warehouse and entered the building, making their way to the back corner of the large room. Tippy was sitting at a large table full of food-- roast pig, fruits, vegetables, breads, wine and mead.

"Khayin!" Tippy exclaimed.

"We're here on business, Tippy, and we're a little crunched for time."

Tippy looked shocked. "How did you's get here so fast, Khayin? I's just sent you's to that island a few hours ago, you's couldn't have gotten here so..."

"You know one of these days I'm going to ask how you knew about my friend Kira here, but right now I need to see that coin I gave you earlier today," Khayin said straight to the point.

"Wha...why would you's want to see that?" Tippy asked.

"I'm also looking for a girl named Rosa. I believe I saw her here this morning." Khayin didn't waver in his speech. He knew if he spoke quickly and with authority Tippy was more apt to listen. "And when I find said girl I need you to port us to Tuxtla Gutierrez. There is a circle there, so it should be an easy port."

"And why would I's do all this?" Tippy got some of his composure back.

"Because then I won't turn you in for the bounty that's on your head," Khayin said with a smug smile.

Chapter 22   The Bounty

"What bounty? I's smell bullshit. I's would know if there was a bounty on my's head." He crossed his arms over his chest.

Khayin pulled a rolled-up piece of paper out of a side pocket of his saddle bags, throwing it at Tippy. It landed on the table in front of him, missing the plate of food. Tippy picked it up and unrolled it.

"Wanted: Tippy 20,000 chips."

This better work.

"This is fake. I's would have heard," he protested.

"Really? It was a private contract. The client asked for me personally. If you don't believe me you can check with Codex?" Khayin pulled out his phone. "I'll even call her for you."

"No's!" he snapped. "No's. No's need to do that." He looked at the poster again and shook his head. "Fine." He snapped his fingers and the coin appeared between his thumb and forefinger. Tippy flipped it to Khayin.

Khayin snatched it out of the air, closed his eyes and took in a deep breath. He opened his hand and looked down at the coin, flipping it over to the side with the man's bust. A barrage of images flooded his mind that almost made him flinch. The images meant nothing. No clear story. No clear memory, but the face he remembered. Somehow that face was etched into his memory. He couldn't place it.

He felt a hand touch his arm. Khayin opened his eyes to see

Kira. She looked concerned.

"You OK?" she whispered.

"Yeah sorry. I'm fine." He gave her an appreciative look and nodded. "OK, Tippy. The girl. Where is she?" Khayin tossed the coin into the air and caught it. "And I'm keeping this."

Tippy scowled. "But..." he grunted. "Fine."

Is it me or Codex that he is afraid of?

"She came heres with her boyfriend, some guy with ties to Mexican cartel. I's kicked him out of my's city, but she was pretty for a human and I's made her an offer to stay here." He grinned, then he frowned. "She didn't stay; she ran away."

"Where, Tippy? I don't have time for your games." Khayin's muscles tensed.

"And I's swear to you's that I'm not playing any." He shook his head. "I's don't know where she's went, but I's can tell you's where they stayed before she's came to me's."

"Where'd you send the boyfriend?"

"My's first mate led him's to the north end of town and watched him's walk away." Tippy relaxed.

"OK, where'd they stay before you got a hold of them?" Khayin asked.

"Hotel Panama."

"Seriously?" He shook his head.

"Yes. Why?" Tippy looked perplexed.

"Nothing." Khayin looked at Kira. She shrugged. "OK. When I bring her back here you are going to port us."

"Fine," he said with a little whine.

Khayin and Kira left the same way they had come. Millennium was scouting the city, giving Khayin another pair of eyes. When they reached the hotel Khayin caught a glimpse of Rosa heading out of the city. He told Millennium to follow her.

"Got her." Khayin said. Kira looked at him. "Millennium's tracking her. She's a few blocks north." He firmly grasped Kira's arm. "We need to do this quickly. We can't let Tippy examine that poster too closely." She just nodded and the two of them started after their target.

They weaved through the street, while dodging tourist and

merchant alike. Khayin wasn't in the mood to be discreet, and he made no attempt to blend in. Millennium gave him a good description. She wore a blue sundress and had her long black hair tied back into a tail. Khayin could see her with his own eyes. He caught Kira's attention and motioned for her to cut Rosa off.

I just might be warming to the idea of a partner. I could get used to this.

Rosa looked behind her and must have spotted Khayin because her walk turned into a sprint. He cursed himself for not being more careful. She turned down the first alley she saw, and Kira ran after her. Khayin sent Millennium to follow. Khayin continued north, only stopping to look through his falcon's eyes. Kira was gaining on her. The alley was dirty, but less populated. Trash was piled mostly in the back alleys and unused streets.

The two women ran. Rosa jumped and knocked over trash. The new obstacles didn't slow Kira down. Rosa ran west a few more blocks before turning north. Khayin saw where she was headed and ran to try and cut her off. He got there just in time to see Kira reach for Rosa and miss. Rosa looked back at Kira and almost ran into Khayin. She managed to slip by him, but the detour allowed Kira to catch up and tackle her.

Rosa kicked and yelled. "Get off me!"

Khayin looked at Kira and he smiled. "Why didn't you use any magic?"

"The chase was too much fun." She smiled back. "I would've if I thought she might have gotten away."

Rosa squirmed, but Kira was the stronger of the two. She had her pinned to the ground. Khayin squatted and grinned. "I'm going to take a wild stab and say you're Rosa." She spit at him and missed. "You gave us some exercise. I didn't really need any today, but you gave my friend here a taste of the old bounty hunter trade, so I thank you for that."

"Who sent you?" Rosa asked through clenched teeth.

"Your mother," Khayin said. He stood and Kira pulled Rosa up off the ground.

"How much to say you never found me?" Rosa asked.

"Sorry, you're not going to buy me. Your folks were good to

us." Khayin pulled a cigarette from his tin. He started to make his way back to Tippy's, while Kira followed with Rosa. "What's so bad about mom and dad?"

"They didn't like my boyfriend, Roberto," She snarled.

"And where's he now?"

"I'm not tellin' you."

"I honestly don't care; I'm just tryin' to prove a point. If he loves you, where is he?" Khayin lit and took a drag off his cigarette. It felt good.

"Tippy kicked him out of the city. He couldn't come back." She said defensively.

"What stopped him? The guards that are posted every few feet or the invisible fence that surrounds the city?"

"That's not fair," she spat.

"No? I'm sorry, but if someone tried to separate me from the one I love...death couldn't stop me." He took another drag from his cigarette. "You know what? I really don't care. Pretend we never had this conversation."

"Fuck you, pendejo." She tried to kick him and failed badly enough to lose her balance. Kira caught her.

"Come on, Rosa. We're not the ones you are mad at. Khayin is only doing his job." Kira tried assuring her.

They walked the rest of the way in silence. The ogre let them in without a fuss. Rosa became a little fidgety the closer they got to Tippy's, but Kira kept her in check. The day was getting late. The sun was about to set. Khayin was getting more and more restless. Tippy was sitting on a couch with a girl on either side.

"Khayin!" Tippy nearly shouted with wide eyes.

Khayin shook his head. "Tuxtla Gutierrez," he said.

Tippy frowned. "Yeah, yeah. You's no fun, Khayin." Tippy got up and motioned for them to step into the water.

"How about next time I see you, I'll come dressed as an ogre." Khayin, Kira and Rosa stepped into the water.

Tippy's face lit up. "Would you?"

"Yeah, sure, why not?" Khayin looked down, making sure the three of them were in the little channel. "There's no water by their farm. Where exactly are you sending us?" Khayin was a bit worried that Tippy was going to screw him somehow.

"To the circle you's mentioned. There is a Nexus point there, so I's don't need water on the other end to do it, just as long as there is water here's." He winked and they were gone.

Khayin didn't vomit this time. He was thankful, as he didn't want to appear weak in front of a bounty. Before they could even take a few steps, Khayin saw Luis and a couple of his sons approaching. They carried weapons, but they didn't have them aimed at them this time.

"Rosa!" Luis yelled.

Her head hung low and her bottom lip shot out in a pout. Kira tried leading Rosa, but the girl was proving difficult, refusing to move and when she did only with very short steps. Luis took his daughter roughly by her arm. She yelped from the pain. Khayin could see Kira's hands ball up into fists, so he put a calming hand on her shoulder. She nodded.

After a moment Luis turned his attention to Khayin and Kira. "You have some unfinished business with my wife. She's expecting you."

Khayin nodded and they proceeded to the Barragan home. Mrs. Barragan was sitting in a rocker in the main living space of the house. She motioned for the two to take a seat and they sat on the couch.

"Did she give you any trouble?" She asked.

"Nothing we couldn't handle," Khayin replied.

"Good. The rest of your payment is on the end table there." She pointed at the little table next to where Kira was sitting.

Khayin motioned for Kira to take the bag. She was about to open the bag when Khayin shook his head. Kira stopped.

"It's alright. She can count it," Mrs. Barragan said with a warm smile.

"No. I trust you. She's a little new." Khayin smiled at Kira, assuring her that it was alright.

"Then that concludes our business. Will you be staying for dinner?" She inquired.

"I'm afraid not. We're needed elsewhere." Khayin stood. "I thank you. It was a pleasure doing business with you." He bowed.

Kira stood as well and tried to bow but it came off a little awkward. Khayin pretended not to notice.

"Well, be sure to tell Mistress Tao I said hello." Mrs. Barragan smiled and nodded.

"I'll do that. Farewell." Khayin turned and left.

Chapter 23 The Mistake

Vegas was in chaos. People ran through the streets haphazardly. Buildings were on fire. Women and men were weeping over loved ones dying or dead in their arms. Armed guards patrolled and coordinated emergency response teams. Among the dead were Nueden Security, battlemages, mercenaries and of course citizens of Vegas.

Khayin and Kira appeared in the middle of The Strip. There had been a battle and they stood in its aftermath. After a moment's pause to choke down what he last ate, Khayin sprinted toward Codex's place, with Kira close behind. They bobbed and weaved their way through the street and stopped at the alley. Khayin noticed that The Port Authority was ablaze.

"Kira, go check on Mistress Tao," Khayin said in a huff.

Kira nodded and ran. Khayin took off down the alley, noting that he didn't see the usual guards outside the door. Something didn't seem right. He inspected the alley more closely than usual and found nothing. The door to Codex's place was unmarred. He found no signs of struggle, but that didn't make him feel any better. Just as he was about to open the door his phone rang.

"Codex!" Khayin practically yelled into the phone. "What happened? I'm at your door now."

"Aww...isn't this touching," said a male voice Khayin didn't recognize. "I have your girlfriend and if you want to see her again you'll come to Nellis Air Force Base." The line went dead.

Khayin didn't wait and he didn't go after Kira, but immediately ran to the north end of town. He saw a stable of horses and buggies. The stable master was tending to an injured horse and didn't see Khayin. Khayin jumped onto a mare, bareback, and rode to the northeast toward Nellis. He was fueled by pure adrenaline.

It didn't take him long and he knew he was walking into a trap, but his love for Codex pushed him forward. Nellis hadn't been used as a military base for over two hundred years and had been picked over for anything useful by scavengers since. Most everything was covered in rust. Planes and other vehicles became windows into the past and the majority of hangers and buildings were missing roofs, doors, and even walls.

The front gate was guarded by a couple of the Black Tempest Mercenaries. Khayin glared at them as he rode by. He dismounted and walked the horse without incident to the main hanger where he saw a gathering of other horses and more mercenaries. He left his horse and walked into the hanger.

The hanger, for the most part, was still intact. A well preserved jet sat at its center. There was a group of people standing next to the plane. Khayin counted eight and half as much behind him. He saw no sign of Codex. His heartbeat started to quicken.

He walked toward the group of eight and stopped about twenty paces from them. Two battlemages, five mercs armed with automatic rifles and one tall, lanky man in a white suit stood in a line before him. Mr. White must be the voice on the phone.

"Thanks for coming on such short notice," the man in white said. "I'm Dorne. And you are the infamous Bounty Hunter Khayin." He extended his hand for a shake, but Khayin just looked at it, then him. "Ah, well. As you can see we don't have your girlfriend here. What's her name? Codex. Yes. She is quite the handful. Very pretty too. You have a soft spot for the cute ones, don't you? Maria couldn't stop talking about you."

Khayin could feel his face turn red and he tried to fight it back. *He better not have hurt her*. His hands curled into fists.

"Good. I was hoping I'd find something to rattle you. You'd be pleased to know she held out a lot longer than Jesus, but in the end..." He shook his head as if he were sorry. "But enough of the depressing stuff. I bet you are running through scenarios as to how you are going to get yourself out of this obvious trap. Quite frankly I'm surprised you fell for it."

This fucker will die for messing with Maria. "I didn't. I just wanted to see your face." Khayin pretended to examine Dorne's face more closely. "You know you should get those ears looked at. The Dumbo thing doesn't suit you." *I shouldn't have come alone. Damn, that Kira, she has gotten into my head. I never make rash, emotional decisions.*

Dorne scowled. "Name calling? Is that the best you can do?"

"No, I just don't think you're worthy of my best."

"Khayin, I expected better." He frowned. "Do you know who I work for? Do you know what I can do?"

"I don't care, but I can guess. There are, at the very least, two individuals above you. You act extra smug and more brutal out in the field, because no one is watching over your shoulder. The constant supervision really gets under your skin, so you take it out on other people. I bet you're even the interrogator, because it makes you feel more powerful, when really, you are just impotent."

Dorne smiled.

"People like you. You're nothing special." Khayin looked him up and down. "In fact, if your mother were still alive I bet you would be calling her every night before bed for that extra affirmation. You hoped that your wife would've been able to give that to you, but that didn't happen, so instead you torture and hurt people to prove to yourself that you are important or powerful."

"Careful, Khayin" Dorne said softy.

"You're fascinated with magic, but could never wield it. Just another reminder that you are insignificant." Khayin prodded.

Dorne's eyebrows furrowed and face tensed.

"The one thing I can't figure out is, what happen to your mom? Your mom, not your dad, because, well, come on, you're totally a momma's boy. She didn't die of old age, 'cause you're young. Did she die of heartbreak, because of how pathetic her son turned out to be? Or, maybe she killed herself because she couldn't bear the thought of you loving her in a not-so-mother-and-son way." He looked at Dorne through squinted eyes. "Did you have a thing for mommy?"

"Shut up," he yelled.

"Or maybe, she did reciprocate that love and you couldn't get it up? Your mind says yes but your body says, 'What the fuck are you doing?'..."

"Shut up!" Dorne screamed. "Take him!"

Khayin immediately dropped into a squatting position, pulling out two pistols and shooting two mercenaries between the eyes as four soldiers tried to grab him and missed. Everything above the victims' lower jaws blew apart. Skull shrapnel pelted the other two soldiers who were now covered in their companions' blood and gore.

The soldiers with assault rifles laid suppression fire to keep him from running. Dorne definitely wanted him alive. So much for playing dead to get rid of them. The battlemages shot off bolts of magical energy and missed as Khayin rolled toward them, catching them off guard. He shot one mage in the head and kicked the other mage into the suppressing fire. The battlemage was reduced to a bloody husk in a matter of seconds.

He knew he was to be bait, so he decided to take out as many as he could. The two blood-soaked soldiers took aim and shot Khayin, one in the right arm and the other in the left leg. Khayin winced and was knocked momentarily off balance as pain shot through him. He dropped the pistol in his right hand, taking a desperate shot with his remaining gun. The bullet hit its mark and ripped through the soldier's throat.

Khayin was shot again. His left shoulder erupted in pain. He tried to stand, but his wounded leg protested and he fell to the floor. Khayin looked up to see that the remaining guards surrounded him. He started to laugh and, despite the pain, he laughed hard.

Dorne kicked him in the side. "What are you laughing at?"

"You." He grinned. "You're pathetic and you've got no idea who you made into an enemy today."

"I have you surrounded and lying in your own blood," he

sneered. "You are no threat."

Khayin laughed louder, which brought on more kicks. He felt a couple of ribs break. He coughed, but still laughed, which caused more coughing. He was kicked again. This time a broken rib punctured a lung. He laughed again.

"What is so funny?"

"I am nothing compared to my friends." He went into a hacking fit. There was a coppery taste in his mouth.

Joshua Dorne bent low and pulled a syringe from an inner pocket, sticking Khayin in the arm. "This will put you to sleep so I don't have to listen to your mouth anymore. I'm sure the Chief would love to meet you. And if I'm really lucky that witch of yours will come running to save you." He pushed the plunger and within seconds Khayin was out cold.

Chapter 24 The Base

Kira raced to The Port Authority. Her heart kept pace with her feet as she dodged the dead and injured and hurtled those she couldn't dodge. Before she had even reached the entrance to the building, Codex exited with Tao in tow. Codex was coughing from the smoke. Kira ran up to help support Tao and the three of them got clear of the burning building.

They stopped and rested a few doors down and across the street from The Port Authority. Tao was unconscious and Codex was checking her vitals. Kira looked up and down the street, making sure they were safe. No one noticed them and most were tending to their own problems. She looked back at Tao and Codex.

"She's breathing," said Codex.

"Khayin went looking for you at your office. He sent me here to check on the Mistress," Kira explained.

"We should head there. I don't think they'll be back, but my place is better protected." Codex started to lift Tao. "Help me with her."

They both draped an arm around their shoulders and carried her. They made their way through the chaos of the street and entered the alley. Kira noticed that the two guards who were there the last time were gone.

"Codex, where are your guards?" Kira wondered.

"I sent them to follow that Dorne fellow. They should report back in a few minutes. Can you get the door?" She wheezed.

Kira turned the handle and slid it open. The hall immediately lit up. The short corridor ended in another door. Kira grabbed Tao's dangling arm and the three of them entered. The door shut on its own behind them. Codex led through the lobby and down a twisting hall that took them to her living space. The place came alive as soon as they entered. Lights turned on and music came from a box. They laid Tao down on a couch.

"I don't see Khayin." Kira whipped her head round quickly scanning her surroundings. "Do you see Khayin?"

"I didn't see him on the way in. Hold a sec." Codex left and checked a thin box with a glass panel. It light up with words and pictures. "He never entered. Looks like he got a call on the phone I gave him and he left. That doesn't make any sense. I never called him. No one else should have that number. Who has that number? Why would they call him? I have a bad feeling about this." Codex grabbed a similar phone to Khayin's, punched some numbers in and put it to her ear. "Nothing." She looked worried. "Kira, wait here. I'll be right back."

Kira stayed close to Tao. She couldn't find any outward injuries and she wondered what exactly had happened. She seemed to be breathing fine and Codex said her heartbeat was normal as well. She brushed Tao's long black hair back and she examined her neck. That was where she noticed a tiny pin prick.

Codex burst through the door and her face was red. "I don't know how they did it, but they got one of my phones. That's how they called him. They must have a skilled wizard with them. Dammit, how could I be so careless? Did I have one on me and I dropped it? No. How would they have known that it was mine? They had to have gotten into my inner sanctum, but how? I took all precautions. No one can get through my defenses. I must have left a door open. That is the only way. Yes, that's got to be it. I was in a rush when all the commotion was happening and I left without arming my defenses. That has to be it. They couldn't possibly have someone who could crack my security. But if that is what happened then it is my fault that Khayin is in trouble. He can't take on that whole army. But, what if..."

"Codex," Kira said sharply. "Can you track him somehow? Do

you know where that army went?

"Yes and no." She punched a couple of different numbers into the phone. "Huey, what's going on?" Kira couldn't hear the other half of the conversation. "He just arrived and they just let him in. OK, stay put. I'm going to send you some help and the three of you are going to break him out." She closed the phone and looked at Kira. "Khayin went to Nellis Air Force Base. I'm going to send you to Huey and Dewey's location."

"OK, send me." Kira straightened up.

"Do you need a weapon?"

Kira smiled. "I am a weapon."

Codex smiled back. "Good, bring our boy back."

Kira nodded and Codex snapped her fingers. Kira was gone.

****

Huey and Dewey were hiding behind a wrecked plane. The base was large, but Kira noticed some mercenaries at the front gate. They looked to be leaving. There were two horse-drawn buggies and everyone else was on horseback. *This isn't going to be easy.*

"OK, Khayin is probably in one of the wagons. Everyone else is expendable." She looked at the two brothers. "What're you two capable of?"

They smiled and shed their human guises. Two massive ogres towered over Kira. "If you can distract the wagons, we can eliminate the soldiers," Huey said.

"They'll probably have some battlemages," Kira said.

"If Khayin didn't take them out already. There was a fight inside the hanger. He wouldn't have been taken easily." Huey flashed his enormous teeth.

She knew that. That's what she liked about him, among other things. "Alright. I'll lift the wagons and place them well out of the way, but you have to keep them off me. I won't be able to defend myself."

"No problem, little lady," Dewey said. And the two of them charged the front gate.

Huey and Dewey ripped the gates from the hinges and used them like fly swatters, hitting horses and riders alike. The militia didn't have time to prepare. They saw the ogres coming, but were unable to get out of the way. Some fired their weapons, but nothing slowed the brothers down.

Kira could feel her adrenaline rise. Her magic filled her. Her skin began to tingle with the energy and her tattoos swirled into a menacing pattern. She stepped out of cover to get a clear view of the wagons. With a raise of her hands she Pulled the wagons high above the ground. She moved them through the air and put them down just a few yards from her and well out of the way of the carnage the brothers had started.

She tapped a little deeper into her will and ripped the doors off the wagons as soon as their wheels touched down. Metal squealed for only a moment before they snapped. Kira Pulled the first two people she saw in the doorway of one of the wagons. She let their bodies hang in the open air for a couple of seconds. Neither of them were Khayin. Kira widened the gap between them and then slammed them together as hard as she could. The bones shattered; she could hear them--the distinct sound of a skull cracking and bones breaking.

The pain was first, then the sound of gun fire. Kira saw a man in a white suit with a handgun peeking out of the wagon to her left. She let the bodies drop. Her right arm was screaming with pain. She grimaced. The gunman popped off another couple of rounds. The first went wide but the other grazed her right leg. She didn't have time to react to her injuries. She Pulled the gun from his hand and tossed it aside. Biting her lower lip, she pushed back the pain. She violently Pulled him from his hiding space and threw him a hundred yards into the mayhem of Huey and Dewey.

Kira ran to the wagon on her right and saw an injured, unconscious battlemage. She backed away from the wagon and her blood began to boil. Her hands curled into fists. Her rage fueling her magic, she Pulled and the wagon imploded, crushing the mage inside. Kira spun and marched toward the last remaining wagon. She peeked inside and saw Khayin lying unconscious on the floor. Her magic pulsated and her reflexes quickened. Kira grabbed

Khayin and dragged him as far as her muscles allowed. She briefly turned to watch the ogre brothers causing their mayhem and used the precious moments they gave her to escape.

She was worried for them and her tattoos expressed as much. "Please get home alive," she whispered, before she turned her attention on Khayin.

She shook him. Slapped him. Yelled at him. But nothing woke him. She grunted in frustration. Kira then noticed that not all of Khayin's weapons were on him, so she ran back to the wagon and took everything she could find, including some rations and canteens of water.

Khayin was still out when she returned. She Pulled him to help lift him and she carried him to Sunrise Manor, a mile off base. The minor city was just as abandoned as Nellis. She managed to find one building intact enough for shelter. She was weak. The magic was draining her and she hoped that Dorne and his men wouldn't try tracking them down. Kira barricaded and warded all windows and doors. The building must have been home to squatters at one time, because she found old clothes and blankets. She made a makeshift bed and laid Khayin down on them.

She rummaged through his stuff and found the container with the healing balm, applying a generous amount to both Khayin's wounds and her own. She watched Khayin as he lay there, barely making any sound at all. Her stomach churned and her heart beat irregularly when she thought about him too long, and that scared her.

Her sister was behind this. Her sister wanted her dead. That was no surprise to her, but what had gotten into her head to kill their whole tribe? All the tribes. She and her sister were the last of their people and soon there will be only one. Kira meditated and waited for her friend to awake.

Chapter 25   The Verdad

The smell of mildew and mold permeated the air. It was a cool evening, jacket kind of weather. Khayin opened his eyes and felt a little groggy. Remnants of the sedative lingering in his system made him feel a little nauseated. It was night and he saw Kira huddled close by shivering. He took a large blanket, laid it over her and he watched her till her body stopped shaking.

The building was small and remarkably preserved. He checked his wounded leg and arm that were now just bruised and sore. His chest still ached from the beating he took, but his ribs had healed. *Well, if there is a bright side to my immortality, it's the healing.*

A small ray of daylight shone through a crack in a boarded-up window. Khayin decided not to disturb Kira's barricades and wards. He looked down at her. *Fuck! What did I get myself into? What is it about this girl that's got me all...* He shook his head.

Kira's eyes slowly opened and she stretched. Khayin looked away in time, he hoped, to not appear to be creepy. He heard her shuffle into a sitting position. He turned around as she rubbed her eyes. Khayin walked over to the pile of his weapons and equipment. He found some food rations that he didn't recognize and grabbed them.

"I thought we might need them," Kira explained. "I wasn't sure how long you were going to be out so I grabbed everything I could from the wagon they had you in." Khayin nodded and tossed her some. "That was kind of dumb of you, you know."

Khayin nodded again and sat down on the pile of blankets and clothes. "How long was I out?"

"Through the night." She broke open the food. "You were shot twice, had a broken rib and they sedated you. I figured you'd probably be out awhile."

"Thank you," he said sincerely.

"Of course." She smiled and he liked it. It was a pleasant progression from the scowls she had worn when they first met.

"Well," he began, "since we're here with no distractions, I guess I owe you some answers."

"No, you really don't owe me anything." She looked down and away from him. "I still feel like shit for killing you. I shouldn't have lost control like that." She looked back up at him, a small tear rolling down her cheek.

Khayin got up and moved to sit beside her. He put his arm around her shoulders and gave a light side hug. "Hey, I'm right here and speaking. I'm not a zombie or a vampire. I'm...hell, I don't know what I am, but I'm here. I'm not mad at you. If you're looking for forgiveness, you've got it, but I don't think it is all that necessary." He smiled.

"You're not a what?"

"That's what you take away? All right, when we're done tracking down your sister, I'm taking you to the movies, starting with Star Wars, of course." He tried to joke through his frustration.

"So, how old are you?" she asked.

"Nice and direct, good first question, and before I answer, I hope you will answer some of mine later." She nodded. "Alright then." Khayin broke the embrace and let out a heavy sigh. "I don't know how old I am. There's a good portion of my life missing, probably because of the curse. I do have vague recollections of a life before the gods."

"What?" she gasped.

"Yeah, the gods are nothing more than ancient humans with lost magic. They grew so powerful that people started worshiping them as gods. Most of them have inflated egos." Khayin took out his cigarette tin and started to roll a couple of cigarettes. "I think I wound up pissing one off. I don't really remember, on account of losing that part of my memory?"

"Were you one of these 'gods'?"

"No, but killing one made me public enemy number one for a while. It was that god's death curse that made me what I am. I live as long as they do, without all the magical perks." He handed one of the cigarettes to Kira.

"So you've wandered the world for millennia?" She lit the tobacco-filled paper with the tip of her finger.

"Many, but I didn't disappear when magic left the world like everything else that was affiliated with magic. Science became the new god and with it a prejudice that spread rapidly." He let her light his as well. "Knowing and using any kind of magic marked you and you were hunted down and killed. So, a group of powerful wizards banded together and cast a very powerful spell that shrouded any and all magic, including creatures that relied on it."

"What is science?" She looked confused.

"Science is the study of, well, everything that isn't supernatural. They started to create things--objects to mimic magic, like all the electronics you see Codex using. That used to be the new magic and in turn became their new gods." He took a long drag. "Then the old magic returned and, well, this happened." He gestured all around him.

"But who did my sister align herself with? A phone?"

Khayin laughed. "I don't think so. I don't know."

"Lilith said she made a pact with the gods for power," she said.

"Lilith? Who's that?"

"The Dragon-Mother." She breathed in a lung full of smoke. "She said she knew you."

Lilith? THE Lilith?

"Stories can be powerful. They were used as entertainment and teaching. In fact, ancient primitive tribes used stories to tell their past rather than hard facts, which makes discerning actual history hard. Some figures in these stories became so popular that people began to worship them and thus make them real, some say."

"There is a figure named Lilith from several of these ancient stories that your Lilith may fit. She didn't much care for men, or at least she wasn't too happy with the way women were treated like second class citizens. Sometimes worse, a lot of times worse. I have met that Lilith." He paused in thought. "It would make sense for that Lilith to create her own tribe that hated men, though she never mentioned having worshipers. Maybe she didn't want to let on that she was a god?" He said the last bit in a very hushed tone, more of a spoken thought than anything else.

"Weird that we'd have a connection like that," Kira said.

"I don't know if I'd call it a connection, but it's definitely weird." He scratched his head and stared off into the distance.

"Lilith and Muma both took different identities through the ages. Did you?"

He snapped his head back to her as if just remembering he was having a conversation with someone. "Umm...yeah. Some have called me Ziusudra of Shuruppak, Parashuram, Tithonus, Cain from the Christian bible and the Jewish Torah, The Wandering Jew, Sir Galahad." He chuckled. "Count of St. Germain, some have even referred me to as Gilgamesh. All stories of beings who were thought to be immortal. Are any of them true? Am I tied to these names? Maybe. Stories get twisted over the ages." He leaned forward.

"Anyway, to be honest I really don't know." He flicked some ash from his cigarette. "A drawback of being so old is that time passes differently for me. Something that happened just yesterday could seem like a very distant memory and sometimes the opposite is true."

"What about that guy you saw on the coin?" she asked. "Was he a god?"

"Yeah, I think I may have to take a trip to Atlantis. There's a reason he came to me in a flash image. Hmm..." He thought a moment about the face. It scared him, but it also stirred up hate and rage. He shook his head. "All right, what about you? Talk, Princess."

Kira told him about her tribe, the slaves, her sister and

mother. She even told him about the slave boy. Khayin could tell it wasn't easy for her to talk about it, from her shifting anxiously and causing her to snuggle even closer to him. He saw her a bit differently. She wasn't as cold as he had first thought. The telling of her story made recent events, including the midnight rendezvous, make a lot more sense. He lightly stroked her back.

"So, you still haven't explained how you were caught by the infamous Bounty Hunter Extraordinaire Juan Rodriguez?" He was wide-eyed and raised his voice on the latter part of the question as if he were making a grand announcement.

"My mother was the Crone, the spiritual leader of the tribe, as you already know. Other sisters, when they reach a venerable age, become teachers, guides, and mentors. That includes the Crone's predecessors." She paused. "One such mentor was Sister-Mother Helga. She was very much loved and respected in the tribe. Her word was second only to the Crone's. Anyway, my sister had always been jealous of me. I was next to be the Crone and my power was growing fast. She had hoped that my little escapade with Quinn would have ruined that." She tensed slightly when she mentioned Quinn's name.

"Brianna killed Sister-Mother Helga, and made it look like I did it. She was quite convincing. She wore my clothing doing it and then she stashed those garments in the bottom of my foot chest. She used my Gnoxel Knife to slit her throat. In my opinion she made it 'too' obvious, but the tribe believed her, and at first, so did my mother. There was to be a trial. The trial would have been just for show. It had already been decided that I was going to die." She grabbed the cigarette tin from Khayin's hand. "Wow, it wasn't until our trip to my homeland that I remembered any of this. Lilith?" The name was barely audible.

"It wasn't uncommon for a sister to die at the hands of another sister, if it were under the law, but murder never was. If I had done it I would have proudly taken my punishment, but I knew Brianna was behind it. I wasn't going to let her win. So, I ran." Kira started to roll a cigarette. "I loved to explore when I was younger and I knew that island better than anyone. I lived off the land for weeks. My sister knew that eventually I would go to the mainland, so she hired bounty hunters." She finished her roll and pocketed the tin.

"One of them finally got me. Actually, it took several of them and they drugged me. Drugged me to the point that I can't remember how I ended up with the Mexican. I was in and out of consciousness for a month or so, maybe. It was all really foggy. I was able to use my magic to cleanse my system of the toxins when they finally stopped giving me the drugs. And shortly after that I met you." She smiled a warm smile.

She has a beautiful smile.

He drew her in closer and she rested her head on his shoulder. "Why'd your sister send bounty hunters? Why not send assassins? She needs you dead. Why go through all the trouble of capturing you? And what's up with those tattoos, they're moving now?"

Her tattoos shifted and her face flushed red. "Are they ugly? It was a result of my encounter with Lilith."

"No, not ugly at all, more mesmerizing actually."

She smiled and sucked in a lungful of smoke. "I don't know why Brianna is trying to capture me." She paused to blow out. "Maybe she needs to kill me herself. With her own hands. Like she did our mother."

Khayin thought about it. "Makes sense. I'll guess we'll have to ask her when we see her. But right now, we should check in with Codex. She is probably worried sick." The warmth of her body was comforting and he didn't want to let go.

"One of these days, gorjcha, you'll have to tell me how the two of you met." Kira said.

****

The walk back to Vegas was uneventful. The Strip had been mostly cleaned since the last time Khayin had seen it. There were no vendors of any kind on the streets. Everything was quiet except for the sound of brooms and other cleaning tools. They didn't waste any time and made their way quickly to Codex's place.

They walked down the alley and saw Dewey standing outside the door. As soon as Dewey saw Kira he rushed her. He took her off guard and he slammed her against the wall. Before Khayin could react, Kira Pulled, pinning Dewey to the opposite wall.

"What the hell, Dewey?" Khayin yelled.

"Witch left us to die. Huey not come back," he snarled. "Huey now dead."

"My goal was to get Khayin and get him to safety," she retorted. "You and your brother were the distraction. You knew that."

"Huey dead, 'cause you not come back to help." He seethed.

"Khayin was unconscious and hurt! I couldn't leave him." She still held him to the wall. "I truly am sorry about your brother." A single tear rolled down her cheek.

Khayin walked over to Dewey and put his hand on the big guy's arm. "I'm sorry about Huey and look, Kira is too. Killing her isn't going to help." He tried to sound soothing. "If you kill her, then I'll have to kill you. Hasn't there been enough death?"

"Dewey not happy," the ogre pouted.

The ogre relaxed and Kira set him free. Dewey turned his back to the two of them. Khayin and Kira hurried through the door before the big guy changed his mind.

Chapter 26   The Box

The hallway was well lit, yet no light source could be seen. Kira and Khayin walked down the familiar corridor and they stepped through the door at the end, which deposited them in the main lobby of Codex's office. Stephen wasn't behind the desk and the lobby was empty. Kira noticed that there were no doors except the one they had come from.

A light flashed on the desk. They approached and saw a box, what Kira would later find out was a speaker, and a switch. Khayin flipped the switch.

"Khayin, is that you?" came Codex's voice from the speaker.

"It's me, Baby Doll," Khayin said brightly.

"Oh thank the gods above, below and in the sun. I was worried sick. First Tao was injured, then you go running off trying to be some kind of hero? I had to send Kira after you. Is Kira there? Of course, she's there. Hi, Kira. And then Dewey comes back without Huey. The two of you disappear for a day. I can't reach you on your phone. Is it broken? Did those bastards steal it? I'll get you a new one, don't worry. Tao is fine, by the way. Then Rocco was flipping out so I had to give Stephen the day off. Now no one is manning the desk. And the work just keeps coming and I have to do everything myself. I'm trying to figure out how that Dorne bastard got into my inner sanctum. MY SANCTUM. Ooh, that pisses me off. They break in and steal stuff, now I have to figure out what they took, so I can disable it. I put a kill switch on all my stuff just in case this shit happens. Ugh! So, how are you?"

"I'm good, but I'd feel better if we were talking face to face."

"Oh, sorry," she replied.

There was a clicking sound and a door appeared to their right. Kira remembered this door; it was the door to Codex's living quarters. Khayin flipped the switch on the box and the two of them went through the door that opened on its own as they approached it.

The room was lavish and just the way Kira remembered it. Codex sat in a large cushioned chair with her feet kicked up. She was sipping from a glass that had some kind of pink liquid in it. Despite her relaxed posture Kira could see Codex's muscles flinch and twitch with anxiety. As soon as she saw Khayin enter the room Codex leapt from the chair and embraced him. When they released each other Codex punched him in the mouth. It was no little punch. Khayin's head snapped back from the impact.

"What are you, some kind of idjit?" She stomped with her high-top canvas shoes. "Trying to be some kind of hero? You know why there aren't any heroes? They die. Heroes die. That's what they do." Her hands were on her hips, curled into tight fists. "I appreciate the sentiment and I know you can't technically die, but I'd hate to find out what someone could do to you when they discover that little secret, especially some egomaniac wizard or god. You ran off alone to face off against a small army. I know you've been alone for most your life, but you've never had the Black Tempest after you. Not for a long while anyway. Dammit! You had me worried. Kira was worried too, you asshole." Kira shot her a look and Codex pretended not to notice. "You know Huey died trying to rescue you." She said the last part with a little more control.

"I know. I'm sorry." Khayin glanced around the room. "Where's Tao? Is she OK?"

"She's fine." Codex gave him another hug then grabbed his arm and threw him onto the couch. "Sit." She then faced Kira and wrapped her arms around her in a very warm embrace. "Thank you," she whispered. Kira took the only remaining seat, next to Khayin on the couch. "So, what's going on?" She didn't wait for an answer. "Mr. Brown Eye was in my house and he has caused a lot of chaos and death in my city."

"Mr. Brown Eye?" Khayin asked.

"Yes, Mr. Brown Eye. Unless you prefer Asshole, or Douche, or Anal Face?" she said in all seriousness.

"Nope. Mr. Brown Eye will do." Khayin smirked.

Kira found a little amusement in Codex's anger. "We need to end this. And I need to know what is going on. So, one of you two is going to fill me in." Kira looked at Khayin, who only shrugged. "Well?" Kira shrugged back at Khayin and Khayin just stared at her. "Oh for fuck's sake." She looked at Kira. "Girl to girl, woman to woman. Your tribal secrets are safe with me. You don't have to give me any intimate details about you and Khayin."

Kira's head shot up in shock. "What?!" She looked at Khayin then back to Codex. "We...didn't..."

"Oh, please. Don't insult me. And if you really didn't, what the hell are you waiting for? You two obviously are into each other," Codex said, sitting back into her large chair.

Kira's face was a brilliant shade of red. Her heart fluttered and the butterflies were flapping madly in her stomach. She was flustered and lost her train of thought. Instinctively she tried to move further away from Khayin, but there was nowhere to go. She saw Codex smile.

"It's alright, darling." Codex said in a soothing voice. "I don't always have a filter."

"She never has a filter," Khayin corrected. He got a look of warning from Codex.

"In this world we don't always have the luxury to take our time on things. Whatever those things may be. 'Take life by the horns' they used to say. Though I have no idea who 'they' are. But I digress. What do I need to know? And if you want to talk about other things when you-know-who isn't around, I'm always up for some girl talk." She said the last part in a whisper, smile and a wink.

Kira bit her lower lip. *What the...I didn't expect this. I'm not even entirely sure what I feel. My family and tribe are all dead. Life as I knew it is dead. I'm being forced to live in a world that's completely foreign and my best friend is a man. This is all messed up. But, he isn't just a friend, or at least I don't think he is.*

Kira looked at Codex and began her tale. She was on such a roll and so absorbed in the story that she forgot who was in the room and spilled everything, even the night that made her relationship with Khayin awkward and ultimately evolve. Codex sat in silence, which was a little weird to Kira. She had never been in a room with Codex before where Codex wasn't talking. Codex remained stoic and only smiled where Kira knew she'd smile, making Kira realize she had told her a detail she meant to keep to herself. Oh well, no secrets now.

"I'm with Khayin on the Lilith theory. I've never met her, but it would make perfect sense that your sisters worshiped her, or sought her counsel, however you want to see it. There is more to it than, 'It's not my time'," Codex mocked. "I think there had to be some ancient bargain, but she would never have agreed to the slaughter of all of her followers. Something went wrong and whatever deal she struck was preventing her from taking any action, hence why she gave you her life's essence." Codex tapped her index finger on her ruby lips. "She did more than make you the next Crone, darling, she gave you her power. Her immortality."

She got up from her cushy chair and walked to another part of the room. She opened a big white box and pulled several bottles from it.

"I'm mixing myself another drink. You two want anything?" she offered.

"I'll take..." Khayin began.

"Whiskey, I know." Codex finished. "What about you, darling?"

Kira had no idea. "Whatever you are making for yourself will be fine."

Codex smiled.

A few moments later she reentered and offered the drinks to each of them. Codex crawled back into the chair. When she was comfortable she sipped her drink and looked back at Kira and Khayin. Kira was intrigued. She liked Codex, a strong, powerful woman in a world that seems to be run by men. She took a small taste of the concoction that Codex had given her. It was sweet. There was a hint of raspberry and chocolate, and the alcohol wasn't overpowering. The beverage was sublime.

"So, your sister is in league with the big Nueden Corporation, but we don't know who the big boss is. I'm guessing female, 'cause I don't see your sister following a male. Not after what you just told me anyway." She took another drink.

"I don't like wild cards," Khayin said. "Too many unknowns."

"I agree, but we don't have a lot of options." Codex paused a moment in thought. "Does your sister know of your capabilities?"

"No. I really wasn't aware until what happened on the island." A wave of sadness washed over her and she shuddered.

"Did you do anything that Mr. Brown Eye could take back to your sister?" Codex inquired.

"Nothing she hasn't seen before."

"And your sister can raise the dead," Codex said.

"Not just raise, she can bring back the living. She restores the soul to the body, healing the body completely in the process. But the healing part is only when she resurrects, her magic cannot heal otherwise." Kira was jealous of her sister and mad that the gift was wasted on such an evil soul.

"Hmm...Seems to me we have two options." She looked at them both in turn. "One, we wait for them to come and attack. Or, two, we go on the offensive and attack them."

Kira looked at Khayin. "Look, I'm not happy about it either." Khayin looked as though he was disgusted. "You know when the last time was that I was in a war, or went looking for a fight?" Both women shook their heads. "Me neither."

Kira started to get nervous. *Is he going to bail on me now? After everything we've been through. He can't even die. What is he afraid of?*

"Balls!" he yelled. "I'm not going anywhere, Kira. Please wipe that look off your face."

Kira didn't know she had a look on her face. Her tattoos must have betrayed her. She was momentarily embarrassed before she realized she needn't be. She took a longer sip from her drink.

"The survivalist in me says to run. I know, I'm effectively

immortal, but that's not the point. I've been able to fly under the radar for most of my life. The idea of going up against a god is not appealing. You can't just go and fight one, let alone kill one, without other gods knowing. We'll be opening ourselves up to a world I've been avoiding." He swallowed the entire glass of whiskey in one gulp.

"Option one won't work. We'll be putting innocent lives at risk and your sister won't come here, or her master. Option two isn't very appealing either, but it's all we've got left. If there's a silver lining, it's that they won't be expecting it, especially if it's just the two of us." He winked at Kira.

"Whoa! Wait one stinkin' minute. You are not leaving me out of this. They attacked my home, my city. I deserve payback just as much as the next guy." She shot out of her chair, stood and bent down in front of Khayin with her face mere inches from his. Codex's voice was slightly higher in pitch than normal and she was talking even faster. "My girlfriend was attacked, I lost Huey, and Rocco and Stephen are freaked out. Nope, no way, not a chance. They waltzed into the city like they owned it. Unencumbered, unresisted. Mr. Brown Eye came in here all smug and flaunting his feathers like some damned peacock. This is my town. My people. They look to me for protection. They look to me to make sure their livelihood isn't threatened. I've spent years on my reputation and I'll be damned if I let some snot-nosed little piece of shit come into my town and act like 'I' am nothing. I'll go to Chicago and I'll burn that city to the ground. They will rue the day that they messed with me and my friends. My family. I'll open the earth beneath them and swallow that hellhole up. I'll wipe it from the face of the earth. I'll..." Tears were streaming down her face.

Khayin stood and embraced her, burying her face in his chest and effectively cutting off her words. "And that is exactly why you need to stay here." Her eyes, pooled with tears, were red with rage. She stared at Khayin. "This town needs you here. Let us be your angels of death." He cupped her face with his hands. "Baby Doll, nobody can kill better than me. This may be personal for you now, but think of Kira. It can't get any more personal. Who else could get this done?"

Codex nodded, then buried her face in his chest again. After a minute she let go of Khayin and stood before Kira. She hugged her and kissed her cheek. Codex pulled away, but kept her hands on Kira's shoulders.

"I can't imagine what you're going through, but I hope we both find some resolution in this." She stepped back and looked at them both. "We'll need to figure out a plan, but first, let's get some rest."

Chapter 27 The Table

The pain was excruciating and Dorne could feel his bones scraping against each other. Blood oozed from every orifice. He was sweating and it made gripping things difficult, if not impossible. He dropped the teleporting stone as it was only made for one-time use. His breathing was labored and he needed healing badly.

He limped his way to the back entrance of the Nueden building. Dorne wanted to avoid the hospital. The doctors would make a report and send it and the bills to Nueden and he knew he was in deep enough trouble; he didn't want to add to it. Dorne unlocked the door and followed the corridor until it ended in a large open room. The elevator was on the other side.

Dorne struggled, but eventually made it. He looked behind him and noticed the trail of blood. I'll have to send someone down here to clean that up. He coughed and noticed blood in his hand. He had to get to the lower levels. He stepped into the elevator and pressed the button for sub-floor fourteen, Medical Research. The door dinged and the whole thing jerked into movement, causing a shock wave of pain to shoot through his body.

The doors opened and he spilled out onto the floor, his legs no longer able to support him. A group of scientists and researchers ran over and helped him up, carrying him over to a chair. A young woman gave him a cup of water that he gladly accepted. He swallowed the water in one gulp and let the cup fall from his hand to the floor.

The room was sterile white and devoid of any decoration. He sat in a chair that was part of a group of chairs that rested along a wall. He couldn't focus on anything more, nor could he make out who the woman was that started barking out orders to everyone, but he could make out her voice. *Ah, the famous Dr. Faulkner.* Then everything went black.

****

He was lying on a table with an IV in one arm and a tube for a blood transfusion in the other. His body ached, but there was definitely a difference from when he had first come in. He slowly opened his eyes and saw he was the only one in the room. The room was not accommodating. The table on which he lay sat in a corner. The rest of the room consisted of tables, chairs, medical and scientific equipment. He could feel his strength returning. *How long was I out?*

Dr. Faulkner and another woman entered the room. The doctor was tall, nearly six feet, and she made no effort to enhance her looks with make-up or fancy hairstyles. She wore her long hair pulled back tightly in a tail. He had never seen the other woman before. She had blond dreadlocks that fell down below her waist and had tattoos on her face. She was shorter than the doctor. Though Dorne was no wizard he could feel the magic pulsating from the shorter woman.

"Is this him?" the blond asked in a strange exotic accent.

"Yes, he…"

"Good, you can leave," the blond said, cutting off Dr. Faulkner.

The doctor didn't protest and left. The tattooed woman approached Dorne and appraised him. She circled the table that he was lying on, inspecting the IV and the blood. She got close to his face and stared into his eyes.

"Joshua Dorne, is it?" It was a simple question that demanded an answer.

He didn't know what to make of her. He began to sweat, and

he had to concentrate not to tremble. "Y..." he swallowed, "yes."

She smiled. She was mere inches from his face. She smelled of rosemary. Her eyes were big blue orbs. Under different circumstances he might have flirted with her, but something told him that that would be a horrible idea. She sniffed him and her nose wrinkled.

"Did you see my sister?"

Sister? What sister? I don't even know who you are. "Uh..." he swallowed again.

"Yes...sister. Red hair. Tattoos like mine. My sister, did you see her?" She started to rub his groin.

What is she doing? Shit! If I wasn't so terrified I'd be getting aroused. Wait, shit, no.

She smiled again. "Glad I have your attention now." She reached under the blanket and took him in her hand. "Did you see my sister?" she repeated.

"Y...yes." He was terrified and turned on at the same time. His body trembled. "She attacked our caravan. Her and a couple of ogres."

"Hmm...Ogres you say. Interesting." She continued to massage him.

"They were trying to rescue Khayin." A wave of pleasure shot through his body.

"Trying? I think she succeeded." She breathed heavily, her hot breath on his face. "What did she do? Her magic, I mean. How did she accomplish the rescue?"

"Some kind of telekinesis. She was quite powerful. We had no defense for it. She lifted our wagons away from the fight with the ogres and took on the occupants of the wagon by herself." He was panting. "She made short work of us, despite being shot by me. She lifted me in the air and threw me to the ogres. I barely made it out of there alive." He was having difficulty talking as the sensations increased.

"Was that all you saw?" she purred.

"Yes, I swear," he managed to say. She stopped abruptly.

His panting ceased. She withdrew her hand and pulled away from him. His interrogator walked over to another table filled with medical tools. Dorne couldn't see what she was doing. He heard the sound of metal on metal; it sounded like she was inspecting the tools then laying them back down. She turned to face him.

"I hear you are quite the accomplished torturer," she said with a wicked grin.

Dorne wasn't sure if it was the encounter he had just had or the lighting, but he was enraptured by her. "My methods produce results," he said with all the bravado he could muster.

She approached him. She walked like a dancer--deliberate, precise and elegant. Her eyes entranced him. And if she wasn't as captivating as she was he probably would have noticed the long dagger she had pulled from her belt. In one swift movement she plunged the knife into his chest and through the heart. He heard the tip of the blade hit the metal table on which he lay.

"I also heard you tortured a young woman recently. I'm sure she wasn't the only one." He could barely hear her now. He felt his life flowing from him and into a pool beneath him. "You don't get to do that to women, you sick fuck."

That was the last thing he heard.

Chapter 28   The Mom

Khayin awoke to shouting.

"No, Mom. I will not come stay with you. Everything is fine here. I have Khayin and Kira with me and Tao is not far away. I'll be fine. I just wanted to be sure you were OK... No, nothing happened... No, I'm not into Kira, she doesn't even swing that way. Geez, can't I just have friends over without you psychoanalyzing everything? Gosh, mom, why do you have to be like this? I wanted friends to stay over. My city was attacked. Why can't I have friends stay the night?... No. Tao had to check on her employees... Of course, I care for her. I asked her, and she said she was fine. Now all of a sudden you recognize our relationship. UGH! You are sooo frustrating." Codex stomped around the room. Her face was red and turned an even brighter shade when she saw Khayin. "Yep...yep...yep, I...yep...yep, I...yep...yep...I love you too." The phone made a crisp snap noise when she shut it, ending the conversation.

"Good morning," Khayin said with the cheesiest grin he could muster.

"Shut up," Codex spat as she walked by, giving him a light shoulder bump.

"You know, I don't think I ever met your mother. What's her name?"

"Nope." She walked to the kitchen and to the coffee she had made earlier.

"Nope what?"

"Just nope." She turned in his direction. "I love you, Snuggly Bear. Too much to subject you to my mother." She turned back around and grabbed some mugs.

"Can I at least have her name?"

"Nope," she said in a short clip. "I know how good of a tracker you are and you have tracked down people with less. Sorry, Snuggly Bear. This is one subject that is off limits."

"Fair enough." Khayin took a seat at the kitchen table, completely amused by the spectacle he had just witnessed. "What's for breakfast?"

"There's fruit on the table in front of you. And behind you on the counter I have some bread and jam," she said as she carried over the coffee.

"So...you're not going to serve me?" he asked with a grin.

"You're cute. Now unless you want to lose some teeth, I suggest you get your own damn breakfast," she said with an even bigger grin.

"I was only kidding," he said half-heartedly.

"I wasn't."

"What did I miss?" asked a sleepy-eyed Kira. She stretched as she entered the room. She sat down across from Khayin and Codex slid her a cup of hot coffee. Codex gestured to the sugar and Kira waved her off. "Black is good."

"Codex is trying to get back some semblance of control after getting yelled at by her mother this morning. So, she's taking it out on me. Though I probably did ask for it." He looked at Codex. "I'm only trying to help. I figure if you're barking at me it might make you feel better."

"Did you just say I was 'barking'?" she asked.

Khayin couldn't tell how upset she was by that remark. "In the cutest way possible, of course."

"Anyway," she smiled at him, "today is the day we assault Chicago."

"I don't know if 'assault' would be the word I'd choose," said Khayin. "Maybe infiltrate?"

"Sure, whatever." She rolled her eyes.

"Can you get us in there, or do we have to get there on horseback?" He sipped his coffee. "It's quite a trip."

"No, silly, I can port you to just outside the city. There's some kinda interference that keeps me from porting directly into the city. It'll be up to you to get inside. That shouldn't be too hard. You've been there plenty of times; it ain't like the city has walls." She grabbed some melon that she had cut earlier. "Your biggest problem are your faces. We could try a glamour, but if the Boss truly is a god, she'll see right through it, and maybe even have a counter spell prepped for her lackeys to see through it too." She paused. "Your best bet is to just go as you are. Wear some hoodies or just try to blend in."

"But where do we go when we get inside the city?" Kira asked.

"The Nueden Corporation building. The building itself has only two stories made up of offices, which is where you'll find the boss's office. It'll be somewhere on the second floor. The building also has many sub-levels. I'm not sure how many, but that is where they do all their nasty stuff." Codex's phone beeped. She looked down at it then looked at Khayin. "I have to take this, it's Tao."

"Go ahead," he said.

She flipped open the phone and put it to her ear. "Hi, Pookie. How is everything? Everybody OK? How are you? Do you need me to come by? I can be there before you can blink... OK, but we can get together later? Yay... Oh... Yeah, they're here. They stayed the night. I'm about to port them to Chicago. We have to put a stop to this. I can't have Chi-Town come into my home and wreak havoc... What? No. Just them. It will be easier and I can stay and defend here just in case they get stupid enough to attack me twice... No, no, they have yet to see what the two of them can do together, I..." Her words cut off when she entered another room and shut the door.

"Well, this is it. Are you ready to face your sister?" Khayin was nervous for her and he noticed her tattoos jump radically for a second before calming to their usual mesmerizing pattern.

"Physically and magically I am at my best. Emotionally? I don't know." Her eyes were little slits and her tattoos swirled slowly.

"Hey, I'm there for you. We'll tackle this thing together," he said warmly as he reached across the table to lightly touch her hand.

"Lilith mentioned you had the means to kill gods." She took a sip of her coffee.

"Did she now?" It was more of a statement than a question. "I've been avoiding those beings for the majority of my existence. Luckily they tend to mind their own business. They are lazy and usually stay in their own territory. The gods try to stay clear of conflict with other gods. They are powerful and they don't need worshipers, though they are a big boost to their egos, which make them all the more dangerous. You can't kill them by conventional means. They heal too quickly." He drank the last of his coffee.

Kira leaned forward, holding her cup with both hands.

"I acquired a dagger in my travels. It's said that it holds special properties. The legends say it was used to kill a god of death. Now the dagger has that god's blood infused with the blade, which gives it a darker hue. And they say it is indestructible. I've never really tested that theory, the indestructible part." He tapped the blade sheathed in his boot against the leg of the table.

"So...you've killed a god before?" She almost appeared to be shy asking the question.

"A few."

Her eyes went wide. "You say that like it's no big deal. People worship those beings for a reason. They..."

"They what? Have the power to control weather, make crops grow, blah, blah, blah." He shook his head and slammed his fist on the table. "They are no different than you or me. They just discovered magic that they're not willing to share. Some are good, some are assholes, and believe me, I didn't kill any that didn't deserve it. People should have free will, control over their own destinies. Most of these beings can't live without mucking around in other peoples' affairs. And that includes Lilith and Muma." He hated the gods, and his face was starting to flush as a bead of sweat formed on his brow.

"I'm sorry, I didn't mean..." Kira reached across and grabbed his hand.

"No, it's my fault. I get worked up over it. I don't know all the details, but it's because of the gods that I am what I am. It's because of them that I can't die. It's because of them that I am forced to outlive my friends. My world is death, Kira. You know how hard it is to fall in love when you know you're going to watch the one you love die of old age?" He fought back a tear. "Balls," he whispered. She squeezed his hand.

"OK, let's change the subject. How do you suppose we get into the city?" She attempted to sound cheerful. Khayin appreciated it.

"We walk in," he said plainly. "We'll stay in the shadows as much as possible. I don't think they'll be expecting us. Getting into the Nueden building is going to prove a little more problematic, but I won't be able to form a plan until I see the place. We're assuming your sister is going to be with this Boss. Fighting the two of them together may prove difficult. You may have to fight your sister while I take on the Boss. Again, something else that we'll have to wait and see." He chuckled. "What a great plan."

The sound of a door shutting and the shuffle of feet came from behind Khayin. "What plan? You made a plan? Let me hear it. How could you make a plan without me? I wasn't going to be long on the phone. Tao was just checking in, making sure everyone was good. She's good, by the way. I know were wondering. But really, how can anyone be good after the attack? It's like being violated. At least that's how I feel. You feel that way? Even if you don't, you must feel something, 'cause you ran off like a bat out of hell. But that was probably 'cause you thought they had me. That was really sweet. I always knew you were a sweet man. You only act tough and non-approachable. You even got a woman who grew up hating men to like you. I think the two of you would be perfect for each other. Scratch that, you two are perfect for each other. Don't fuck it up, Khayin." Codex poked him in his shoulder, and her sharp pointed nail nearly broke the skin, even with his shirt on.

"What?!" Khayin was confused. "How'd that become about me and... Never mind."

"So, about this plan?" Codex asked, returning to the original subject.

"You mean the plan that there is no plan," Kira replied.

"Now it's my turn to be confused," said Codex.

"We don't have enough intel to make a definitive plan. We'll have to finalize when we're there. Make decisions on the fly." Khayin sat back. "I find I work better without a plan anyway."

"You're just going to wing it?" Codex asked a little annoyed. "You're going to face a powerful witch and a god, and you're going to wing it? You can't die Khayin, I get it, but Kira can. You need to think about her."

"What do you think I've been doing since I met her? I haven't been able to think straight with her constantly invading my thoughts. What else are we going to do?" He stood up. "Do I put her in danger by following a plan, a concept completely foreign to me? Or do I put her in danger by not having a plan?" He let out a sigh of frustration. "We'll have the element of surprise. They're not going to expect us to just walk in. Besides, we have a powerful witch too," he said, as if that was enough to settle the dispute.

Kira looked at him, and her tattoos moved in a hypnotic pattern. He liked the new look; he was definitely falling for her. "You can't stop thinking about me? What are you thinking about?" Kira was boring holes into him.

Those eyes. Khayin looked away, ignoring her questions.

"You're insane." Codex crossed her arms in front of her chest.

Khayin walked over to his bags and rummaged through them for his weapons, starting to put them on. Kira got up and did the same. He eyed a couple of oversized hoodies and decided not to take one, but he did throw one at Kira.

"Put this on and pull the hood over your head." She looked at him quizzically. "You're going to stick out like a sore thumb." Khayin finished, answering her obvious question.

"What about you?" She held up the hoodie and gave it a quick once-over.

"Then again it probably won't matter. If they recognize me, they are going to know you are with me and I don't want to wear anything that is going to interfere with me reaching my weapons." He sighed. "Alright then, let's do this." He was nervous--not for himself, but for Kira. He looked at her and smiled. He wanted to be strong for her and he was, but he wasn't confidant that she would come out of this alive.

Codex smiled. "OK, now the port will drop you in the backyard of an old house of mine. The back door should be unlocked. Now you two hold hands." Their palms touched and their fingers slowly laced together.

I could get used to this.

"Ahh...aren't the two of you cute."

"Codex..." He didn't get to finish.

Chapter 29 The Photo

It was mid-afternoon on a Friday and they were about a mile out of Chicago. The seventy degree weather was perfect with no humidity. Kira and Khayin both carried a backpack. Kira had just thought it was a weird looking bag until Codex showed her how to wear it. The port put them in a suburban town, in the backyard of a large house. All the houses were large to Kira and in pretty good condition.

"The success of Chi-Town attracts. People kept these homes in good shape." Khayin motioned toward the house. "Let's go take a look."

Kira followed Khayin to the back door of Codex's house. The entrance seemed to be two large glass doors that slid along on rails. Khayin tried one and it was locked, so he knocked. *Why did he knock?* When there was no answer, Khayin grunted and knelt down, pulling his bag off his shoulder. He rummaged through and found a little folded piece of leather that had tiny metal tools inside. He grabbed a couple and then proceeded to put them into a hole on the handle. After a few moments there was a small click and he slid the door open.

"Ta-da," he said with a broad smile. "I know magic, too."

Kira shook her head and brushed past him into the house. She found herself in the kitchen; she recognized the stove and other appliances. The counters were cleared off and the refrigerator was empty. Making her way into the main living area, she noticed a long couch and two cushioned chairs.

"They put a computer screen on the wall?" Kira said pointing to the large screen.

Khayin chuckled. "No, that was a TV, or television. People used to put on elaborate plays and record them for other people to watch on screens like those." She thought about that a moment. "When we are done and we have defeated your sister and her master, I'll take you to a place that has an even larger screen."

"For that Star Wars play?" She said hesitantly, not entirely sure if she had the name right. She was pleased when she saw him smile.

"Exactly." He put his bag down on one of the chairs. "We should probably lay low until night. We'll be less likely to be seen. I'm going to take a look around upstairs." He left the room and climbed a set of stairs by the front door.

Kira followed suit, she set her bag down and explored the floor she was on. There were two fully furnished bedrooms along with a bathroom. Other than a complete lack of dust, it didn't seem that anyone had lived there in quite some time. Kira found two other doors, one that led to a large empty room that Khayin later explained was called an attached garage, where people kept their vehicles, and another door that led to another set of stairs leading down to the cellar.

The stairs down creaked. They were made of wood and had been replaced several times over the years. The cellar was dark, save for daylight that trickled in through block glass windows. She felt a powerful magic in the cellar. Several tables lined the walls. All had different wizard tools laid out in neat rows. In the corners of the cellar stood candelabras atop tall stands. The setup was similar to Lilith's work room.

She headed back toward the stairs, but altered course when she noticed an alcove underneath them. It was darker than the rest of the cellar and the light from the windows barely reached the little nook. She was about to ignore it when something caught her eye. There, partially covered in dust, cobwebs and dirt, the little amount of light that did manage to break through reflected on a glossy piece of paper. The paper was a photo of a woman and a young girl. Kira flipped the photo over to find writing on the other side. She couldn't make it out, as it was in a language she couldn't read. Kira flipped it back over and studied the photo again. That looks like Codex. She stuffed the picture in a pocket and left the cellar.

Kira and Khayin both finished their exploration at the same time. They retired to the living room and Kira pulled the photo from her pocket, handing it to Khayin as the two of them sat. Khayin chose one of the large chairs while Kira flopped onto the large couch and stretched out her legs.

"I found that in the cellar. It wasn't locked up or hidden or anything. It was just lying on the floor covered in dirt. It was probably dropped and forgotten. There is some writing on the back, but I couldn't read it." She crossed her arms behind her head.

Khayin looked at the picture for a long moment, then he flipped it. Khayin recognized the writing on the back as Moabite.

"'Me and Anat'," he read aloud.

"Do you know this Anat?" She looked at Khayin. His face was all scrunched up in thought.

"There was an old god that went by that name, but the name got very popular in twentieth century Israel." He studied the picture more. "She can't be THE Anat, can she? How'd Codex know her? She hasn't shown her face in..." he whispered. He looked up at her. "Mind if I keep this?"

"Sure, I figured you'd want it, at the very least to ask Codex about it." She twisted to lie on her side so she could see him better. "What do you know about her? Something we should worry about?"

"Virgin goddess of war and strife, from a long dead religion. The gods don't just disappear when no longer worshiped. They lose some of their power, sure, but they don't disappear. Let me rephrase that--they don't just cease to exist. Anat did disappear. No one knew where she went. Most of the other gods don't care. I met her very early on in my life and she'd pop in every once in a while like she was checking in on me. I think she's tied to my curse somehow, but I could never ask her. Every time I tried to talk to her she'd simply disappear." Khayin seemed to drift off.

"Well, hopefully you'll be able to get some answers from Codex," she said as she closed her eyes. "I'm going to take a little nap."

"Sure," he said sounding very distant.

****

It was evening when Khayin woke her. Kira rubbed her eyes with the heels of her hands. She let out a big yawn as she stretched. She found Khayin strapping on his weapons and getting ready to leave, so she grabbed her bag and pulled out the scarf Muma had given her. She turned it around so that the beads and decorations rested against her as to prevent it from making noise. She could feel the magic within it.

"Let's do a little recon," Khayin said. "Shouldn't be a far walk, but bring whatever weapons you think you may need." He looked at her scarf. "Where'd you get that? I've never seen it on you before."

She smiled. *He's noticing my outfits now, huh?* "The gypsy woman Muma gave it to me." She touched it, feeling the fabric between her fingers. "There's magic in it, so I thought I'd wear it today. Every little bit helps, right?" Khayin only shrugged.

"I don't trust her." He was heading toward the front door. "But, she helped you and showed no sign or reason to trick you. Did she tell you how it worked or what it does?"

"No, I figure it will let its nature be known when the time is right." She followed him out the door.

There were no lights in the street. Candlelight and the occasional glow rocks could be seen shining through the windows of the houses on the street. Khayin and Kira stood on the front porch, letting their eyes adjust to the darkness. The moon was full and bright in the sky. It was a clear night. There was a small breeze, but otherwise it was a very calm evening. Khayin started down the street toward the city.

"So, I didn't bring it up earlier, but Codex has a house this close to Chicago?" she asked.

"Yeah, second home, I guess. As clean as it is I'm sure she's there on a regular basis." He pulled out his cigarette tin and offered one to Kira. She gladly accepted.

"There were magical tools in the cellar."

"I've never seen the place before, nor did I know that she comes out here. Makes sense though." He held out the cigarette for her to light it. "We're close, but she likes her privacy. There are a lot of things I'm probably not privy to."

"Have you ever asked her more about herself?" she wondered.

"You're intrigued." He grinned. "She's quite impressive. And there's definitely more to her, but I respect her enough not to ask. I figure if she wanted me to know she'd tell me."

"How long have you known her?"

"A while. She's older than you might think. For as long as I've been a bounty hunter, I've worked with her." He was looking straight ahead. The tip of his cigarette glowed when he inhaled.

"How long have you been a hunter?"

"A century or so, and I'll keep doing it until I get bored, or unless something else comes up that is more interesting. Codex keeps trying to convince me to settle. Maybe one day I will." The street was vacant and had been since they had left Codex's house.

"Do you have a home?" she asked.

"Not really. I'm rarely in one place long enough. I do have an old bunker outside of Vegas that I keep stuff in. It has the furnishings of a home in case I need a place to lay low, but I don't know if I'd necessarily call it home."

The city was not hard to find in the distance. They were still a ways out and Kira was impressed. She thought Vegas was a marvel, but Chicago, even from their position, was lit up bright. Tall buildings loomed over head. She was already fascinated. She couldn't wait to see it more up close.

"The city looks impressive," she stated.

Khayin looked at her with a smile. "It's considered the most advanced city in the Americas. The wizards, artificers, alchemists, and cybermages spent decades working together to make it what it is. Too bad we're not here as tourists. Maybe I'll get a chance to show you around when we are done."

She looked up at him and smiled. "I'd like that."

They walked a few more blocks in silence. She started to get anxious. She had no idea what to expect and the anticipation was killing her. Part of her wanted to face down her sister, but the other part wished she didn't need to.

The city before them became larger and brighter and Kira's hands began to shake. She looked at Khayin, who was just staring ahead. She tried to draw on his strength. She closed her eyes. *If he can be strong, so can I. I'm better than my sister. I am the Crone.* She opened her eyes before she inevitably tripped on something while walking with her eyes closed and just watched the city envelop her.

They entered Chicago on the west side of the city. The Nueden building was only a couple miles east. They were making good time, though she realized that keeping time wasn't necessary. She saw horseless metal carriages, some parked while others moved in an orderly fashion down the street. Khayin told her later that they were called cars, leftover from the age of science. The further they walked the more awestruck Kira became. The city was truly a marvel.

"Khayin!" A male voice shouted from behind them. "I can't believe you'd come waltzing on in here with a price on your head."

Chapter 30   The Kiss

Khayin didn't need to turn around. He knew the voice and a shiver ran up his spine, but not from fear. The bounty hunter behind them was the slimy sort. 'God's gift to women' he'd call himself. Khayin really didn't want to turn around.

"Balls," he cursed. "Hey, Jax, isn't it past your bedtime?" Khayin said as he faced the man.

Jax sat high up on a horse staring down at them. He wore a duster and a pair of six shooters on his belt. He had a mustache, which Khayin liked to call a porn 'stache, and short cropped brown hair. The worst part was that Jax always managed to smell of way too much cologne. He leered at Kira. Khayin felt Kira move closer. She was so close their bodies touched, which Khayin was fine with.

"Khayin, when didja take on a partner? I've always thought you were a lone wolf." Jax grinned.

"Are you jealous? You always talk a big game, but you never seem to keep any women."

"Why'd I wanna keep em? They're good for a roll in the sack, but after that they just get in the way, slow me down." Jax leaned to try to get a better look at Kira. "She's an exotic one." He pointed and frowned a little. "Not sure about the tattoos though. Kinda slutty if you ask me."

Khayin was getting irritated, but he was happy Kira wasn't up-to-date on slang and probably had no idea what a slut was. Khayin reached around and pulled her closer, his hand resting on her waist. She didn't resist.

"Mind your manners, idjit." He held her a tad tighter, and still she didn't resist. "She's a lady and if she's traveling with me you'd better believe she can handle herself."

"Is that why she's clinging to you?" Jax craned his neck to put her in full view. "Come on out, little girl. I won't bite ya. Too hard." He chuckled a sinister chuckle.

Khayin laughed.

"What's so funny, shithead?" Jax spat.

"You." Khayin laughed even louder.

"Stop laughing!" he demanded. Jax pulled a pistol from its holster and pointed it at Khayin.

"You're a fool if you think that I'm protecting her from you." He had calmed himself enough to speak clearly. "On the contrary, Jax ol' pal, I'm protecting you from her."

As if the two of them had planned it, Kira's eyes began to glow and with a raise of her hand she Pulled Jax from the saddle of his horse. She Pulled the pistol from his outstretched hand and the gun hit the wall of an adjacent building. Jax dangled motionless ten feet from the ground. There was a look of sheer panic on his face, his eyes were wide and he started to visibly sweat.

"She's a witch." Jax barely said. Khayin could almost see Jax turn paler.

"What's wrong, Jax? Are you afraid of magic?" Khayin taunted.

"I'm not afraid of no magic, but she's a witch." His voice began to tremble. "Witches ain't natural. They in league with demons."

"The mighty Jax has turned into a sniveling baby. I thought you were past that superstitious mumbo-jumbo." Khayin shook his head in pity. "It's been over two hundred years, Jax."

"I'm fine with magic, Khayin, but witches ain't natural." He tried to sniff up some run-away snot. "Put me down and I'll leave you be. I swear."

Khayin was actually beginning to enjoy the spectacle before him. He had always hated Jax. He was a fine hunter, but Jax was a notorious womanizer and he could get overly abusive with his marks. He let Kira hold him there a moment, to milk it for all that it was worth.

"Alright, Kira. Lower him." She did so and Khayin disarmed him. "Let him go." Kira dropped her hold of him and Jax fell the last foot or so to the ground, landing hard on his tailbone. "Where's the contract? I want to see it." Khayin stood over him.

"In my saddle bags. Please keep the witch away from me." He tried scooting further away from Kira, and Khayin snickered.

He walked over to Jax's horse and rifled through his saddle bags. He found food rations, rope, a canteen, and other traveling tools. He opened a side pocket and found a folded piece of paper. He withdrew the paper and studied the picture of himself along with the offer of the reward for capture--25,000 chips. Closer inspection revealed the same watermark he had seen on Kira's poster and no Syndicate seal. He held it up for Kira to see.

"At least they got the likeness right," he remarked.

The light of the moon wasn't enough for her make out what was on the poster, so she got closer and took it from him. She examined it for a moment and snorted. She shoved it back at him.

"What?" he asked as he took it back.

"You're worth more than me?" she whined.

"Seriously?" He laughed. "Maybe we should take it up with your sister or the Boss."

"Shut up." She smiled. "Does he have a poster for me as well?"

"I didn't see one. You're welcome to look." Khayin gestured back to the horse.

She shook her head. "What are we going to do with him?" She was now standing over Jax, who looked as though he may pee himself.

"Leave him. I doubt he'll come after us." Khayin thought a moment. "Although..."

"What? I don't think I like the sound of that." Kira looked at him over her shoulder.

"Maybe we let him capture me. Turn me in."

"What?! Are you serious?" She gave him a scrutinizing eye. "Because that has to be the dumbest thing I have heard you say yet."

"No, no, hear me out. This'll get me in past their defenses.

They won't kill me; they'll need me for bait," he explained.

"Bait?"

"For you. They ultimately want you."

Jax tried to get up, but Kira kicked his legs out from under him. "So, splitting up is your idea of a plan?"

"Yeah. Why not? They'll be so busy interrogating me that you could sneak in. It's Saturday. There won't be that many people working." He wasn't at all confidant, but it was the best plan he could come up with.

"It's still crazy," she mused as she shook her head. "What makes you think that they'll buy it?"

"Buy what?"

"That he was able to capture you." She shot Jax a look that made the hunter stop in his tracks at another attempt to get away.

"Your sister doesn't know me and I doubt the Boss does either. I'll spin them a nice web of lies, and sprinkle in some truth. They'll have no choice but to fall for my charm." He grinned ear to ear.

"You're telling yourself a lie right now," she teased.

Khayin frowned. "Hey, that hurt."

"Get over it. Look, Mr. Charming," she said in a very sarcastic tone, like she didn't believe he could be charming, "my sister hates men. No amount of charm is going to sway her."

"Really." Khayin said a little perturbed.

Khayin walked over to Kira, standing mere inches from her. His shoulders were back and his back was straight. He gently pushed her dreads away from her face, lightly caressing her skin. He felt her goosebumps under his touch. He let his hand slide to the back of her head, ever so slightly brushing her ear. She let out a small whimper. Khayin's other hand, at the small of her back, firmly but affectionately pulled her body against his. He tilted her head back and leaned in very close. Her eyes were closed. He let their noses touch as his mouth faintly grazed her lips. Her mouth opened in a tiny moan. He could feel her hot breath and moist lips. He had to stifle a moan of his own. Then he let go and backed away.

"I say I've got a few tricks up my sleeve." Khayin was all

smiles. He knew he wouldn't be able to charm her sister, but he had been dying to know how Kira really felt about him. She stood with her eyes closed for another moment before regaining her composure.

"I think you broke her, Khayin." Jax said, still sitting in the road.

"Shut up, Jax." Khayin snapped.

"You think I'm going to go along with your little plan?" Jax tried to sound as though he had any say in his situation.

"Yeah, I do."

"Yeah, you're right. I'm with her though. I think your plan is crazy, so I'm actually anxious to see it." Jax still watched Kira, not moving.

"You'll get a nice payday and you'll get to walk away. Kira will be watching, so if you try anything stupid, she'll track you down and turn you into a toad." He put in as much bravado as he could to nail the point home. She glared at Jax.

"OK, Khayin, you've got a deal." Jax said as he got up.

"You do this without a hitch and I'll forget all about you trying to capture me."

"No problem." Jax made his way over to his horse.

"Give me a minute," Khayin said to Jax as he moved over to Kira.

They walked a few feet away. When they stopped, Kira slugged Khayin in the upper arm. Her face was struggling. She twisted it to look angry, but Khayin could see the smile she was trying to hide. She glared at him. He stifled a laugh and glared back. He was happy he broke away when he did; there was definitely something there.

"You bastard! What was that about?" she huffed.

"I was proving a point," he said simply.

"And what point is that? You can't just do that. You caught me completely off guard."

"I didn't see you try and stop me."

"I was confused, and..." she trailed off. "Dammit. Don't do that again."

"Alright, if that's what you want. I'll never try to kiss you again." He tried to hide his amusement.

"That...that's not what I meant. I..." He could see the conflict on her face, and her tattoos looked like they were at war with each other. "Fuck you," she huffed. Khayin just laughed.

"Brianna isn't going to fall for your seduction. She hates men, remember?"

"I remember, and I wasn't planning on 'seducing' her?" he countered.

"Then..." she started.

"That was for your benefit. I didn't want you to think I was just some brute who only knows how to kill or maim people." Kira just stood there and Khayin swore that he could see the wheels turning in her head.

What am I doing? I can't fall for her. It won't end well. But, shit...I don't care.

Khayin walked up to Jax, who was now back on his horse. He reached into Jax's bags and pulled out the rope, untangling it and holding it out to him. Can you tie a good knot? It's got to be convincing. Also, you may want to disarm me." He smiled. Jax jumped off his horse.

Khayin started to remove his weapons and hand them to Jax, who stuffed them in his saddlebags. He also took Khayin's bag and attached it to his. Kira helped with the ropes. They tied Khayin's hands together and behind his back. They then wrapped his torso, pinning his arms against his body. It was extremely uncomfortable.

Khayin's eyes met Kira's. They were close. "In my right boot," he whispered. "There is a dagger. Take it, keep it close and bring it with you when you rescue me." Before Kira could react, Khayin leaned in and kissed her. Their lips met only briefly before Jax tugged them apart. "Wait until dawn before you do anything," he said in a slightly louder voice.

"OK, love birds. Let's get this show on the road," Jax cackled.

Kira stood motionless once again. Khayin could only imagine what was going on in her head, but he figured that if this was going to be their last night together, he wanted no regrets. Kira grabbed the dagger before Jax pulled him away. She stayed back and trailed them, keeping to the shadows. Khayin watched her for as long as he felt was safe before finally turning his attention to Jax and the road.

Jax kept a nice slow pace for Khayin, but he knew that the bounty hunter would speed it up the closer they got. They walked that way for a couple miles until they were able to see the Nueden building. Jax stopped and jumped off the horse. He walked up to Khayin and the two of them stood face to face.

"What is it?" Khayin asked.

"Why the Nueden Corporation? They're a medical and alchemical research company? What did you do to them for them to put a contract out on you?" he asked.

"Does it matter? That's just a cover--a clean business to mask a dirty one. Who cares? The chips are good, right? Why should you care?" Khayin responded rhetorically.

"Good point." Jax hit him square in the face. "We have to make it look like you put up a fight." Jax said smiling.

"Oh, good thinking." Khayin kicked Jax in the groin doubling over the bounty hunter, then kneed him in the face.

Jax spit out blood and coughed uncontrollably for a few seconds. When his hacking was done he stood up and hit Khayin again. Khayin shook his head when he saw Kira out of the corner of his eye. Jax hit him a couple more times before he got back onto his horse. Both men were bloody and both were smiling.

Jax pulled up in front of the Nueden building and hopped off his horse. He grabbed the bags that had Khayin's weapons and the rope that held Khayin captive. Jax led him to about 30 paces from the glass doors and stopped. He looked at Khayin. Khayin nodded.

"I've come for the bounty on Khayin! Open up!" Jax shouted.

Chapter 31 The Alley

Kira was still in a daze when she watched Khayin and Jax leave. Her flesh tingled. She felt warm and fuzzy and she had no idea what to do about it. *He kissed me. And I let him. What does this mean? Does he?...No...Can it be?...No. Fuck. What does it mean? It's because he thinks we're not going to make it through this, or me at least. That's got to be it.* She was rationalizing with herself, trying to explain what had just happened.

Kira followed the men to the Nueden building. She stuck to the shadows in hopes of not being spotted by anyone from the corporation. The streets were deserted. Cars had been parked along the sides of the roads and very little litter could be seen. Kira was impressed by how tidy the city was. Vegas was nice, but Chicago took it a step beyond. She remembered Panama and how dirty it was. It had seemed like people there just didn't care.

They had walked a couple miles when she saw Khayin and Jax stop. She was nervous and a little scared, being in the city alone, so she didn't want to take her eyes off Khayin until she absolutely had to. Jax got off his horse and the two men conversed. *What are they doing?* Then she saw Jax hit Khayin in the nose. Blood came gushing out. She stepped out of hiding, but then Khayin kicked Jax between the legs and kneed him in the face, crushing his nose as well.

Jax got up and struck Khayin again. Her adrenaline pulsed and her temper began to flare. She had had enough and she started toward them, but saw Khayin look at her and shake his head. She stopped. What are they doing? Then it dawned on her. They both needed to look roughed up. She nodded, even though she was certain Khayin didn't see it and she slid back into the shadows.

Kira followed them for another mile or so until the two hunters stood in front of the glass doors of the Nueden Corporation building. Jax shouted, announcing his arrival with a bounty. Kira made her way around the side of a nearby store, being sure to stay out of view, but positioning herself to be able to witness the exchange. She couldn't hear anything, but the moonlight was enough to make out what was going on. The area became really visible when Nueden Security turned on the lights and walked outside.

Five men dressed in matching uniforms appeared from the building. They were armed with clubs and large guns. She'd seen guns like them before at the Air Force Base. She had seen what they could do and she wanted no part of it. Words were exchanged before one of the men left and headed back into the building. Khayin and Jax stood waiting with the remaining Nueden employees. The six of them, and Kira, waited for several minutes. After what seemed an eternity the man that had left returned with another man. The newcomer wore a different uniform with medals on it. He wore a hat and had a face full of hair. He was obviously important.

More words were exchanged before Jax handed the first man the rope and received a bag from the man in uniform. Jax nodded, handing him Khayin's bag of weapons before shaking the important man's hand. The hunter climbed back onto his horse and left. Kira decided to do the same. She wanted to be sure she couldn't be seen in case they saw through Khayin's ridiculous plan. She felt jittery and she could feel that her hands wanted to tremble. She ducked back around the corner and out of view, following the road on the other side of the store. The road took several turns, so Kira was sure to take mental pictures along the way so she could find her way back. Now she felt truly alone.

Kira found an alley behind a restaurant and decided to sit and wait for an hour before she did any reconnaissance. She was lonely in her solitude and she wanted to cry, the weight of everything that she had been through threatening to burst. She had always struggled with her emotions. Her sister was a master of controlling them, but Kira had to learn to hide them. She often thought that others in her tribe did as well, but her sister, she knew, truly didn't feel. The only emotions she saw in Brianna was envy and hate and she only showed them when she was doing something cruel or selfish.

Kira meditated. She crossed her legs, inhaled a deep long breath and exhaled through her nose. She focused on her magic; it flowed through her and she felt it tickle her skin like a cool breeze lightly caressing her flesh. Then she felt Khayin's touch. His hands gently brushing her face and hair. Her eyes snapped open, effectively breaking the meditation.

"Well, that's not going to work." She sighed. "We will definitely need to talk about what happened when this is all done." She shook her head, as if to shake something loose. She stood up and paced the alley.

The area behind the restaurant was fairly clean. There was a large metal trash receptacle next to the back door. She thought about possibly changing her appearance--her dreads were a dead giveaway and of course her tattoos could identify her in a second, but she hadn't the faintest idea how to cover them. That's when she felt it.

Kira looked at her arm and saw the sleeves of a jacket and not her hoodie. She looked at the rest of herself and was amazed to see that she was wearing a Nueden employee uniform. She immediately reached up to touch her head. Kira gasped. Her hair was shorter and fine and...blonde. This was no illusion; it was an actual transformation.

What did I do? How did this happen?

She was trying not to panic. She started to think rationally, realizing that when she had thought about a disguise, she had felt magic. But, where did the magic come from? *Think, Kira. The sash from Muma. Did she foresee this? Did she know about my upcoming confrontation with my sister? Only one Crone every couple of generations was born with the gift of foresight and Sister-Mother Helga was it. Shit! This is starting to come together.*

"Oh, Brianna, you are so going to die," Kira seethed.

She began to pace and she tried to concentrate on her normal self. She willed the sash to change her back. It was a mental war at first. A wrestling match of sorts, as she pictured herself fighting another version of herself. She started to perspire. It wasn't this hard to change the first time. But she knew she had to learn control, otherwise it would change her every time she thought about it, even when she didn't want it to. She reverted back to her own self after her magic sparring match. She willed it back to the disguise with much greater ease.

I wonder what else this thing can do?

Her mind was a jumble. Fear, anxiety, and the feelings that Khayin stirred up were a chaotic mess in her head. Kira closed her eyes and thought of her home. She envisioned the bodies, the destruction, and ultimately, her mother. How had the Crone known Kira would return? Lilith, the Dragon-Mother? Kira kept her focus on her sisters, the Crone and Lilith. Revenge fueled her.

How could Brianna have done this? She had to have gone mad, killing everyone for the promise of power. What's she the Crone of now? I don't know who this Boss is either, but she will die as well.

Kira had to get control. She slowed her breathing. She focused on only one thing. *Stick to the plan, Kira. Rescue Khayin, kill Brianna and the Boss. Simple enough. We kill my sister, a powerful witch and a god. No problem.*

She pulled out the dagger that Khayin had given her. She turned it over in her hands. Kira could feel the dark magic radiating from it. There was barely any weight to it at all. The blade was crude and made of human bone from hilt to blade. Kira surmised that it was carved from a single bone. It was about a foot and a half in length and the handle was wrapped in strips of leather or some other skin, which looked as old as the blade itself. The pommel was the distal of the femur. She saw writing etched on the dagger blade in a language she didn't know.

This is the weapon that kills gods. I bet Khayin has a story. This kind of artifact just doesn't fall into one's lap.

She wrapped the dagger in an unused shirt and tucked 'The God Killer', which is how she had started to think of it, into her carrying bag. She decided that she didn't want to carry her backpack with her, so she left that behind after she transferred a few small items to her carrying bag. She had really nothing else of value for the rescue attempt, aside from herself.

Kira left the backpack beneath a nearby trash receptacle and she exited the alley. She made her way down the dark streets and around the back of the Nueden building. As she suspected there was a door in the back as well. She continued to circle the building, making an effort to note guard posts, other entrances, and lit rooms. The two floors above ground were dark; she saw no sign of life. She also noticed no guards. She shivered.

She made her way back to the rear door and checked if it was locked. The handle didn't budge. She really hadn't thought this through. She had no spell to unlock it and she didn't have Khayin's skill of picking it. She stood there a moment in thought.

I could try breaking it, but that will make a lot of noise, as will forcing it off its hinges with magic. I could wait till dawn and walk in the front door. She looked at her arms and the rest of her uniformed body. *I look like one of them. Great, Kira, you're an awesome partner. You can't even get into the building.*

The door opened and Kira jumped. In the doorway stood a uniformed guard. He looked as shocked as Kira felt and probably looked. The two of them just stared at each other for a long moment. He was about six feet tall and broad shouldered. He wore his hair short and his face was cleanly shaven.

He spoke first. "Who're you and why are you standing at the service door?"

Kira glanced down to see if her jacket had a name tag. "I'm Kim," she read aloud. "I'm new. I was told to come first thing in the morning. I know I'm early. I tried the front, but there were no lights and it looked deserted, so I decided to see if there was a different entrance." She flashed him a big toothy smile.

"Ugh! Newbies." He moved out of the way. "Come on, I'll

show you to the lockers."

Holy shit, it worked.

Kira walked past him. She put a little sway in her walk and she looked over her shoulder. "Thanks."

He checked out her ass. "Um, yeah. No problem. I'm Sam." He shut the door behind him.

Chapter 32   The Room

The whole building was alight and was nearly blinding. Coming from the dark of night Khayin would've liked to cover his eyes, but had to settle for first closing them, then squinting, and then eventually opening them back up altogether as his eyes adjusted. He was flanked by two armed guards, who insisted on partially dragging and leading him through the building. There were two more armed guards behind him and they all followed the man in the more elaborate uniform.

They passed the information desk in the lobby where two more guards kept watch. To the right of it was a set of stairs leading up to the next level. To the left was a door to offices, Khayin presumed. Beyond the desk was a single elevator and a door that led to another set of stairs. The elevator isn't the only way up and down, good to know. They led him to the elevator. The main man said nothing and Khayin decided to keep his mouth shut for the time being. He figured he'd have plenty of time to talk soon enough.

"Where's Dorne, sir? I wouldn't have disturbed you if I could've found him," said one of the guards in front of Khayin.

"Joshua Dorne is no longer with us. You will answer to me from now on," The head man said assertively.

"Yes, sir!" The guard said sharply.

Khayin decided to call this main man Mr. Head, not because he had a large head but just because he seemed to be the one in charge, for now. Mr. Head pressed the down button for the elevator and they all waited for it to arrive. After a few moments there was a dinging noise and the door opened.

Khayin was always in awe when he came to Chicago. It was a marvel that a city in this age could still run on power--magic power that acted like electricity, but power nonetheless. Why other cities haven't followed their lead he hadn't the slightest idea.

They all stepped through and entered the small elevator; the six of them were packed in like a can of sardines. "We're all going at the same time?" Khayin questioned. He couldn't help himself; the silence was killing him. "Is this part of the interrogation process?"

He was answered with the butt end of a rifle hitting him in his gut. It knocked the wind out of him and he doubled over, which invited another blow and a guard yelling at him to stand up straight. Khayin was surprised the guard could get that much force in the blows in such a small space.

He remained quiet for the remainder of the descent. They stepped into a small lobby with an empty desk. The walls were bare of any decoration. Everything was white. Must be a fun place to work.

Mr. Head approached a door and unlocked it. They entered a long stark hallway with many doors along both sides. There was a chill in the air, though Khayin couldn't tell if it was his imagination, or if the temperature was actually cool. Every door was marked with a number and a letter, ranging from 13A – 13M. They walked to the door marked 13M, which sat at the very end of the hall. After Mr. Head unlocked and opened it they all ventured in.

First appearances would suggest that it was a medical room. There were gurneys and rolling surgical trays. Curtains made partitions segregating the large room. Along one wall was a long table with many different medical and surgical tools. In one particular corner was a single chair with wrist and ankle restraints. There was space around the chair for someone to stand or sit comfortably in another seat if one were there. The interrogation room. These guys don't play around. Impressive.

They roughly dragged him over to the chair. Khayin stumbled and was helped with another blow from a rifle. They stopped in front of the chair while the two guards behind him untied his bonds. As soon as he was freed from the rope they violently spun him. The hands of the guards holding him dug deep into the flesh of his upper arms. They shoved him down hard into the chair. Khayin didn't fight, but that didn't stop the men from being as rough with him as if he was. At one point one of the guards referred to Mr. Head as Chief Rantz, so Khayin focused on making that shift in his head.

The moment he was fully strapped down and restrained, the four guards backed away. One guard took Khayin's hat. Mr. Head stood in front of him. He was a sturdy man with a full beard. His coat was reminiscent of a Marine's uniform. The man had his hands clasped behind his back. Behind the facial hair Khayin noticed a scar that ran along the man's left cheek and behind his ear. The Marine just stared at him.

"So...how does this work?" Khayin decided to break the ice. "You rough me up a bit before the real interrogator comes in? Or are you the real interrogator?" The man remained silent. "I can't imagine you being the 'getting dirty' type. So, you'll have one of your goons over there rough me up. You'll ask questions, in which you'll get no answers, then you'll leave and the real nasty starts."

Chief Rantz's voice was low and gravelly. "Are you trying to be funny? Are you a comedian? Do you want to put on a show?"

"Are those rhetorical questions? Or, do you really want a show? I've never done stand-up, but I could give it a go? Have ya heard the one about..." He didn't get it out. The Chief moved fast and punched Khayin in the gut.

"You are right on one matter, Khayin. I'm not your interrogator. I personally find the act despicable." He punched him again. "But I am here to soften you up a bit," he said, speaking through his teeth.

The scruffy man continued to tenderize Khayin's mid-section. He only stopped to dodge a coughing fit of Khayin's that spat out blood. Khayin was certain a few of his ribs were broken, again. *I wish I had an adamantium skeleton like Wolverine.* As soon as his coughing stopped, the pummeling began anew. The Marine stayed away from Khayin's face. He backed away and stretched his fingers by opening and closing his hand. Khayin spat out blood. The red spittle made a splat on the floor. Tiny red drops fell on his abuser's nicely polished shoes. "With you not hitting my face, are you planning on kissing me after all this foreplay?" Khayin smiled, showing red stained teeth.

Chief Rantz grimaced and landed a haymaker punch to Khayin's smiling grill. Khayin's head rocked back and if the chair wasn't bolted to the floor he would have fallen over. Khayin started to laugh.

"You're so pathetic," he said through his laughter. "Is this what they have you do? Are you nothing but muscle for them?" He spat out more blood. He had almost bitten through his tongue. "You dress like you're important, but you're nothing but a thug."

As a result of Khayin's taunts, the Chief resumed his beating with more fervor. Khayin's face wasn't spared, and he gritted his teeth through the pain. The Marine only paused to catch his breath and rest his now swelling hands. Khayin laughed all the more. The laughter only enraged his abuser.

Chief Rantz charged Khayin with a fist pulled back ready to be thrown, but he stopped short. "Out!" he yelled. "Everyone out!" He stood with his head down and eyes closed. He was heaving. The guards in the room left without hesitation.

Khayin spat out blood. "I can't go anywhere."

The Marine glared at him. "I am the Chief of Security here. And I am a retired General of the Black Tempest Mercenaries. You will address me as such."

"Umm...as Chief or as General?" Khayin was no longer laughing.

"Chief. I am retired and no longer with the Black Tempest. I have twenty-eight successful missions. I've fought against raiders, bandits, and other looters. I have led successful raids on other cities. Detroit was my last, and it was glorious." The Chief started to pace. "Chicago is the most advanced and the wealthiest city in the Americas and probably the world. Everyone wants to live here. You yourself have been here enjoying our hospitality." He stopped pacing and turned his gaze on Khayin. "I am no thug," he said plainly.

"But yet you resort to thug tactics when asked, or is it told?" Khayin teased.

The Chief ignored his remark. "The Boss is a powerful mage. She has brought great prosperity to this city. Chicago would not be where it is today if it were not for her. So I do what I'm asked."

"The loyal lap dog. Do you do tricks? Can you roll over on command?" Chief Rantz hit him again. "Do you even question her motives? Like, why are you kicking the shit out of a bounty hunter that never did anything to you or your precious city? I just do my job, just like you." Khayin knew he wasn't going to be able to reason with him, but he thought if he could keep him talking long enough, his body would be able to heal some.

"She's like a mother to us. Like a mother to me." His eyes narrowed and pierced Khayin. "I will defend my mother. I would lay my life down for my mother. And if she says that you are to be beaten in preparation for her daughter...that is exactly what I will do."

"Her daughter? You mean Brianna?"

"How do you know her name? What do you know?" He was suddenly panicked. It was definitely a different emotion then what he had displayed before.

"So you do follow blindly." Khayin said with a mocking smile. That got him a scowl.

"You don't know me. Don't presume to know me," he hissed.

"I am a free man. A slave to no one. So I am a threat. Do what you are commanded, idjit." Khayin spat. He had had enough of his bullshit.

Chief Rantz's face turned a nice shade of red and stomped his way toward Khayin. He got in his face and Khayin spit in his eye. The Chief took a step back and cocked his arm for a swing.

"Have you had your fun, Lawrence? He's mine now." A woman of Kira's age and build walked into the room. She had long blond dreadlocks and she sported facial tattoos. She wore tight jeans and a spaghetti strapped blouse. She made a shooing gesture to the Chief. "Scat," she said. When she saw Khayin's face, her eyes went big. "What did you do, Lawrence? You were specifically told not to hit him in the face." Her accent was the same as Kira's. This must be Brianna.

She spun around and glared at the now shaken Chief of Security. She marched up to him and stood toe-to-toe. She came only to his chest. She shoved an index finger in his ribs, and the big man looked awkward with her scolding him, like a child confronting an adult.

"I don't have time to deal with your insolence. When I am done here we will have words." She grabbed the Chief's wrist and pushed up his sleeve. Khayin could barely see a row of tally mark scars on Chief Rantz's inner forearm. The small woman added another mark with a sharpened fingernail, as blood pooled and dripped to the floor. "One more, Lawrence, and you'll wish you never took this job. Now go." The Chief left quickly and the woman watched him leave.

The door shut and she turned and walked toward Khayin. She was smiling. *She's got a very pretty smile. That's probably how she lures them in.*

"I'm sorry he hurt you," she said in a very convincing sympathetic tone. "My name is Brianna and we are going to have a wonderful chat."

Chapter 33 The Locker

The door opened to a long hallway, another pair of doors visible at the end. Kira and her companion took the door on the right, which opened to a set of stairs. They descended three floors. On the wall she saw some writing that signified what floor they were on but she couldn't read it. *I'll have to get Khayin to teach me to read.* Sam opened the door and held it for her. She nodded and passed through.

They walked down another hallway and took their first left. A short way down that hall they entered a room that had a wall with metal doors. Kira tried to pay close attention to their twists and turns; the building seemed mazelike. There was nothing remarkable about the rooms they had seen thus far and this room was no exception. The metal doors were of a blue color and the walls were white.

"The lockers." He gestured to the wall of blue doors. "Take an empty one and you can put your stuff in there, or you can hold on to your stuff until you get a lock." He looked down at her. "Did they tell you where to go, or who to meet?"

"No," she replied.

"Figures." He rolled his eyes. After a moment he continued, "OK, follow me. I'll take you to my supervisor; he should know where you're supposed to be." He headed out the door and back into the hall. "I guess I'm not getting a break today," he mumbled.

Kira's palms began to sweat and she suddenly felt like she had

The Malevolent Witch

to pee. They wandered the corridors to the point that Kira lost complete track of where she was and gave up trying. They finally came upon their destination. She didn't know what to expect or what to say. Her disguise was only physical and there was no proof of employment. She didn't feel good.

The small room was big enough for a single desk. There were piles of papers and other assorted junk that Kira couldn't identify. The old man behind the desk had his head down and was writing in a book or journal.

"Yes, what is it?" He had an accent Kira was unfamiliar with.

"New employee, Mr. Benjamin," Sam answered.

"Right, right. They're early. Take 'em up stairs to the Boss's office. We're short-staffed so you have to do it, Sam. The Boss ain't in yet, so you may have to stay with her until she comes in," Benjamin said never looking up. "Are you still here? Go. Get. You're dismissed."

Sam left the small office and Kira followed. They wound their way back through the halls and ended back where they started. The two of them entered the stairway and ascended the stairs five floors. Kira walked out onto the building's second story. They stood in a large open space. There were no chairs or any other kind of furniture and the far wall was all glass. The majority of the glass was frosted. The only part that was transparent were the doors.

There was some writing on the glass. Kira thought they might be a couple of letters that formed another letter or just some kind of symbol. Sam proceeded forward, opened the glass doors and held the door for her. Those doors opened into another room with a desk at the far end. The same symbol that had been on the glass was also on a wall behind the desk. On either side of the desk were openings to a larger room.

A young woman stood behind the desk. She hadn't put any make-up on and her eyes were puffy with sleep. She wore a white blouse and a pencil skirt that stopped just above the knee. She had natural black hair and her skin was brown with a slight reddish hue. She was sipping something when Kira and Sam entered the room.

She pulled the cup away from her lips before she spoke.

"Sa...Sam. I...I didn't expect to see you this early." She was trying to hide her face with her hair and by turning away. Kira could see a hint of rose blossoming on her cheeks.

"Good morning, Lucy," Sam said in the sweetest voice Kira had ever heard.

Aww...ain't this cute.

"Umm...why...why are you up here? And who is the girl with you?" she asked with her back facing them.

"That's kinda why I'm here. Her name is Kim and she is new. I was told to bring her up here." He scratched his head. "Do you know anything about it?"

"I..." She turned back around, while being sure to keep her hair covering her face. "Give me a second. I think I heard the Boss say something about having one of the security detail posted up here. I knew they weren't gonna send you so I didn't pay it much mind." She rummaged through some papers on her desk.

Sam looked at Kira and smiled. "It would be a boring gig up here, but Lucy is fun and I'm sure the two of you will hit it off." He looked up and away, then to the floor. "It sure beats working downstairs. You won't get bugged too much by Mr. Benjamin. He's an asshole." He said the last part in a barely audible whisper.

"Ah yes," Lucy said. "I don't have a name, just that a female was requested." She looked at Kira, still trying to keep her face partially hidden. "That must be you then." She smiled at Kira. "Welcome aboard." Lucy shifted her attention back to Sam. "You'd better go before the Boss comes in." She dared to make eye contact and they briefly met each other's gaze.

"OK, see you later, Lucy." He turned to Kira. "Good luck." Sam left through the glass doors and into the stairwell. Lucy watched him until the door blocked her view.

"So, you're Kim. I'm Lucy." She extended her hand for a shake and Kira obliged. "Did they tell you anything about what your assignment will entail?" Kira shook her head. "Figures, and your first day is on a Saturday. I can't even believe I'm here on a Saturday. Alright, let me go freshen up and we'll try to figure it out together. I'm sure the Boss herself is going to want to talk to you since I didn't get any other information. This secrecy shit gets annoying sometimes." Lucy walked around the desk and behind the wall. "You can put your bag on the floor behind my desk if you'd like. I'll be back in a minute," she half-shouted from the other room.

Kira was unsure what to do. *Should I stick around to see the Boss, or should I go find Khayin? What if my sister comes in? I wonder if she'll recognize me even with this disguise.* She checked her reflection in the glass wall. Her sweaty palms didn't go away and she was thankful that her hands were the only part of her that were sweating.

She nearly jumped when she heard the small ding of an artificial bell. She heard a couple pairs of footsteps approach the glass doors. She stood up more straight and brushed her uniform with her sweaty palms. Her heart raced and she tried to center herself with a little meditation. She took a deep breath and exhaled, and when she opened her eyes she saw Mistress Tao standing in the open door. Following close behind her was the same hairy-faced man she had seen outside. He was carrying the limp form of Codex.

Chapter 34 The Sister

Khayin felt the tingling sensation of magic. It mostly gathered in his face as it mended the broken blood vessels and cuts. He didn't know how he felt about this. He knew it wasn't a kind gesture and that Brianna was setting him up for something more awful.

"I thought you couldn't heal." Khayin voiced his confusion aloud.

"Naturally? No, this is a spell." She was all smiles. "It is a simple incantation. I can't regenerate limbs and such, but broken bones, scrapes and bruises? Sure."

He dared to study her face. Brianna and Kira were twins. They weren't identical, but they shared many characteristics. They both had blue eyes, high cheek bones and full lips, but despite Brianna's current toothy smile, Khayin could see her perpetual frown.

"Trying to find my sister in my face?" she asked.

"You two do look remarkably alike." His face felt much better and her touch was much more soothing than painful. She smelled like Kira. A shiver of pleasure ran up his spine. I'm doing this for Kira. Keep your head in the game.

"We're sisters; of course we look alike." Her grin widened.

"What're you hoping to get out of me, Brie?" Khayin snarled.

She snapped her hand back from his cheek and she let slip a minute grimace, but she quickly recovered her smile. Brianna bent low to reveal that she wasn't wearing a bra. Khayin struggled to keep his eyes on hers.

"You have a very old soul," Brianna said. She looked down at her loose blouse then back to Khayin. "It's OK, you can look." Khayin kept his gaze to her eyes. She stuck out her lower lip. "Don't you find me attractive?" Khayin didn't react.

"Huh," she sighed as she straightened up and turned her back to him. "What do I hope to get out of you?" She turned to look at him. "Not one for small talk, are you? I was hoping to get to know you better. After all, you are spending an awful lot of time with my sister." Her eyes bored holes into him, but Khayin didn't sense any malice. "Tell me, Khayin, who are you really?"

"I'm a bounty hunter who's just trying to get by in this messed up world," he said in a pleasant tone.

"Oh, you're just being modest." She smiled and waved like she was batting something out of the air. "That is your cover, er, your escape. Who is the 'real' Khayin?"

"If you know so much about me, why ask?"

"All second-hand information, honey." She clasped her hands in front of her and swayed her shoulders. "Enlighten me, please, I will be so grateful." She batted her eyes.

"Your act won't work on me, sweetheart." Khayin was conflicted. He wasn't sure what she truly wanted and he didn't want to give her anything that would help in any way.

"Listen, can we be honest with each other? If I give you some answers will you give me some as well?" She stood with her arms crossed in front of her chest.

"As long as I reserve the right to not answer."

"You're hardly in a position to negotiate, honey, but since torture won't yield anything at all this will probably be the only way I'll get something out of you." She pressed her index finger to her lips. "OK, let's have a conversation. Though let me apologize first that we can't share any wine together. I don't trust you enough to free one of your hands. You understand?" Khayin nodded. "What do you find so attractive about my sister?"

"Really? This is what you want to talk about?" Khayin replied. He knew he shouldn't be confused by her intent, but he was having a really hard time trying to read her.

"Sure, why not? I can't stand her, so maybe if you can give me something that may be redeeming..."

He decided to play her game. "She is smart, independent, and she has great survival instincts."

"And she's hot. It's OK, you can admit it."

"You speak English well, where did you learn it?"

"The Boss helped me refine it, but I spent years learning your language from traders that visited the island." She twisted one of her dreads between her thumb and forefinger. "Do you know or use any magic?"

"Personally? Yes and no. I'm not a mage, but I use some magical items," he replied. He didn't know how to take her. He knew some of what she was showing was an act, but some was actually her. *Could she be a decent person if circumstances were different? What happened to her to make her so..?*

"I like your earring," she stated. "It translates for you. Pretty handy."

She walked over closer to Khayin and sat cross legged on the floor in front of him. She continued to play with her hair, looking up occasionally and slowly batting her long lashes.

"Where are you from...originally?" She was examining a bead that was woven into her hair.

Khayin just watched her. The witch before him and her sister Kira were the last of their people and from what he had witnessed so far they couldn't be more different. Sure, she was playing nice, but he knew she was only stalling until Kira showed.

How is Kira? I wonder if she got in yet. Maybe I should have done this by myself. How long am I going to have to entertain this girl?

"What's wrong, honey?" She was looking at him. "Trying to come up with a convincing lie?" She winked at him.

"It's really a shame, you know." They locked gazes. He could get lost in those eyes. "You and your sister are the last of your people and you both want each other dead." She radiated sexuality and was not nearly as shy as Kira to use it. It didn't help that Khayin liked blondes.

"My sisters, our people, had outlived their usefulness. They were behind the times. They lived in the past and showed absolutely no intention to grow, progress, and evolve. And I didn't see that changing even if my sister took on the mantle of the Crone." She paused and squinted, then a smile spread across her face. "So, I did what I had to do, but Kira proved to be more resourceful than I had anticipated. She found herself an ally that no one expected." Brianna toyed with Khayin's pant leg, every so often lightly touching his calf. "You haven't answered my question."

"The honest answer is, I don't know," he said plainly.

"Educated guess? I can't simply believe you never researched it for yourself."

"Somewhere in the Middle East, maybe. I honestly don't remember. I don't even know who my parents were."

"Fair enough." She had moved on to stroking his leg.

"So how'd you do it? How'd you manage to slaughter not only your tribe, but every other tribe on the island?" He tried to ignore her soft, delicate touch, but the fact that she smelled like Kira and looked like Kira made the endeavor very hard.

"Ooh, good question," she purred. "Planning. Careful planning," she cooed. "And I had help. The Mother, or the Boss as she's more commonly known around here, helped.

The Mother...

"OK, but you still didn't answer the question." Khayin shifted in his seat. They certainly hadn't chosen a comfortable chair for him. It was made of metal and had no cushion.

She placed her hands on Khayin's knees and opened his legs. Brianna moved in closer, placing herself between his legs, moving her hands higher. A wave of pleasure ran up his spine and he bit his tongue to fight it off. Her eyes focused on the fly of his pants, but she made no other move. She slowly looked back up to his face.

She's a monster. She practically committed genocide. She's in league with a petty, spiteful god and she kills without remorse. She's using you. She's not Kira.

"We used some mercenaries to distract. We attacked from

every beach. Magic was used to camouflage our approach on all fronts and no one suspected me at that point. Surprise was on my side." She was dangerously close to his most sensitive areas. Khayin started to think of Star Wars. He started to recite lines of dialogue in his head. "We knew we would lose a lot of men. Sacrifices had to be made. I mean what else are men good for, besides for a good fuck?" She massaged his thighs.

Distract yourself, distract yourself.

'That's what your uncle told you. He didn't hold your father's ideals. Thought he should have stayed here and not gotten involved.'

'You fought in the clone wars?'

'Yes, I was once a Jedi Knight the same as your father.'

"The battlemages were our secret weapon though. Oh, my sisters put up a valiant fight and we lost a great number of our mages, but they were successful in the end." She reached her destination and it took every ounce of will for Khayin to suppress what his body clearly wanted. "They broke through the Crone's defenses, leaving her open for me."

She made no move to open his pants, but she lingered and played. "The Mother...er, Boss and I fought the Crone till eventually I overcame her. I took her mantle and I took her life. I always hated that bitch." Her caresses became rougher, which Khayin was thankful for. The image of Jabba the Hut in his head was dangerously close to morphing into an image of Princess Leia in the metal bikini and if that happened he would've lost it entirely.

Brianna stood up suddenly, grabbed his manhood tightly, and began to squeeze. That was a pain Khayin never got used to. He winced, but didn't cry out. She got very close to his face, their noses nearly touching. He almost closed the gap and kissed her just to see what she'd do, but then he thought better of it. She didn't say anything for a long minute. She squeezed just hard enough to hurt but not incapacitate.

"I don't know what kind of spell she cast on you, but I will learn what I need to know. Where is she?" Her grip tightened. Khayin tensed, his muscles constricted, and his teeth were clenched.

"Why do you need her? Why can't you just leave her alone?" He managed to ask through the pain.

"Simple." She let go and walked away. "I hate her. She was the chosen one. The Crone actually loved her. Real love. That emotion was never expressed amongst ourselves. Loyalty, respect, even fear, but never compassion. And when we turned thirteen I passed my Gnoxel and was given the gift of life. Do you understand what that means? No other sister in over two centuries was ever given that gift. I can bring back the dead. Not like a necromancer, but restore the actual soul." She stopped at a table that held some medical instruments, but Khayin couldn't see what see was looking at.

"My sister," she spat. "She couldn't do anything. Nothing but cast a simple spell, and she passed her Gnoxel without displaying a shred of natural magical talent." He could hear her breathing from the other side of the room. She nearly panted with anger. "And our 'mother' still placed her above me." Brianna suddenly calmed. She grabbed something from the table and held it from Khayin's view as she turned to face him again.

"So this is a jealousy thing?" Khayin tried not to chuckle. "Really? You're more mature than that, aren't you?"

She smiled and Khayin could instantly tell it was not a happy smile. It was the kind of smile one would see on a serial killer. He didn't fear for his life, but he feared what she would do to him instead. She sashayed across floor.

"You don't get it. In our society it was the difference between ruler and servant. Sure, I may have been placed higher than the other sisters, but she never forgave me for what happened to her precious boy-toy. I would never rule at her side." She looked up to the ceiling. "Nope, Kira had to die, but I couldn't do it, no, no. So I devised a plan."

"Yeah, you killed Sister-Mother Helga and framed your sister. I've heard this story." Khayin shook his head in disgust. Jealousy turns people into despicable human beings.

Her face lit up. "Oh goodie. How did she find out?"

Khayin didn't think it would hurt to tell her. "The Crone

recorded a message on a magical stone of some sort. Told Kira of your betrayal and everything else."

"Well, not everything. You still don't know who the Mother is do you?" She was delighted.

"No, we don't," he confessed.

"And you thought you'd come marching in here anyway, with no plan, and maybe catch us by surprise? You have no idea what we know about you, Khayin," She taunted.

"Usually not having a plan is the surprise; it makes me less predictable." He grinned.

"What makes you any less stupid than I? You accuse me of immaturity and yet you pick a fight with a god, with no plan of attack? I hope you weren't relying on the fact that you can't die, 'cause boy do we have a surprise for you." She had an 'I win' expression that Khayin quickly disliked.

What the hell? Man, I have a bad feeling about this.

"How does 'the Mother' fit into all this?" He was fishing, but he hoped she was too busy gloating to not answer.

"You haven't figured that out yet? I don't know if I want to spoil the surprise. I will say this: she had a quarrel with Lilith, our Dragon-Mother. She just needed an 'in' to try to draw her out. The Mother took a great risk invading that island." She giggled. "I can't believe you haven't figured it out. Who else would know your secret? Who would be able to break into your friend's home and steal a communicator to draw you out? And what other god would have a feud with Lilith?"

She paced, swaying her hips in a mesmerizing pattern. Khayin shook his head. He began to sweat. For the first time he felt nervous. He stared at the floor and his hands were curled up into fists. He racked his brain.

Lilith, Dragon-Mother, founder, creator of the Schadovitch. She originated from Jewish stories of creation. Adam's first wife.

"Where is Kira, Khayin?" She was beginning to sound impatient.

The Mother, actually a mother? The Chief talked like she was his mother. Why would she have conflict with Lilith?

"Khayin, honey, where is Kira?" She put some sap into her

The Malevolent Witch

voice. Brianna closed the distance between them. She walked around his chair and stood behind him.

Eve? Adam's second wife. The Christian mother of creation. Shit...Eve. Khayin's eyes went wide.

"By the gods I think he figured it out." Brianna plunged a syringe into his neck and emptied its contents. "Khayin, where is Kira?"

"Fuck you." He started to feel drowsy.

"Maybe." Brie said, answering his retort. She walked around to face him. "The Mother wants to see you."

"I'm not telling you where she is," Khayin said defiantly. The drug she had injected was making him sluggish and light headed. He wasn't even sure his words came out clearly.

She moved in very close again. Her lips lightly brushed his. "Hmm...I wonder what my sister sees in you." She kissed him. It was soft at first, but quickly became more deliberate. She forced her tongue in his mouth and straddled his lap. He was too weak to fight it. Brianna slowly broke off the kiss. "I wonder how my sister would feel if I took you here and now?" A wicked grin crept across her face.

Brianna started to sway her hips to unheard music. She kissed him. *Don't do this.* He tried to voice his thoughts, but nothing came out. Her movements became more passionate. Her kisses became longer as if she didn't need to breathe. Brianna's nails were like talons and she tore at his clothes, leaving bright red lines of blood in their wake. She ripped his vest and shirt off like they were tissue paper. She dug her nails deep into his chest. Blood began to ooze from his injuries and she rubbed her body against him without a care.

Brianna nibbled his ear. "I think you're ready, honey," she whispered. He couldn't fight. The drugs didn't knock him out, but left him conscious and unable to move. His mind was in a fog. "You tried so hard, didn't you?" she said in a mocking purr. She bit his ear, drawing blood and then licked his wound.

She leaned in close to his bleeding ear. "Don't worry, honey. I promise you'll enjoy this."

Chapter 35 The Office

It took every ounce of willpower not to audibly gasp in astonishment. Kira felt every hair on her body stand at attention. *Mistress Tao? How did we miss this? And what did they do to Codex?* She tried to remain calm. *Keep it together, Kira, keep it together.*

Tao walked past Kira without a glance. The man in the fancy uniform followed behind with Codex draped over his outstretched arms like he was carrying a bundle of firewood. He did look at Kira. He never stopped walking, but he gave her a full examination with his eyes. Kira shivered.

Kira let out a breath she hadn't realized she was holding and exited the lobby. She almost began to hyperventilate and she broke out in a cold sweat. *I should leave. I should leave and find Khayin.* It wasn't hard to convince herself. Kira looked back at the door Tao had entered and she started to leave.

"Where ya goin, Kim?" Lucy asked.

Kira stopped. "Umm...I need to use the bathroom," she lied.

"It's over there, silly. That's where I just was." Lucy pointed at the bathroom door.

Kira turned around and headed toward the bathroom. "Thanks." She shook her head. "Dummy me, I mustn't be fully awake yet," she said with a warm smile.

She walked over in front of the mirror and stared at her transformed self. She turned on the faucet and splashed water on her face. The water didn't mess up any of the enchantment and she looked as if she hadn't gotten her face wet at all.

"Fuck, what do I do? What do I do?" She leaned on the sink and nearly pressed her nose against the mirror.

The door opened a crack. "Ah, Kim," came Lucy's hesitant voice.

"Yeah?"

"You are needed in the Boss's office."

"OK, I'll be right there," Kira responded. The door closed.

Breathe, Kira, breathe.

Kira dried her hands and ran them down her non-existent uniform before she exited the bathroom. Lucy sat behind the reception desk and Kira smiled at her. Lucy smiled back.

"Good luck," Lucy said.

"Uh, yeah, thanks." She entered the office.

It was nothing like Mistress Tao's Port Authority office. The windows were tinted black and there were both candelabras and magical lights. The majority of the office had a desk and chair and some other pieces of furniture to sit on. Kira saw that Tao would run business and casual meetings in the same area. The whole thing looked rather tame but for one corner.

In one corner of the room stood a table cocked slightly on an angle. Codex was strapped to that table. She didn't appear to be awake, and a cold shiver ran up Kira's spine. Knots twisted in her stomach. The uniformed man was tightening the straps while Tao watched. There was a full instrument tray next to the table. Kira could see several knives, but the rest were obscured by Tao's form.

"You must be new," Tao said in a non-Japanese accent. Kira couldn't place it. "Come here so I can get a look at you."

Kira walked forward. The uniformed man now stood next to Tao and Kira stopped a few yards in front of them. They both eyed her.

"Turn around," said Tao. Kira turned her back to them. "She'll do, Lawrence."

"I don't know who she is, Boss. I've never seen her before," Lawrence said.

"I asked for a female security guard and here one is. You

didn't send her? You can turn around, dear." Kira turned to face them again.

"I didn't hire her."

"Maybe Dorne did?" Tao countered.

"Perhaps, but we can't ask him now can we?" There was a bitter tone to his voice. "Plus, I always screen new hires. And I always get paperwork before they start. I haven't received any paperwork and I ain't never seen her before." He started to raise his voice.

"Come to me, dear," Tao said in a very tender voice.

Kira gripped the strap of her bag to stop her hands from trembling. *This is it. Are you ready, Kira?* She looked down at her feet as if to will them to move. She couldn't remember a time she was so scared. She lifted her gaze to Tao and was about to take the first step when the door to the office flew open with a crash.

Brianna stormed in and behind her were two battlemages carrying a limp and bloodied Khayin. They walked in a few feet and dropped him. He was still breathing. A new wave of panic shot through Kira. Khayin was naked and wounded and Kira's mind was a hive of swirling chaos. She didn't know what to do.

"He wouldn't talk," Brianna squawked. "Stubborn mule." She looked back at his prone form on the floor. "She has got to be here somewhere."

It was that last sentence when Kira felt every eye in the room suddenly fall upon her. She swallowed the lump in her throat. Tiny droplets of sweat started to bead up on her brow. Kira stared at her sister and her sister stared back. This was the first time she saw Brianna in...well, she couldn't remember how long it had been since she had seen her sister.

"Who's this?" Brianna asked pointing at Kira. Brianna was covered in blood and Kira guessed it was Khayin's. Her hair was clean, as was her face, but everywhere else was painted a dark shade of red.

"The new security I asked for," Tao responded.

"And I told you, I didn't hire anyone yet. I have a stack of apps on my desk. I haven't even looked through them." Lawrence was beginning to sound perturbed.

"Who are you, dear?" Tao asked.

"Kim," she practically whimpered. Shit, my cowardice is going to find me out.

"Who hired you?" Tao probed deeper.

"Joshua Dorne," she said with a bit more confidence. She knew that name at least. She just hoped they would buy it.

"Bullshit!" Brianna shouted. "Grab her!"

The two battlemages that had come in with Brianna were on Kira in a flash. She barely had time to blink. Each mage seized an arm and held her tightly. Kira tried to remain calm, but all she saw was Khayin's bloody form and Codex lying unconscious on the table. She went through her options, which unfortunately weren't many. She could attack, but she counted five against just her. She didn't think she'd get very far.

C'mon, think, Kira.

"Drop the facade, Kira. I know it's you," Brianna sneered. The Chief's head swiveled from Brianna to Kira and back. Tao stood silent. Brianna approached Kira and stopped a foot away. She slapped Kira hard. Her nails tore flesh away from her cheek and blood began to bead up in the wounds. "I want to see your face," she seethed.

"What did you do to Khayin?" Kira tried to ignore the pain and locked gazes with her sister.

Brianna slapped her again on the other cheek, resulting in the same bloody tracks. "You don't get to make demands. You are in my house now." She punched her in the stomach. Kira was stopped just short of doubling over; the mages held firm. "Drop your disguise, bitch."

Kira straightened and resumed the stare. She willed the disguise to drop and Kira stood before them all in her natural form. Her short blonde hair grew out to long blood-red dreadlocks. Her eyes went from brown to blue and the pale face remained pale, but sported tattoos. Blood ran down her cheeks. "What did you do to Khayin?" she asked, careful to enunciate every word.

A wicked grin slowly crept across Brianna's face. "I fucked him till he couldn't stand."

All Kira saw was red, and rage was the color. Brianna didn't get the chance to react to her sister's sudden fury. Kira lashed out. The magic swelled and burst like an over-filled balloon. The two battlemages holding her flew in opposite directions and only stopped when their bodies hit the walls. The shattering of their skulls reverberated throughout the room. Brianna was knocked backward and smacked the wall behind the table that held Codex's limp body.

Chief Rantz pointed a gun at Kira and pulled the trigger. A loud bang filled the air and Kira felt the impact of the bullet in her shoulder. She turned her wrath to the Chief. Kira Pulled and lifted him into the air, she jerked his body in one direction and his head in the other. The neck snapped with a loud crack and she released him before she tore the head completely off.

A flicker of a battlemage was all she saw before a clawed hand tore at her stomach. Kira screamed in pain and her hand immediately covered her wound. She didn't see the mage. How many more are in this room? She saw the flicker again out of the corner of her eye and again the clawed hand scored, this time across her back. The pain almost brought her to her knees. Her bag fell to the floor.

The next flicker was followed by a full body tackle. The figure straddled her bloodied stomach and came into view. It wore the same black Lycra and skull mask as the others. The mage was able to land one solid hit to her face, breaking her nose. Her face exploded in pain and blood poured down her face as Kira Pulled, sending the mage across the office. It landed hard on Tao's desk, breaking both the escritoire and its back. Kira began to shake and breathe rapidly.

In the commotion Brianna grabbed a knife from the tray next to the table and held it to Codex's throat. "Stop!" Brianna screamed. "One more move and I'll slit her throat."

Tao walked over and picked up Kira's bag. She opened the bag and dumped its contents. The shirt-wrapped dagger clunked onto the floor. Tao cocked her head to the side. She bent down, picking up the bundle and unwrapping it. Her eyes widened as her hand gripped the handle and she held it out in front of her.

Kira, bloody and battered, stood in the middle of the room. To her right she saw Tao with 'The God Killer' and in front, she saw Brianna hovering over Codex. Khayin was behind her. She was breathing heavily and her face was streaked with blood and tears. Her pain would have been excruciating, but the combination of adrenaline and magic made her numb.

"Wait!" came a strained but clearly audible voice from behind Kira. Kira turned to see Khayin sit up.

"Oh, we're all here," Brianna purred. "Now the party can begin."

Kira was conflicted. She wanted to run to Khayin, but she didn't want Brianna to kill Codex. She looked from Khayin to her sister, then to Tao and back. Tao was examining the dagger. Khayin struggled to stay sitting up. *What did she do to him?*

"I've got an idea," said Brianna. "I want you to slit Khayin's throat, or I will slit your friend's." She smiled that same sadistic smile she used to when they were kids; it had always meant something sinister. Kira shivered. "But with that knife." She pointed with the knife in her hand at the dagger in Tao's.

Panic seized Kira. Her muscles tensed and her eyes went as wide as saucers. *The God Killer? Will that actually kill him? What if it does? No, I can't.* Tao walked over to Kira with a smile and tossed the dagger at her feet.

"Don't get any smart ideas," Brianna said, the knife at Codex's throat again. Kira saw a flicker standing next to her sister.

I'm too weak to take on both; one of them would kill Codex. *Shit! I'm screwed.*

Tao backed away before Kira could pick up the ancient dagger. Kira hesitantly picked up the blade then looked at Khayin, back to the dagger, and again at Khayin. Her palms began to sweat and the dagger became slick. She looked at her sister and saw that Tao had moved over to stand next to her.

"You kill Khayin and I'll let Codex go." The light in the room reflected off the blackened blade. "I promise. If you don't believe me just ask Khayin; he'll tell you I keep my promises." She giggled.

Kira walked over to Khayin, dreading every step. She knelt down beside him and looked into his eyes, pleading and hoping that this was all part of an elaborate plan he had neglected to tell her about.

"I want to apologize," Khayin said.

"For what?"

"This was a really stupid plan." He tried to laugh but just wound up coughing. "You've been clouding up my head from the day I met you. I haven't been able to make a rational decision since. Don't take this as me blaming you for our situation, really. This is all on me." He laughed some more and his body nearly went into convulsions. Kira maneuvered behind him, cradling him.

Kira looked at Khayin. "I can't," she whispered. "What if it really kills you? I can't lose you."

Khayin smiled and she felt a warmth wash over her. "I've lived a long life and I wouldn't be able to live another day of it if it cost me Codex." A tear rolled down her cheek. "It's OK. I accept this. I'm tired of watching my friends die. I just never had the strength to do it myself."

"I'm waiting," Brianna said with a higher inflection. She dug the tip of the knife into Codex's throat, drawing a small trickle of blood.

"I can't do it. I just can't." The tears fell more freely now, and she could hear her sister laughing, which brought in the memory of Quinn. Her sister laughed then, too. She gripped the dagger tighter.

Maybe he will heal faster than bleeding out. Maybe he can survive this. Then all I'd have to do is stall for time.

The memory of her childhood trauma flashed back and the idea of slitting Khayin's throat became nearly impossible. "I...can't. I think...I...am...in love with...you." Her words were a whisper.

Khayin flashed that smile again. "I love..."

"Oh, for the love of the goddess, do it already." Brianna plunged the knife into Codex's shoulder. Kira winced as Codex twitched with the pain, even in her state. "C'mon, big sister. I know you can do this; you've done it before. Don't make me hurt this little bitch." She twisted the knife and blood began to pool beneath Codex.

Kira raised the dagger and put the blade against his throat. She was sweating and her heart beat rapidly. *Please, Lilith, or whoever, please...* She slowly slid the razor edge across the bare flesh of Khayin's neck. Blood poured and Khayin's body slumped to the floor.

Chapter 36   The Mother

Kira dropped the dagger and Khayin's lifeless body lay in her arms. Her whole world crashed in around her as she heard her sister's laughter in the distance, but she felt no more rage and the only red she saw was blood. All her hope was gone. The light flicked out of Khayin's eyes too fast, and Kira knew he was dead. Kira sobbed and her body shook.

A pair of hands grabbed and lifted Kira from the floor. She took a moment from her grieving to look over her shoulder. It was Lucy, who brought Kira before Tao and firmly held Kira's arms to her sides. It wasn't hard; Kira didn't have any fight left in her. She dared a peek at Khayin and immediately wished she hadn't. There was so much blood and he looked so pale.

Kira slowly lifted her head to face her sister and Tao. She caught a glimpse of Codex lying still, blood slowly dripped. Brianna was smiling and Tao's face remained calm. Kira could sense an air of satisfaction from her. Kira decided to focus her attention on Tao and tried to block her sister out.

Tao's face softened and her cheeks blossomed into a rose color as a wide smile spread on her lips. Her face started to elongate and all of her Asian features faded away. She grew another six inches and her black hair turned a sandy brown. She wore a cross on a chain around her neck.

"We were never properly introduced." She stuck out her hand in the customary American greeting. Kira didn't take it. The

Mother shrugged. "My name is Eve."

Kira was flummoxed. *Eve? Who the fuck is Eve?* "Is that name supposed to mean something?"

There was a minute flash of anger, but Eve recovered. "The mother of creation? Adam and Eve?" Kira just looked at her. "Second wife of Adam?" Kira still said nothing. "Your Lilith was the first wife of Adam." Finally, a light-bulb.

"You know Lilith, the Dragon-Mother," Kira said.

Eve grimaced. "Yes, yes I do. I've been hunting her for a while."

"Why? What did she ever do to you?" Kira wondered.

"She exists," she spat. "She thinks she is better than me, than Adam, than our god. My god commanded that she was to die."

"Your god?" Kira was starting to feel all of her injuries. She tried not to show any physical signs of discomfort, but was failing miserably. Her courage started to seep back. "Aren't you a god?"

"Technically yes, but I was created just like everyone else--by the one true god."

"What? This isn't making sense. Who is this "one true god"?

"There is one god that created everything. The world, people, animals, everything."

"And why am I just now hearing about this? You're delusional." Kira looked at Brianna. "You bought this bullshit?" Her sister just glared at her.

"Enough. You will not disrespect my god. You are truly a daughter of Lilith." Eve spat on the floor. "My god demands retribution and it will be paid."

"Well, guess what. She isn't here. She's already dead. And you caused the death of everything I loved." Kira's hands balled up into fists and her tattoos began to swirl chaotically, glowing brightly. She was weak, but her anger started to give her strength.

Eve smiled.

"What?" Kira demanded. "What could possibly be so funny?"

Eve chuckled a little. "Darling, Lilith is here."

"What?" Kira was thoroughly confused.

"You." Eve shoved a perfectly manicured nail into Kira's chest. "Right there. Don't you feel it? You are Lilith. I felt it the moment I stepped into my office. I was waiting for Brianna before I did anything."

Kira shook her head. *It can't be, but yet...I feel it. I feel her. I feel them all.*

Every tattoo felt like a presence, as though she carried the souls of her ancestors and they were represented by her glowing marks. She could hear them speak to her--not voices, more like intuition--like they were guiding her, fueling her, giving her more power. Something about meeting Eve and killing Khayin with the God Killer woke her up. Kira felt alive.

"My plan worked. Lilith gave you her essence--gave you her immortality. You are the Dragon-Mother. And you walked right into my domain. I could have stopped you when you and Khayin needed to get to Panama, but I needed Lilith. You were the key. Lilith wouldn't give herself to Brianna, so I hoped she would either give it to you or come out of hiding altogether." Her smile widened.

Kira scanned the room, but tried to make it look like she was confused. She counted four others, aside from Khayin, Codex and herself. Eve, Brianna, Lucy and the lone battlemage. *I've got to do something. They're not going to let me walk out and Codex is already as good as dead. I killed Khayin for nothing.* Her body wanted to hyperventilate. She needed to suppress the growing panic. *If I'm to die, I'm taking as many as I can with me.*

She channeled her fear and anxiety and converted it to rage. She looked at Eve. Kira's eyes glowed a brilliant blue and her tattoos flared and shifted chaotically. She Pulled and sent Eve crashing against the far wall. Kira felt a sharp pain in her back. She spun to face Lucy with a knife in her hand, looking wide eyed at what she had just done. Her mouth dropped open as her body was flattened to the floor, like a giant thumb squashing a grape.

Kira briefly saw a flicker, but couldn't respond to it before she felt a slash of claws on her lower back. The cuts were deep and Kira had already lost a lot of blood. She could feel her energy flowing out from her wounds and she nearly dropped to her knees when the battlemage made a mistake. The mage materialized in front of her to cast a spell. Kira smiled and chuckled.

Eve stood up and marched toward Kira. With a look, the battlemage disintegrated in a cloud of dust. Eve turned her eyes to Kira, who could feel Eve's power. It took every bit of willpower Kira had to stop it. She started to sweat and her muscles tensed. Eve looked just as stressed. Kira felt Eve's power intensify. Kira's nose began to bleed as the two women became locked in a magic wrestling match.

Kira was fueled by revenge as she thought of her sisters, of Codex, and finally of Khayin. She reached down within her for something more, she could feel the power of her ancestors wane. She thought of Khayin.

Did he say he loved me, too?

Her love for Khayin and the love he had for her gave her the strength she needed. She Pulled and she could see Eve's facade crack. The Mother's shins broke and she fell to her knees.

Kira felt a sharp pain in her back, but this time it hurt much more. Her eyes went wide and all magic ceased. She felt a twisting in her and then a bursting pain through her chest. She looked down to a hand protruding through her rib cage and holding her heart. She coughed up blood, along with her last breath.

Chapter 37   The Dagger

Eve watched as Brianna plunged her hand through Kira's torso, her sharp talons gripping Kira's still-beating heart. She counted the last few beats and let out a loud breath. Brie pulled her hand back, still clutching the bloody mass. Kira slumped to the floor, lifeless, as blood started to pool beneath her. Eve reset her own broken bones with a loud snap and massaged them while weaving healing magic into her legs. After a moment she stood up and brushed herself off.
"Well," Eve began, "that could have gone better."
"We only faced my sister." Brianna stared at her sister's heart. "I had no idea how powerful she had become." She looked at Eve. "We're lucky the drugs and that dagger worked on Khayin."
"Lucky indeed, but no worries. What's done is done." Eve looked around the room. "We'll either have to clean up or move." She was quite proud of herself. She had been planning the confrontation with Lilith for millennia. She was happy it was finally over. Now if she could only get rid of Brianna.
Brianna dropped her sister's heart with a splat. She turned and looked at Codex. "What do we do with her?" Brie asked.
"I like her," Eve said. "Maybe she can see reason. She could be a valuable asset."
"I highly doubt that. She loved Khayin. The way you talked about the two of them I could swear they were related in some way." She tapped her index finger on her ruby lips. "No, I think we

should probably kill her too."

Eve didn't like the thought of that. She had grown rather fond of Codex and there was so much more she didn't know about the woman. She looked at her unconscious body lying on the table. Codex was an enigma and Eve knew there was still more she could learn from her, like who her mother was.

"Let me think on it for a few," Eve said.

"If we don't let her wake up soon we'll have to feed her through a tube or something." Brie said in an unhappy tone.

"We have time. First I think we need to get this place cleaned up. We'll probably have to promote some people as well." Eve made her way over to Khayin's body.

"Not just promote, but we'll have to recruit." Brie countered. "Let's get more women this time; there was way too much testosterone in the building."

Eve stood over Khayin's body, breathed in deep and puffed out her chest. Both Lilith and Kira'Tal were dead. She hated the idea that Brianna had had to save her from Kira, Eve had totally underestimated her. She saw the dagger lying on the floor near Khayin's lifeless hand. Eve squatted down and reached for it. Just as her fingertips touched the blade, Khayin sprung, grabbing her arm and pulling her into the dagger that was now in his hand. It sank deep and pierced her heart from under her rib cage.

"I'm back," he said in a little sing-song. Khayin gave the dagger another push, sinking it deeper.

Eve spit up blood. The pain was like nothing she had ever felt before. It was...pleasurable, an actual kiss of death and in her ecstasy she was nearly overwhelmed and forgot where she was. She hacked up more blood, which brought her back to reality. She was dying. Eve looked into Khayin's eyes.

"I curse you, Khayin. Your..." His head slammed into her face, cutting off her words.

"I don't think so, bitch. I ain't falling for that again."

She went into a coughing fit. She felt her life pour out of her, onto Khayin and the floor beneath them. She felt at peace. Everything around her started to fade and the last thing she saw was a pale horse with a figure dressed in black sitting upon it.

Chapter 38   The Eye

The blood in his veins felt like fire. He didn't take time to inspect the room. He only had a second, he knew, before Brianna would attack. He pushed Eve's body off him and pulled the dagger from her with a wet slurping sound. Brianna stood wide-eyed in momentary shock. He threw the dagger with all his strength.

The bone blade sank deeply into Brie's shoulder, knocking her off balance. Khayin quickly got to his feet and charged.

Brianna wasn't prepared for Khayin's naked bloody form tackling her to the ground. She tried to lash out with her talons, but he pinned her arms under his knees. Khayin straddled her. He jerked the dagger free and held it to her throat. His heart raced and his resurrected body protested every movement.

"Don't say a word." Khayin growled. He refused to allow her to speak any magic.

He took stock of the room. To say it was a mess would have been an understatement. He started to count the bodies when he finally saw Kira's lifeless form. He saw the hole in her back and could feel his face turn red. He hadn't felt such rage since...since...

A multitude of images flooded his mind. His body jerked, but he controlled himself enough to keep Brianna pinned to the floor with his knees and dagger. Images of his long dead wife Rebekah, his daughter Adelaide, the brutal attack on his home and on them began to flash through his mind. He started to sweat and his eyes welled up with tears. The anxiety was almost too much and it took everything for him to remain in control. He screamed at the top of his lungs. He was so loud that Brie cringed and tried to back away.

Khayin hadn't seen his family's faces in millennia. They had been blocked. By the curse? Suddenly, he was seeing images of their deaths and the men who caused them. He saw himself kill every man. Khayin saw the bearded man. He remembered the bearded man. He remembered what he did. He remembered his name...Molek.

"I killed you," he seethed.

"Wh...what?" Brie managed to say.

Khayin, pulled from his reverie, looked at Brianna. Her face was smeared with make-up, blood, and tears. Her eyes were bloodshot and panicked. Tears ran down the sides of her face. Khayin could see the terror. She was breathing heavily and erratically. He stared at Brie. She looked helpless and he wondered if he should feel pity for her.

"What happened here? Who killed Kira?" He barely recognized his own voice as he asked the question. He felt as though he was possessed. He pushed the blade harder against her skin, drawing a small line of blood.

"It's what it looks like." She sniffed a couple times and choked back some sobs. "After Kira slit your throat...we...talked. Then Kira fought." She paused, probably waiting for a reaction, but Khayin didn't give any. "She managed to kill everyone in the room, except Eve and me." She drew in a long breath and released it. "She threw Eve clear across the room, she took out the apprentice Lucy, and then she and Eve had a magic sparring match. That's when I struck."

Khayin saw it in her face--she didn't want to continue. He put a little more pressure on her throat. "Speak, bitch. I want to hear it all."

Her tears started to run freely once again. Khayin's face flushed with a ferocity that he had forgotten he was capable of. "I...I...tore out her heart."

Khayin pulled the blade away and replaced it with his hand. Her neck was so small that one of his hands almost wrapped neatly around it. He squeezed. Khayin cut off both the circulation and air to her brain. He watched as her eyes began to bulge. Then he stopped. He leaned in a little closer.

"Bring her back." The edge was gone. His tone was almost pleading.

Brianna's expression changed. She no longer gasped for air and Khayin could see a bit of her confidence seep back. "Fuck you." And she spat in his face.

Khayin still held her by the throat. He raised the dagger and cut out her left eye. She screamed that nearly shattered the windows, and Khayin got close to her ear. "Bring her back," he repeated with more vigor.

"You will kill me regardless, or she will, so fuck you," she said defiantly.

Khayin strained to control himself. His muscles tensed. His naked flesh was slick with sweat and blood. He was stressed near his breaking point. Remembering his family and their tragic deaths with Kira lying dead behind him was almost too much to contain. His breathing became more rapid. He looked behind him at Kira's form. He took a deep breath and exhaled through his nose.

"I will let you live." He couldn't believe his own words and he knew Kira would hate him for it. "Bring her back and I'll let you have your life. You have my word."

"Your word doesn't mean shit to me."

"You don't know me, so I'll let that slide. You bring her back and I'll let you go. I won't pursue you. I can't guarantee she won't, but I'll discourage her for as long as I can." He let go of her throat and pulled the dagger away. "Deal?"

He offered her his hand to seal the deal. She looked at it with her remaining eye and struggled to get away from his grip. He moved one leg enough for her to free her hand. She took his hand and shook it firmly.

"You have a deal, Khayin. After tonight I never want to see you two again." She gave his hand a quick squeeze before letting go.

"The feeling's mutual." Khayin got up. "Is there anyone else here I need to worry about?"

"No, there are a few doctors and scientists, and maybe a handful of security, but I doubt they heard anything. If they had they'd be up here by now."

Brianna stood up and retrieved Kira's heart. She walked over to her sister's body and knelt beside it, turning Kira over onto her back and placing the heart into the open cavity in her chest. Brie's face looked as if it were in conflict with many emotions. She put her hands, palms down, on Kira's body.

"This is going to take a few moments and she will need a minute or two to fully recover when I'm done. I'll use that time to leave." She explained.

Khayin glared at her. "I will track you down and do things to you that will leave you begging for me to end your life if you screw me over."

Brianna only nodded. She closed her eye and began to hum. The hum then turned into a song. The melody was captivating and her voice was mesmerizing. *How can a voice so lovely and a woman so beautiful be so utterly evil?* Brie started to glow a pale yellow and the light engulfed Kira as well. Kira's body started to rise, hovering about a foot from the floor. Khayin watched as Kira's wounds started to knit close. The massive hole in her chest grew new flesh and soon looked as if nothing had happened.

The whole process took several minutes. Khayin found Chief Rantz and stripped him of his clothes, getting dressed in them himself. They didn't quite fit, but it beat walking around in the nude. He walked over to Codex to check on her as well. She was breathing, but Khayin noticed that she looked different somehow, like he recognized her face in a different way. He was studying her and trying to figure it out when he heard a gasp for air. Kira's chest began to rise and fall. Brianna slowly brought her body back to the floor. The glow that surrounded the sisters dissipated, and Brie stopped singing, opening her eye.

"It is done," she panted. She looked exhausted. "May I..."

"Go," Khayin said, cutting her off.

Brianna didn't waste any time. She got up quickly and ran out of the office.

Khayin knelt down next to Kira and held her. He sat watching her until her eyes fluttered open. For what seemed like several minutes they just gazed into each other's eyes. A warm smile spread across Kira's face and Khayin smiled back. He didn't want to fight his feelings any longer. He supported the back of her head with his hand, brushing her cheek with his other. He leaned in close until he could feel the heat of her breath. She whimpered, and their lips met. Khayin felt her tremble. It was tender at first. He pulled her closer. She reached up and ran her hand through his hair. He let out a soft moan and Kira replied in kind. Their lips parted, the kiss deepened and the two of them got lost in the moment.

"OMG, OMG, OMG, I'm so proud of you two!" Codex exclaimed, and the moment was broken.

Chapter 39 The Uniform

Kira, still in Khayin's arms, glared at Codex, but the beaming smile on Codex's face melted away any animosity. Khayin was still gazing at her and Kira soon forgot that Codex was even there. She pulled him in close for another kiss, not ready to let him go, when Codex interrupted again.

"Not that I don't want a front row seat to your smoochfest, but I'm still strapped to a table and are you two sure there is no one else in the building?" Codex asked sounding a little annoyed.

"Yes, of course." Khayin replied.

He helped Kira up into a sitting position and then stood up. He walked to the table and cut the restraints on Codex's feet and wrists. She slid off the table and wrapped Khayin into a deep hug. There were tears running down her face. Kira didn't want to interrupt their reunion, so she began a search of the room with her eyes.

"So tell me what happened," Codex said.

"My plan worked, kinda," Khayin replied with a half grin.

"What do you mean?" Codex asked. Kira looked at Khayin as well. She had been wondering the same thing.

"You said nothing about a plan, other than turning yourself in." Kira said.

"I had a feeling they were going to try and kill me with that dagger," he explained. Kira started to feel her blood begin to boil. "And I thought they might have you do it." He nodded toward

Kira. "That's why I didn't say anything, I wanted your reaction to be authentic."

"What?!" She was pissed, and her eyes and tattoos flared. "You made me go through that on purpose."

"Well..." He started. Kira began to march toward him. "Your sister and Eve had to buy it, so there was no room for error. And I had a pretty good idea that the dagger wouldn't kill me and if I would have told you that, your act may not have been totally genuine." His eyes were pleading. "I'm sorry."

"Wait a minute! You had an 'idea' that the dagger wouldn't kill you?" Codex finally piped in.

"Well...I know it's enspelled to kill gods, but other than that there really isn't anything remarkable about it, other than the fact that it's old. I figured since I'm not a god..." he didn't finish the sentence.

Kira decided to check the lobby--she needed to clear her head. She didn't want to be angry at Khayin. She knew they had both been in an impossible position. Kira didn't notice anything out of the ordinary, so she proceeded to the elevator and stairs. The door to the stairs was locked from her side so that no one would be able to enter the lobby or office without a key. She pressed the button for the elevator and nothing happened. There was no power. She returned to the office and took account of all the fallen. She couldn't find her sister.

"What about the 'kinda' part?" Kira heard Codex ask.

"Um, Khayin?" Her eyes darted around the room. Her heart began to beat a little faster and her breath became shallow.

Khayin and Codex made their way over to Kira. Codex stopped and stood over the body of Eve. Codex nudged her with her foot.

"What's up?" Khayin replied.

"Where's Brianna?"

"Kira," Khayin began.

"We've got to find her. She's too dangerous. She could sneak up behind us. Is she in here somewhere? If she is, why didn't she attack?" Her head snapped back and forth erratically. "Khayin, where is she?" Her voice was panicked.

"Kira," he stood in front of her and placed his hands on her shoulders. "You were dead."

"I was? I mean...I was." She looked at him. There was a tenderness in his eyes. She liked that; it calmed her a bit. "Where is she?"

"Kira, you were dead. Think about that a moment."

I was dead? I was fighting. I had a magic battle with Eve. Then there was a sharp pain in my back and I felt something burst through my chest. A hand. A hand that held a...heart. Shit! My heart. That bitch! She killed me.

"That bitch killed me," she finally spoke. Khayin's eyes turned sad. He pulled her close and embraced her. "Khayin, where is she?" He didn't answer. "She brought me back didn't she?" Khayin still said nothing. "And in exchange for my life, you let her keep hers." Kira could feel him nod his answer. She backed away, and he let her. "How could you?" A single tear rolled down her tattooed cheek.

"Wouldn't you have done the same?" he asked.

She hated her sister, but she couldn't honestly say that she'd let Khayin remain dead if she could use her sister the same way he did. She hit him in the upper arm and hugged him hard.

"Thank you for bringing me back. I know it must've been hard."

"The decision to bring you back wasn't hard. It was letting her live. She didn't do it out of the kindness of her heart. I don't think she has one." She looked at his face. "It took some convincing."

"What'd you do?"

"I took one of her eyes." He smiled. "That was the 'kinda' part. I didn't mean for you to die. I was hoping I would've come back faster. In the past, a slice to the throat didn't take as long. I'm guessing the magic in the dagger made it take longer. I'm sorry."

The warm feelings came back and her heart was aflutter. She gave him one more tight squeeze and let go. Khayin and Kira walked over to Codex, who was now bent low, examining Eve's face.

"You alright?" Kira asked.

"Tao?" Codex responded.

"Eve, actually. But yes, we knew her as Tao." Kira squatted next to Codex and placed a hand on her shoulder. Codex did nothing to acknowledge it.

"I'm so sorry, Kira. If I would have known..."

"How could you have?"

"It got you killed and almost Khayin." She turned to look at Kira, tears streaming down her face. "That was probably the closest he has ever gotten to an actual death. How..."

"Brianna and Eve threatened to kill you and Khayin said he'd rather take a chance with his own life than to lose you." She saw a smile on Codex's tear streaked face.

"I don't deserve him as a friend." Codex hugged Kira. "You'd better take good care of him."

****

The three of them searched the office thoroughly, looking for any artifacts that Eve may have had. The only thing of use was an old piece of parchment with latitude and longitude coordinates on it. Khayin pocketed it. The three of them decided to stick together and searched the rest of the building. The entire second floor was Eve's office. The first floor held several offices, two of which were Joshua Dorne's and Chief Lawrence Rantz's. Neither of them had anything of significance.

They stopped in the main lobby of the Nueden building. Codex looked at Khayin and shook her head.

"What?" he asked.

"Your clothes. Where are yours?" She stood with one hand on her hip and she kept looking him up and down.

"Long story." Khayin replied.

"Yeah, that won't do." She pointed at him swirling her index finger around in the air. "Go see Penelope at Penelope's Attic. It's here in Chicago. Tell her Codex sent you."

"I don't have any chips on me." Khayin argued.

"Tell her I sent you." She smiled.

"OK. But what about my weapons? I think they may be here in the building, but I have no idea where."

"I'm going to stay and search the rest of this place. If I find them, I'll hold'em for you," she said.

"You're going to search on your own? What if..."

"I'll be fine. They got the drop on me because Tao and I were...well, anyway if I had been alert to such an attack, let's just say that things would have gone down drastically different."

"Fair enough." Khayin walked over to her and gently grasped her arms. "We need to talk."

Codex looked up at him with big saucer eyes. A warm smile slowly spread from cheek to cheek. Her eyes started to well up, but no tears escaped.

"I know, Papa Bear. I have so much to tell you."

****

The air got so thick you could cut it with a knife. Codex stared at her father and for the first time in a very long time her 'father' stared back. There were tears in his eyes and he drew her in for a hug. The embrace was deep and full of love. She could feel his body shake as he wept. He let it all out. She wept as well, and the two just held each other for several long minutes.

"How can you...?" Khayin asked in a barely audible whisper.

Codex was overwhelmed. She hadn't planned this and it wasn't the way she'd wanted him to find out. "I know."

"You were..."

"I know."

He pulled away, but still held her. He looked deep into her eyes. "Why now? It's been thousands of years."

"I know." She wiped her tear-filled eyes. "I only recently found out myself." She looked around. Kira was standing just behind Khayin and she looked uncomfortable. "Not here, Papa Bear. I don't want to have this conversation in the lobby of Nueden."

They both took a step back. "And I'm really having a rough time taking you seriously in that getup." She chuckled, and he cracked a smile. "Let me clean up here, before the authorities show up." She looked over to Kira. "Besides, I think Kira needs your attention right now. We'll talk tomorrow."

"I've got no way of getting to you."

"There is a hotel called He Bers down the street. I'll book a room under my real name." She smiled warmly. Adelaide was overjoyed. All she wanted to do was to spend as much time as possible with him, but she needed to investigate the Nueden building before anyone else got there.

Khayin closed the gap between them and kissed her forehead. "I've missed you. Even though this curse blocked you and your mother from me, there's always been a hole in me I could never fill." He opened his mouth as if to say something more, but nothing came out.

She gave him one last hug. "I love you, Daddy." And tears started to flow once again.

Epilogue

The sign above the building was large and bright. Millennium sat upon it staring down at them. Several glass doors provided entry and they entered through one of them to be greeted by a live band. There was a guitar, drums, and a piano, as well as brass and wind instruments. Khayin walked up to a desk-like counter and talked to the man behind it. Kira wandered the lobby. Bright tubular lights highlighted the desks and displays. Pictures behind glass hung uniformly along the walls.

Khayin looked back to Kira and caught her eye. He didn't say anything, but gestured toward the food and beverage vendors. Kira nodded and Khayin got in line. There was a spiral staircase off to the side of the large lobby, also decorated in the same lights. It all seemed so surreal. Kira was in awe.

After a few minutes Khayin met her by one of the many framed pictures. She caught his gaze and she smiled. They walked down a long wide hallway. There were several numbered doors along the way and they entered a door marked seven.

The room was crowded. The smell of butter and salt wafted through the air and the lights were low. The live music playing in the main lobby, she noticed, was being filtered throughout the whole building. She didn't know what to expect, but the excitement she saw on Khayin's face made whatever was going to happen worthwhile.

They made their way to the middle row in the middle of the

room. Kira was holding Khayin's hand. Her hands were sweating and she hoped Khayin wouldn't notice. She looked at him. He was facing forward and one of his knees bounced nervously. She gave his hand a squeeze. He looked at her and he was beaming like a child.

Kira leaned in and kissed him on the cheek. She shifted in her seat and rested her head on his shoulder. The lights went out and the screen in front of them lit up, but she didn't see what was going on. Her attention was on Khayin. The screen went black and Kira watched the show in front of her as blue words appeared. He had given her a pair of artifice glasses so she could read the language:

A long time ago in a galaxy far, far away...

ABOUT THE AUTHOR

M.R. Gross hails from the magical land of Warren, Michigan. He lives with his wife and daughter. When he is not writing he is playing games and drinking craft beer or a glass of whiskey.

NOTE FROM THE AUTHOR

I hope you enjoyed the story!

Please take a moment to leave an honest, constructive review on Amazon or my Facebook page, it will only help me become a better writer and provide you many more stories.

Made in the USA
Lexington, KY
17 June 2017